before anyone else

By Leslie Hooton

TURNER PUBLISHING COMPANY

Turner Publishing Company
Nashville, Tennessee

www.turnerpublishing.com

Before Anyone Else

This is a work of fiction. All the characters and events portrayed in this book are either products of the author's imagination or are used fictitiously.

Cover design: Emily Mahon
Book design: Tim Holtz

Library of Congress Cataloging-in-Publication Data

Names: Hooton, Leslie, author.
Title: Before anyone else / Leslie Hooton.
Description: Nashville : Turner Publishing Company, 2020. | Summary: "As a designer of upscale restaurants, 30-year-old Bailey Ann Edgeworth can go into an empty space and immediately see what it would take to create a beautiful and memorable environment. Unfortunately, she's not nearly as good at designing her own life"-- Provided by publisher.
Identifiers: LCCN 2019025024 (print) | LCCN 2019025025 (ebook) | ISBN 9781684424009 (paperback) | ISBN 9781684424016 (hardcover) | ISBN 9781684424023 (ebook)
Subjects: LCSH: Women interior decorators--Fiction. | First loves--Fiction. | Psychological fiction. | GSAFD: Love stories.
Classification: LCC PS3608.O5985 B44 2020 (print) | LCC PS3608.O5985 (ebook) | DDC 813/.6--dc23
LC record available at https://lccn.loc.gov/2019025024
LC ebook record available at https://lccn.loc.gov/2019025025

Printed in the United States of America
17 18 19 20 10 9 8 7 6 5 4 3 2 1

One cannot think well, love well, sleep well, if one has not dined well.

    —Virginia Woolf

Though one may be overpowered, two can defend themselves.
A cord of three strands is not quickly broken.

    —*Ecclesiastes 4:12*

For the woman who taught me to read and love books
Before anyone else,
For my first editor who uttered the phrase "red ink is love"
before anyone else,
and for doing my brand of crazy with me
before anyone else,
Mama, Sarge, and the CEO of me,
Elizabeth Hooton

Chapter One

A s I walked into VERT, memories washed over me. They filled me with unmitigated delight. But if I'm being perfectly honest, they also filled me with just a little disgust. Two-thirds standing water. One part full-blown tsunami.

I made my way to the bar. The bartender grinned at me and said, "Merry Christmas." He added, "The usual?" Although it wasn't a question. I grinned back. My heart had never been immune to Griffin Hardwick.

If Griffin and I were a married couple, we may have kissed each other when he handed me the cocktail. We weren't married. We weren't even a couple. Were we?

"I would've picked you up at the airport," Griffin said.

"And deprive these patrons of 'Atlanta's most underrated . . . '" I started quoting Atlanta's magazine profile piece on Griffin and my brother, Henry.

"Bartender," Griffin said humbly.

"Mixologist," I corrected.

As I rolled my suitcase into the office, I took another look around. Nope. The green looked faded and washed out. The fixtures and hardware looked downright decrepit. I still disagreed with the vibe of VERT, the boys' first restaurant. They had hired Julian Palmer to create the design. He was the best restaurant designer in the business. I should know. I worked for him in New York. He was a good boss. He believed in "brands" and did an extraordinary job of branding his restaurants. My brother, Henry, and Griffin may have come up with the name VERT, but the next restaurant Julian named BLANC. After that, he came up with their nickname,

1

the Color-Wheel Boys, and it stuck. They were famous not only in Atlanta but around the country as well.

I closed the door to the office and relaxed on the sofa. I took a satisfying sip of my drink, a sidecar. Griffin had first made it for me when I was just eighteen, before anyone else, and it had become my signature cocktail. I fished around in my purse and fingered the piece of paper a little longer than I should have. I couldn't get Griffin's signature drink in New York, but I wanted to be the next Julian Palmer and I couldn't do that in Atlanta, and I wanted *it* more.

But there was Griffin. My heart had a stubborn gravitational pull toward him. Not only had Griffin made my signature cocktail before anyone else, he was the epicenter of *all* my important "firsts." My first driving lesson. My first crush. My first kiss. The first person to recognize that I had design talent. The first man I had ever been with—the same night he concocted the sidecar for me. I allowed the memory to keep me company. As it always had. Comfort food.

⚘

The boys were home from Cornell for the summer. It was the eve of my eighteenth birthday, and Griffin let me be his taster for a few of his concoctions. My brother was out on a date. Cooking, drinking, and women: my brother had a talent for each. Griffin and I were at my house experimenting with things like Maker's Mark and honey-dew and mint sorbet. It was a much better way to spend the evening than being at some lame prom.

"Are you sorry you didn't go to prom?" Griffin asked loudly over the blender, where he was crushing ice for a new drink for me to try. Sometimes I think my men felt guilty that they had not exposed me to the "normal" highlights of childhood.

I considered Griffin's question as I watched him concoct his drink. He took his shaker and combined Maker's Mark and other

2

ingredients. If my brother favored scotch, I tended to prefer good bourbon. I had learned to be picky about my whiskey. I could tell the difference even on this side of eighteen. Griffin placed a martini glass in front of his shaker. I was intrigued. I noticed Griffin rimmed the glass in sugar. I had never seen this before. His question about the prom lingered in the air between us.

"Are you kidding? I'm doing exactly what they're doing, only better. They're drinking cheap beer, cheap wine, or cheap liquor and getting drunk and then heading to the back seat of somebody's car. Not my idea of a good time. Rum and Coke? Where's the imagination in that?"

He handed me the apricot-colored drink. I hoped it tasted as good as it looked.

"A sidecar," Griffin announced. It looked prettier than the pomegranate martini he'd fixed me last week. He placed it in front of me next to the honeydew and mint sorbet. I surveyed the drink before picking it up.

"Cheers!" I brought the glass to my lips. Talk about potent potable. It would become my signature drink for the rest of my life. Griffin Hardwick had made it for me before anyone else.

He walked around the island and over to me. "Go easy, girl," he said and picked up the spoon to finish my sorbet. I wanted to know what the combination of the drink and the sorbet tasted like together, so I leaned in and kissed him. To my astonishment, he kissed me back.

The taste of his mouth and his proximity to me were more potent than any drink he could have fixed me. He pulled back.

"Why can't you be older? Why are no other girls like you?" He was looking at me for an answer, but I'm not sure it was to a question he had posed yet.

"Because, Griffin, I am an original," I said confidently. More confidently than I felt as my feelings churned inside.

He threw his head back and laughed and then resumed kissing me gently. We went on like this for a while. He pulled away. "What are we doing?"

"Exactly what everyone else my age is doing except I hope we'll be doing it in a nice bed." I could tell he was wrestling with himself. Wrestling with his feelings.

"I'm just not sure you know the ramifications."

"You said it needed to be my choice. You said the person shouldn't be drunk. You said—"

"I'm stupid. You shouldn't be listening to me or Henry." He paused. I could see he was pondering what to say next. "You are special. Nobody is like you. Nobody."

"Do you have a condom?" I asked. In that moment, I knew he would be the one before anyone else for me.

We went upstairs to my bedroom where we each removed our own clothes. Griffin only stopped to say, "You have a beautiful body, Bailey. Where have you been hiding it?" I led him to my bed. Our kissing became elevated and urgent.

"Are you sure you haven't done this before?" he asked. I certainly couldn't tell him that from the time I was a young girl I had dreamed about this. As dreams go, this was vintage. Old but precious.

In some ways, it was everything I wanted and needed it to be. In other ways, very surprising. Griffin was kind. And patient. And tender. It was as if he felt the responsibility to make this okay for me.

Around ten o'clock, Griffin was getting dressed when the phone rang. He answered it immediately like he'd gotten caught doing something he wasn't supposed to be doing.

"Oh my God. What? Who? Oh no. You did what? Sure. Of course."

My heart lurched. "What happened?"

"George was chopping onions and apparently sliced the top of his finger off. Your dad came to the rescue and put his finger on ice and took George and the finger to the hospital. George is in surgery now to reattach the finger, and your dad is there with him." He paused for the rest. "Your dad cannot find your brother." We both exchanged meaningful glances. Henry could be off doing something neither of us approved of. It worried me.

"What else did Daddy say?"

"He said he'd be home in the morning and for me to stay here and look after you." A small but telling smile crossed Griffin's face.

"Well, that's a little like putting the rooster in charge of the henhouse, isn't it?" I said. He relaxed again and looked at me.

"Any regrets?" Griffin asked. I knew he wanted an honest answer. One that had been fully considered. I wanted to tell him this had been the easiest decision of my life. And while I had no idea then, it would remain so. In the years to come, my sex life would take many twists and turns before ultimately crashing and burning, along with the rest of my life.

"None. However," I started inching closer to him. He looked aghast at my forwardness, and yet I could tell he appreciated it.

"Really? Well, there may have been one little fact we left out of our biology lesson. You're going to have to give me a few minutes. On second thought, maybe one minute will do."

I just smiled and waited.

The next morning, he put his jeans back on and his customary V-neck T-shirt. It worked for him. It exposed just a few chest hairs to make a girl curious. He looked rugged but also nonchalant. That was quite endearing.

Griffin stood in the threshold of my door as if putting a punctuation mark on the occasion. He just looked at me for a moment and said finally, "Are you sure you're okay?"

I delayed my answer just to keep him standing there. "Yes, I am."

He stood in the doorway a moment longer trying to assess for himself if I was truly okay. I may have had sex with him before anyone else, but the secrets we kept from each other in the years to come were what would threaten our undoing.

"How about some bananas Foster brioche French toast for breakfast?" he asked. Without waiting for my answer, he had already turned around to go to the kitchen to look for bananas.

It was the best French toast I'd had in a long time. The brioche that Henry had baked was out of this world. Griffin ate only some toasted brioche with peanut butter. Not exactly haute cuisine.

About that time, my brother came blowing in. He looked like a mess. If I had been happy about the events prior to breakfast, seeing my brother hungover and dissipated scared me. This moment would mark the beginning of my worry about the men I loved and their addictions. I could tell from Griffin's expression, which resembled a nasty scar, that it concerned him too.

"Dude, you were supposed to be looking after my little sister. Did you sneak out after she went to bed?" When Griffin gave him an inquisitive look, my brother responded, "Griff, you're eating peanut butter . . . "

I saw the look pass between them. Something private. It dawned on me. Peanut butter must be what Griffin eats after sex. Henry had no idea that he had come so close to the truth.

"Hey, bro, let's talk about where *you* were all night." He paused, "I didn't think so. Besides, I'm hungry."

"Sorry. Somebody is certainly touchy this morning, Griff."

I went upstairs to my bedroom. Griffin had left his flannel shirt behind, and I picked it up and smelled it. Then I shoved it to the back of my closet like a keepsake, like a memento from a favorite trip. He never asked for it back. I was truly happy Griffin was the one before anyone else.

There was a gentle rap on the door. It pulled me back to the present. Griffin came in, closing the door behind him. He embraced me and we kissed fully, holding nothing back. He said, "I'm glad you're home for Christmas."

"I don't see any mistletoe," I teased. Griffin fumbled in his pocket and pulled out some dried-up herb.

"That better be a piece of fennel from some fennel soup you made me," I volleyed back.

"Maybe. Maybe not. Where do you want to stay tonight?"

"I haven't even seen Daddy, so I'll just stay with him." We were about to kiss again when Henry barged through the door.

"Are y'all decent? Put your clothes back on."

"Stop that, Henry. It's Christmas," I said. I looked over at Griffin. He was silent. The long frown that snaked across his face told me more. My heart skipped a beat. Then another. I felt a thread of discord being sewn between my two men.

"Merry Christmas, Bailey. I heard you were lurking around. You look so pretty. I'm glad you're here. Griff, can you drive my little sister home? I'm meeting some people." He came over and hugged me and kissed me on the cheek. Then he left.

On the way home, we decided not to discuss my brother. After all, Henry's disappearing act was nothing new. The strain between them was.

Chapter Two

My coming home to Daddy's empty house wasn't new either. Daddy couldn't stand not working. He taught us all to be workaholics. I turned on a few lamps and went upstairs to my bedroom. It was just as I had left it.

Next to my bed was the stack of *Architectural Digest* and other design magazines that kept me company when I was growing up without a mother. Or friends. And later, when my men went off to college. They were old, dog-eared, and frayed like stuffed animals. They were loved. I had found the antidote for loneliness within those sleek pages of sophistication. I also found what I wanted to do by studying the lines and moldings in the pictures. I remember the day, a Monday, when I discovered Julian Palmer. He was featured in a "Dining by Design" article. I even remember the cover. It featured a foyer with a round table. Blue hydrangeas adorned it. He designed restaurants for a living.

Wait. What, that's a job?! Sign me up. My heart, which suffered from low-grade sadness, sprung to life with joy. Exhilaration. I devoured design magazines the way other adolescent girls craved magazines that featured the latest heartthrobs. Who knew my salvation could be delivered monthly? I secretly imagined my interview in the magazine.

"Tell us about yourself Bailey Edgeworth," the question would go.

"I grew up surrounded by good men and good food. I grew up appreciating the smell of hash browns cooking in grease. And cinnamon. And brioche baking in the oven. The smells that wafted from my daddy's kitchen and connected me to the best part of my childhood. Daddy and Henry had butter and sugar coursing through their veins. Recipes sparked their imagination. Well, I couldn't cook my way out of a paper bag." I weighed what I had just disclosed. It surprised me how little my answer had changed over the years. I would continue.

"It was *your* splendid magazine that ignited my own ambition." Maybe I would even describe the issue when I discovered Julian Palmer.

I thought again about the piece of paper in my purse. I was twenty-five, still young enough for something like this to come true. I noticed the other magazines nestled to the side. It was all the magazines that my brother and Griffin had appeared in.

I heard a knock at my door. "Come in, Daddy."

"It is so good to have you home, Bae. I'm sorry, honey. I just let the time get away from me. Everything all right?"

This had been the extent of our conversations when I was a teenage girl. "I am just fine. See you in the morning." I could tell he was grateful for the reprieve. Poor Daddy. Neither one of us expected raising a girl would be so difficult. While my magazines kept me company, they were no match for the rambunctiousness and noise the boys made. The house was silent when they went off to college. So were Daddy and I.

Daddy called me Bae. But he wasn't the first. That honor, too, belonged to Griffin. He had been the first to come up with my nickname, Bae. Was it short for Bailey or for the monogram of my whole name, Bailey Ann Edgeworth? Like the Color-Wheel Boys, my nickname stuck. Little did any of us know that years later in the Urban Dictionary it would come to mean "Before Anyone Else." It summed up the situation perfectly.

Chapter Three

I woke to the steady strum of my men at work in the kitchen. I heard the oven door open and close. I could already smell onions being sautéed. Merry Christmas to me. I jumped out of bed and went downstairs.

I stood on the threshold of the kitchen. All three men were at their familiar posts. Henry, looking no worse for the wear, stood at the stove. Griffin was in front of a cutting board slicing and dicing. Daddy was sitting at the island acting as maestro conducting the workings in his kitchen. He was sipping his cappuccino. Daddy used to make one for me each morning. He called it "starter fuel." Henry looked up.

"Good morning, sleepyhead. We thought you might sleep the day away. I bet you don't want any breakfast," Henry said, turning an eye of the stove off.

"When have you ever known me to turn down food?" I asked. I noticed Henry was already getting out some cinnamon bread.

"Cinnamon toast or cinnamon French toast?" He was already opening the refrigerator. The easy banter that was ours had returned.

"It's Christmas. Let's blow it out," I said, but Henry was already whisking an egg. He hugged me and kissed the top of my head. "Merry Christmas, little sister." Even Daddy leaned over and kissed my cheek. I think my men were more demonstrative in the kitchen because they were just so comfortable here.

Griffin turned around and smiled at me and said, "Cappuccino?" I don't know what he did, but he made the best cappuccino I have ever had. I had sampled them all up and down Madison Avenue, and no one even came close. He put the cup and saucer in front of me, and I noticed that the saucer had a holly leaf and berry. He leaned in and whispered in my ear, "Presentation, Bae. Merry Christmas."

We opened presents before lunch. I always went first. I recognized the box. They always gave me the same thing. I had discovered it during my adolescent years when I was crushing on Griffin. For a tomboy, makeup was just too much for me. The perfume I purchased might be considered odd for a fifteen-year-old girl. It was called Nutmeg & Ginger by Jo Malone. It appealed to me because it didn't smell like a giant gardenia bush had vomited all over me. I may have failed Vixen 101, but my men appreciated it. It smelled like their kitchen. It became my signature scent.

"Bae, they discontinued Nutmeg & Ginger. I hope you like this," Griffin interjected before I opened the box. It was Myrrh & Tonka.

"We splurged and got the lotion to go with it," Henry added. The first year they had given it to me, Henry had groused about the price: "What did you do, Bailey, go to the cosmetic counter and ask for the most expensive and weirdest perfume they made?" But each year, they gave it to me without fail. I sprayed the new fragrance. I loved it.

"Honey, you smell as good as Thanksgiving dinner," Daddy said. These are the kinds of compliments I got from my men. If Griffin had ever told me I smelled like filet mignon, I knew I was on to something. Henry went next.

"Let's see what 'used merchandise' Bailey is giving us this year," he said good-naturedly. We all laughed. I had discovered that I loved estate sales and consignment stores almost as much as I loved designing restaurants—and my men.

"It's vintage," Daddy and Griffin proclaimed as they had every year since I discovered the allure of "repurposed" antiques.

I chuckled. This year, I had broken with my tradition. Not only had I given Henry something new, it technically wasn't even out yet. "You just might be surprised." Henry looked intrigued. He slid the sprig of rosemary I had tucked into the ribbon. If some cooks favored butter and sugar, Henry thought everything was better with a little rosemary. He opened the package and just stared at it. It was a coffee-table book entitled *Last Suppers*. Famous chefs described what their favorite last meal would be. Henry had been featured in the up-and-coming chef section.

"It still has that new book smell," I said.

"How?" Henry asked.

"I have my sources. Daddy why don't you open yours now?" Henry noticed their identical gifts and moved closer to Daddy.

If Henry preferred rosemary, lavender reminded me of Daddy because it grew in his beloved garden. He rubbed the herb between his hands and took deep breaths. I knew he rolled lavender in his pocket square because, occasionally, he would leave his handkerchief on the kitchen counter and I'd bring it to my nose, hoping the smell would connect Daddy and me.

"Well, Bailey has given us the same thing. Thank you, Bailey," he said formally.

"Check out the bookmark, Daddy," I said. In his interview, Henry said that his last meal would be "anything my father, Hank Edgeworth, fixed me. But I wouldn't be opposed to a side of his famous macaroni and cheese with lobster in a béchamel." Father and son, mentor and apprentice, older man and younger one stared at one another. Their love, admiration, and respect written in the expression they exchanged. I may have given Daddy the present, but it was Henry who had given him the gift. I would've given anything for Daddy to bestow that kind of look on me when I was growing up after the boys left for college. Theirs was a mutual admiration society with only two members.

Griffin smiled at me and interrupted, "Well done, Bae." I appreciated his gesture, but I was also eager to see his reaction to my gift.

I had had his the longest, and I had spent more money on it than anything in the past. I knew it was perfect. I wanted it to be perfect. When I learned his parents never bought a Christmas tree or even bothered to give him a present, I knew I wanted to be the person who did.

He admired the festive wrapping paper as he slid the fennel out and pointed it to me. "For soup I am planning to make you?" he asked. "Nice paper." I could tell he was eager to see the contents.

"Presentation, Griffin," I said. I watched him slide the painting from the wrapping. He didn't say anything at first. Had I rendered him speechless?

"Portofino?" he asked. I nodded. In the time I had known him, he had always wanted to go to Italy. He walked over to me and whispered in my ear, "Thank you, Bae." The landscape and blues of the Mediterranean waters beckoned. It made me happy. I would be the reason he never got to go.

After lunch, Henry begged off cleaning detail because he had "a date." Daddy wanted to go to the cemetery to visit his wife. I don't remember my mother. She died soon after I was born. I stayed behind and helped Griffin clean up.

He was drying the last dish and I was putting some leftovers in the refrigerator, and he came up behind me, embraced me, and kissed me.

"Still. No mistletoe," I chastised him. He disappeared briefly and brought out a small ball tied with red ribbon. "Where did you get mistletoe?" I asked.

"I passed an all-night tree lot and I thought I might give them a little business," Griffin laughed.

I rewarded him by smothering him in kisses, which became increasingly urgent, and we ended up unwrapping each other on Daddy's banquette in the kitchen. As we were getting ourselves back together, Griffin said, "You're still my person, Bae."

We were not new to these acrobatics. Griffin's parents had died several years ago in a fire. They were both passed-out drunk. We had stayed behind when Daddy and Henry went to work. I grumbled at the time thinking, "Great, they've left me here to deal with Griffin's grief because I am the only female."

It had been in those quiet moments that Griffin had told me he had never had a Christmas tree. He never had a Christmas present until he came over to our house. I never even thought it strange that he spent so much time here. He just folded into our family as easily as Daddy folded a meringue onto his lemon pie. I had embraced and kissed him and then I had comforted him on the banquette.

He had moved a piece of hair from my eyes and said, "You're my person, Bae. My family." Then, like now, a proper response had gotten lodged in my throat.

I deflected at the time. "After what we just did, if you and I were family, we would have broken the law in at least forty-eight states." He had laughed and rewarded me with one of his hot chocolates with Bing cherries and homemade whipped cream—topped with a fresh sprig of mint. Presentation.

My heart may have been ready to burst at the seams, but my head cautioned restraint. I had my piece of paper. I had my ambitions. I had my dreams.

I was careful to take the memory of the kisses, the touches, and even the laughter and store them away in a secret compartment in my brain the way Henry stored a treasured recipe in his gray folder that he kept tucked behind his good knives.

Chapter Four

When I arrived back at my New York apartment, a big pink carry-on stood at attention by the door. There were pieces of clothing draped on our sofa, all belonging to one of my roommates, Elizabeth Hoak. You never knew if she had gotten caught up in the throes of passion or if it was just a Tuesday and she had simply run out of time. She practiced law at one of those big NYC law firms and worked all sorts of ungodly hours for all sorts of wretched attorneys. I hardly ever called her Elizabeth. I gave her the nickname "Elle" because she looked like Reese Witherspoon's Elle Woods in *Legally Blonde*.

Elle wore her hair long and blonde, carried a Tory Burch handbag, wore Tiffany sunglasses, finished first in her class at Washington and Lee, and was a barracuda in the courtroom. With all her attention to fashion and accessories, she was like a sister I never knew I wanted.

My other roommate was Regina Cunningham. She was an oncology nurse at Lenox Hill. I think her profession suited her because if you ever received a cancer diagnosis, you would be in excellent hands with Reggie. Yes, I gave her the nickname Reggie. She dispensed advice and hugs as freely and often as you would find our living room littered with items from Elizabeth's closet. If Elizabeth was like a sister, then Reggie was like the mother I never knew I needed.

It was really the first time I had ever been around women. When I went to college at the New York School of Design, I begged Daddy for a place of my own. He and the boys thought it would be more conducive for study. The girls I attended high school with often made fun of me and of the food I brought for lunch as they passed my otherwise vacant lunchroom table for their crowded "popular" table. Fennel soup. Cauliflower soup. Pork belly. What's not to like? In high school, I became accustomed to being alone and even lonely. In college, I studied and experienced life in New York City—a place infused with raucous sounds and brimming with people. I adored the smells, even the yucky ones. Living in New York and studying design finally broke the fever of loneliness and suffocating silence.

Being around Reggie and Elle was a delightful novelty. I routinely discovered their enchanting character traits. For instance, Elle carried a new designer bag almost every month. I learned that some of her cutting-edge fashion and handbags were from Rent the Runway. Regina, on the other hand, was very religious. She attended church regularly. Sometimes, she would leave a man behind in her bed and we were left to make small talk over coffee.

The feeling was reciprocal. They found some of my qualities endearing. I often ate soup to save money, but I would splurge on flowers. Elle asked me about it once, and I simply said, "Life is too short to not be surrounded by beauty." Instead of laughing at me, they began to quote me, which was astonishing. Another time I bought flowers for my bedroom and the living room.

"What, Reggie?" I had said. "Regardless of the question, flowers are always the answer." They delighted in my sayings and sensibilities.

For the first time in my life, I had women for friends. I talked about my life. To those girls in high school, my world looked foreign and odd, but for Reggie and Elle, my stories of being raised by men sounded exotic, like a delicacy in a posh restaurant.

Chapter Five

Over time, I became braver. Reggie and Elle wanted to hear my stories. I told them about buying my first bra and how Daddy took me to the mall. He stood outside with his newspaper and waited until a woman came to fetch me. It was as if I were party to an illegal transaction. The woman was old. She looked like Aunt Bee from the reruns of *The Andy Griffith Show* that Henry and Griffin watched. I know because that's all we watched other than reruns of *I Love Lucy*. Even though I was born in 1988, you would never know color TV had arrived. Aunt Bee ushered me through the cosmetic department where big-toothed, smiling women sprayed me with horrifying smells. As we entered the lingerie department, Aunt Bee started touching my breasts like she was choosing tomatoes for tonight's salad. She selected two bras. What an ordeal. Who in their right mind would want to go to a place and be assaulted by such wretched smells, harassed by overly made-up women, and have their personal space invaded?

My brother took charge next. He took me to Victoria's Secret. A lady, maybe in her thirties, approached me. "What size are you looking for?" she asked.

"I have no idea. This is my first bra," I said, burying the incident with Aunt Bee.

"What made you come here?"

"My brother brought me." I pointed over to Henry, who was fingering neon lime thongs on the periphery of the store. The saleswoman looked overly concerned as she eyed me and then surveyed my brother. Stubble covered his face, and his dark hair was disheveled. We looked so different. My blonde hair pulled neatly back in a ponytail. My green eyes bright and alert. Henry's green eyes bloodshot.

"Honey, are you sure he's your brother? You can tell me. Do you need me to call someone? Like a nice policeman?"

I realized she had some sinister concoction rolling around in her head. This mall scene was definitely not for me.

"No, I just need a bra. My brother brought me because my daddy works all the time, and . . . " I motioned her closer to me, "You see, my mother is up in heaven." You could get a lot accomplished if you were a thirteen-year-old girl and uttered the phrase, "My mother is up in heaven."

"Oh, I see. Bless your little heart." Thirty minutes later, I had purchased a training bra, a regular bra, and a sports bra.

"Thank you so much, Mrs. Conner. I still don't know why your store sells all those lacy things when the sports bra is much more comfortable." I hated that underwire of the regular bra and hoped my boobs did not grow any more.

"Yes, my dear, but our husbands like to see us all lacy."

I wondered what she was wearing underneath her clothes and thought, *Not my husband!* I would be mistaken on that topic. I thanked her. My brother and I left to have a cappuccino. I decided to bring Mrs. Conner one. She looked surprised to see me. "I brought you a cappuccino to say thank you." She looked at me with an odd blend of amusement and curiosity. "Daddy makes me one before school. He calls it starter fuel."

"Who is your daddy?" she asked. Her look was one of complete horror. I could tell her focus had shifted away from my brother to Daddy. "Hank Edgeworth. He owns—"

"The City Café," she interrupted.

"This is just mediocre. You should come by the restaurant, and we'll serve you a real cappuccino. In a real cup, on the house. Presentation, Mrs. Conner. Just like in your store." I pointed to the mannequins and display of push-up bras, and she flashed a knowing smile as Henry and I left.

"Then there was a time that Henry and Griffin told me the facts of life." I then regaled Elle and Reggie about the night Henry and Griffin had taken me aside and told me the facts of life—but not before they had consumed quite a lot of beer. "You haven't heard the facts of life until you have heard them delivered by a couple of slightly tipsy boys."

I remembered leaving my brother's room in sheer amazement that this planet got populated at all. In their male brains, sex was an amazing thing, but it just sounded awkward to me. "Wouldn't you rather go out to a nice dinner instead?" I asked.

As Henry and Griffin concluded their remarks on sex, they asked me if I had any questions. I did. "What about love?" I looked at them.

They exchanged confused looks. I had clearly asked them a question they had not thought of when it came to sex. My brother took the first crack.

"If you ever want a condom, you come to either one of us. Don't let a boy pressure you. Because boys basically want one thing—to have sex. So be protected. And always, it should be your choice. Do not feel pressure." Henry's approach was to basically ignore my question.

This was so not in keeping with the romantic novels I read from time to time. It was Griffin's turn to have his say.

"Wait until you're good and ready. You need to be in control of the situation. It's a big deal. It would be good if he had said 'I love you' first, but make sure when he says 'I love you' he's not drunk." This was Griffin's advice. "Do you want to have sex?"

"Oh, no. I'm fourteen years old." Griffin took his big hand and put it on my shoulder. "That's it. You need to be confident." Where was Judy Blume when I needed her?

Daddy hired a church lady to offer her rendition of the "biblical facts of life" and explain "womanhood" to me. I wasn't thrilled about the whole boobs and hormones thing. If I wasn't thrilled, Daddy stayed in a state of discombobulation. After the church lady finished, Daddy put a chalkboard in a kitchen drawer to address all my "feminine needs." The first week, I wrote down "T.P." Daddy literally bought me a case of tampons. There were enough boxes of tampons to equip the girls' basketball team, softball team, and lacrosse team.

When we were having dinner, I said, "You know, Daddy, T.P. stands for toilet paper, not tampons." Well, at the mere utterance of the word, Daddy looked like he had a sudden case of food poisoning. I think he would have been happier if I had just jumped on the kitchen table and yelled "fuck" at the top of my lungs because he heard that from Henry all the time. After that, any time Daddy bought tampons, he also purchased a case of toilet paper so there would be no confusion or further conversation regarding the topic.

This brought unabridged laughter from Reggie and Elle. I would always end these tales with the mantra "being raised by men is just one step away from being raised by a pack of wild wolves."

I made it all sound funny and harmless. I didn't tell them that when the boys went off to school, the house, Daddy, and I all came down with a low-grade depression. Daddy was scared to look at me. Afraid of what an exchange would mean. Most of the time, Daddy and I moved silently around the house like pieces of driftwood floating aimlessly on the water.

I understood missing the boys. But how could you miss someone under the same roof? Occasionally, I would take one of his pocket squares, just to feel closer to him. I slept in Henry's room. Unapologetically I clutched his T-shirt. Even the lingering smells of cigarettes and liquor reminded me of him and brought me restful sleep. Or if I snatched a whiff of citrus or Dial soap, I would jerk my head around only to find no one standing there. I often closed my eyes and whispered "Griffin." Sometimes I said it like a question. More often, I uttered it as an earnest prayer.

The girls must've had some idea. One night, Reggie took my hand and said, "You have us now. We love you." She just said it. No one had ever said that to me before. Not in my entire life. Not from any of my men. I learned to say it back. I liked it. I was so grateful that they had danced into my life. They became the antidote for loneliness. They didn't care if I had been raised by wolves.

Chapter Six

I was just arriving back in the city by train. I had been designing a cafeteria for Newberry College in Upstate New York. Julian had relegated these jobs to me because of the limited budget and vision. My vision had never been hampered by the scope of these projects. I actually enjoyed designing for school cafeterias. I incorporated my own sensibilities and experiences. I always tried to find an interesting place for a single person to eat that would be cozy and visibly interesting to somehow keep them company if they were lonely. Presentation and beauty always guided me. It didn't matter if it was in the halls of academia or a hot New York nightclub. Beauty should surround you.

February had thrown her dark and frigid cloak over the city. I expected Julian to be long gone when I arrived at the office. His light was on. I still hadn't given him the piece of paper tendering my resignation. We had been so busy.

I poked my head in Julian's office. He was having his customary glass of chardonnay. If it was a yawn past 5 o'clock, his wine glass would be full.

"You're back. Come in. Would you like a glass?" I sat down across from him and declined. I debated whether to give him my letter of resignation.

"We have a lot of things to discuss," he began, retrieving a second glass and ignoring me.

"I'm listening." Julian and I had always had a playful banter, but I deeply respected him.

"Where do I begin? You and I were nominated for an IDA Design Award for BLANC," he started. BLANC was Henry and Griffin's second restaurant. It opened just a few months ago. It was a break-fast and lunch spot. My brother's date-nut scones were a piping hot shrine dedicated to butter and sugar. I had never had a scone that came anywhere close. He received countless requests for his carrot cakes with toasted pecans and coconut. Pair any of those with one of Griffin's cappuccinos and you're done. I would never be ashamed of eating cake for breakfast. Especially Henry's. It was one of life's grandest pleasures.

"And you have been nominated for an individual IDA for the standout work you did at Quincy College. And I haven't even gotten to the best part."

"Maybe I will have a little wine," I said, suddenly feeling celebra-tory. Julian continued.

"You, my dear Bailey, have been nominated for a 40 Under 40 award from *New York Magazine*, and let me get this right: for your aesthetic, creativity, and originality." I leapt up from the chair. This was one of those career achievements I had been striving for. "Now is not the time to be stingy with that wine." We toasted and I sat back down. Julian paused a moment. He knew this was a big deal for me. His office may be littered with awards the way a kitchen may be littered with dishes at the end of the night, but he was very generous, and he knew that if I looked good, he looked even better.

"Who knew designing some liberal arts cafeterias would lead to this?" I said taking a sip.

"Modesty does not become you. Besides, you have this special ability to recognize the vibe of a place. Even cafeterias. You have the eye. You can see. And you go in and create magic." This was high praise coming from Julian. I sat there just taking the moment in and sipping his excellent wine.

"One other little thing." He stopped. He wanted my full attention.

"Don't keep me in suspense," I said, putting the glass of wine down.

"Your men have called and are ready to open up another establishment." My heart beat so fast I thought I might need a defibrillator.

"They didn't mention it to me at Christmas," I said.

"They still know the pecking order around here," Julian reminded me.

"What do they want to create?"

"They want to kick it up a notch. A tasting menu in conjunction with Griffin's wine selection for each course. I need your expertise. You have unique insight." He smiled at his compliment.

Then I said, "NOIR? ROUGE?" We drank our wine while exhausting the color wheel possibilities.

"What was it you wanted to tell me?"

"Nothing. Just that I am on schedule." Julian shot up a dubious expression. I struggled being happy for my men but wondered when I could begin my solo career. At least I had a few more accomplishments to add to my expanding résumé.

Chapter Seven

I ended up telling Griffin and Henry separately. After all, VERT was in full swing with customers demanding food and drink. The girls were both home on this rare dateless and work-driven night.

"Let's crack open a bottle of Sausalito's finest," I started. I began with the boys' news, then the nomination for the liberal arts college cafeteria, and ended with the 40 Under 40 award.

"Why do you always refer to this wine as Sausalito's finest?" Elle asked.

I deflected her question. "I think it's pretty good wine. How was your day?"

In truth, I still navigated some conversations with the girls carefully. It was all still new for me. I was a very private person. I suppose my life had made me that way. Could I tell them about Griffin? What would they think? That we were friends with benefits? A convenient hook up? A booty call? I wasn't sure myself.

I reflected on Sausalito's finest. It was the perfect marriage of food and memory.

Because Daddy had given Henry money for VERT, he had given me money for a trip. I chose San Francisco because of the fine dining, and like Mr. Browning said, one's "reach should exceed his grasp." I had rented a cozy little apartment so I could experience the dining opportunities. Julian had given me a list of restaurants to make it easier.

I was just waking up my third morning in San Francisco when I received a text from Griffin. "Check out your front door." I jumped out of bed, ran to the door, and opened it. Griffin was standing in front of me. "Surprised?" Ordinarily, I hated surprises, but this was one I could learn to like. We embraced and kissed tenderly, then deeply, right there on the doorstep in public view. Clearly, we were not ourselves. Clearly, I was not in work mode trying to impress Julian, and neither was Griffin. Before I knew it, we were together. Our bodies were connecting and exploring familiar terrain. Later, Griffin said, "This is one seedy apartment." I laughed. Here's the thing about Griffin Hardwick: one of his charming contradictions was that he could go weeks without getting a haircut, letting it grow so that you could almost pull it back in a ponytail, but he preferred a nice hotel with good room service. I said, "You should just live in a Four Seasons."

"I plan to check in to one of those shortly. You could've warned me about staying on the fifth floor." He laughed.

"There are some things you can get here that you can't get at a Four Seasons. I think I have a pretty good turndown service."

He looked at me. "You make a good point." I made sure to convince him just a little bit more before we got up, showered, and met the day.

"Would you be opposed to going over to Sausalito for dinner? A buddy of ours has a restaurant that I would like to try."

"Sure." I was game for anything. Hadn't I just proven that? That afternoon, we walked around Sausalito and found it utterly endearing. With its tile roofs and blue water, it reminded me of Italy. The restaurant he wanted to try was called Beth's. Thomas Wilson, who had gone to Cornell with the boys, named it for his wife. The restaurant was unpretentious, featuring fresh seafood prepared simply and deliciously. We ordered a bottle of wine and then another. Griffin cautioned, "Go easy girl. Those bottles of wine cost as much as a night at a Four Seasons." I was horrified.

"You know there are cheaper ways to go if you want your way with me," I laughed.

"I know that. You are my person, Bae, and I like seeing you have a good time." Griffin waved his hand and ordered another bottle. I didn't say anything back to him but instead pretended to pay attention to the notes of pear and tangerine. When I returned to New York, there was a case waiting for me. Griffin always kept me stocked with my favorite wine. My thoughts returned to the present as I poured the wine liberally.

Later, I let those memories fold into the announcements and accolades Julian had bestowed. I was going to receive an honor for designing cafeterias. Life was funny. The things that haunt us are perhaps the things that propel us to create and see something better. Something beautiful.

Chapter Eight

Julian and I met the boys for our initial conceptual meeting for their new restaurant at a small but cozy space near BLANC. From the lack of natural lighting, I guessed instantly. This place would be NOIR.

I knew something was off. Henry was brimming with ideas—only some of them good. Unfortunately, most of his ideas were outlandish. He was loud and sloppy. He may have been overflowing with ideas, but he reeked of alcohol and dissipation. He was puffy and sweaty. I could barely focus on my notes because my gaze kept wandering to his appearance.

After the meeting, Griffin announced, "You guys continue talking. I would like to show Bae something."

"I guess this something will take about twenty minutes?" Henry joked.

"Shut up, Henry." Griffin's fuse had gotten noticeably shorter.

When we were alone, Griffin told me the other reason Julian and I were here. Along with Daddy, Griffin had arranged an intervention for Henry while we were in town. "Your brother has lost control," he said.

"No shit, Sherlock. But do we really need an intervention?"

"I need the intervention. I can't do this anymore. I feel like a twenty-four-seven babysitter. Between the drinking and the women . . . just look at your brother. We are going to have it tomorrow afternoon. I'm asking Julian to participate. You need to think about what you want to say to your brother. How you love him, but you cannot have him in your life like this."

Suddenly I realized, this was the real reason Griffin continued to live with Henry. But still I hesitated. "It seems cruel. Maybe we need a 'Can This Marriage Be Saved?' between you and Henry."

"This is serious, Bae. I don't want Henry to end up like my parents. Do you?"

"Is the new restaurant real or a ruse?"

"It's real. But if we don't get Henry in hand, he will be doing it without me." My loyalty was divided. For the first time, I looked at Griffin. He looked thinner. Wearier. The toll Henry's drinking had taken on him was etched in deep lines on his face. Griffin embraced me. "You can write down what you want to tell your brother." He kissed my cheek.

The next afternoon when Henry arrived at VERT, we were waiting for him. Like an ambush. I hadn't slept a wink the night before, and I was having second thoughts. What I didn't know yet is that it would be worse than I even imagined.

When Henry saw Daddy with us, he knew. "Oh shit. Not some fucking intervention. Griff, you're an asshole." He went behind the bar to get a bottle of scotch. His tone of voice shook me. He was angry. Griffin followed and wrestled the bottle of scotch away from him. Henry elbowed Griffin with such force that Griffin doubled over. Henry grabbed another bottle and threw it against the mirror, which shattered. Glass flew everywhere. Hearing bottles break on slate shattered something inside me. My loyalty was being stretched between my two men and what they were doing to each other.

I was becoming doubtful as to whether I could speak. Griffin held out a third bottle of scotch, offering it to Henry, which made Henry sit down.

Julian started. His voice was clear and firm. He spoke of Henry in the past tense, as if Henry were dead. He said he was one of the most naturally talented and gifted creators and chefs he had ever met in his whole career. But like many geniuses, he had wasted his talent. Wasted. The way Julian said it, it sounded like a crime that was punishable by guillotine. He said he would no longer design for Henry nor would he ever for the rest of his life recommend Henry's restaurants. I was next. Daddy grabbed my hand, and Griffin patted my shoulder. I started to cry but swallowed it.

"I couldn't have asked for a better brother. I have idolized you and Griffin from the very beginning. If I'm being honest, I have been jealous of you. You have so much natural talent." I stopped. Memories mixed with emotions. I continued, "I was always so proud that you were my brother. Not anymore. I hate what you have become. What we become, Henry, is the only thing we can take credit for in life. It is our reputation. It is what we are. You were given all the gifts to become—the possibilities are endless. But what you became is a common garden-variety drunk." I sat down quickly.

Henry applauded. "Well done, Bailey. You spent your life trying to be me. You're a pale imitation. Fuck you, little sister. Sorry, I forgot, that's Griffin's job."

Anger got the best of me. "Fuck you, Henry. Not only are you a drunk—you're mean."

My father rose. His imposing frame divided his two children. He nodded at me. Hank Edgeworth had always been a man of a few words, and today that served him well. He landed some powerful blows. "Your behavior has made you a disappointment as a son. Unless you get cleaned up, you are no longer welcome in my house." He sat down. I noticed how Daddy's disappointment had sliced through the enormous pride he had always felt for my brother. His voice trembled. His hands shook. That's when I finally understood what this had done to my father.

Griffin spoke last. He spoke the longest, and his words were the most eloquent. You could tell his past had found him and was repeating itself in his best friend. It was gut-wrenching to watch him destroy Henry.

"If you don't get your act together, we're done. As friends. As partners. As brothers. I can't believe you would do this to me knowing my history." It devolved from there. Daddy announced he was taking Henry to a rehab across town. I announced that I was spending the night at Griffin's. My declaration garnered not even one raised eyebrow. It was the first time I had said anything about being with Griffin. It was ironic, though, because it would be the first time we would be together and not sleep together. There is no such thing as intervention sex. I felt trapped between my love for Henry and my loyalty to Griffin, sprinkled with a dusting of guilt over the toll this might take on Daddy.

❧❀

An intervention must rank as Dante's tenth circle of hell, right after treachery. It was awful. Griffin and I went through their apartment, cleaning. Henry had hidden scotch bottles in his nice shoe pouches in his closet. Seeing my brothers substance abuse was a horrible thing to discover. I felt sucker-punched and exhausted. I was also hyped up on adrenaline. Griffin fixed an omelet with mushrooms and cheese and put it on a plate between us. We ate it *Lady and the Tramp* style.

"Are we going to be okay? You and me and Henry?" The day had left me so uncertain.

Griffin chewed a mushroom slowly. His deliberateness alone scared me. "I hope so. Take your work. You tear things down only to transform them into something truly extraordinary. I have to believe that is also true with people. I'm sorry you took the brunt of Henry's anger."

"It's fine. I'm twenty-five years old."

"But you were right. We do make a good team. The three of us. I have to believe we're better together. You could move back home."

"My career and my life are in New York. I still need to establish *my* reputation." The unintended heaviness of this conversation coupled with the events of the day wore us both out.

As I got ready for bed, I noticed a wicked bruise the color of an overripe eggplant on Griffin's stomach. "Are you okay? Do you want ice?"

"It's not the first tussle your brother and I have had."

I was worried about Griffin. I started crying. Griffin embraced and consoled me. I didn't want to cry, but I couldn't stop, and Griffin didn't ask me to.

"Don't ever do anything like this to me," I said.

"Not to worry. I've never even been drunk."

"Never?" I asked, as he wiped my tears away with his shirt sleeve.

"I've had to sip wine for my job. But nope, I have never been drunk. It would take something really life-shattering for me to want to get drunk."

As I crawled into bed next to him and turned out the light, I had twin thoughts. I thought of my brother across town, but I also wondered what constituted life-shattering. Unfortunately, I would later find out.

Chapter Nine

Julian sent me on my first solo trip to Atlanta armed with a satchel full of ideas. Henry still acted guarded when I returned. It had been six months since the intervention, and Henry had stayed on the straight and narrow. I stayed with Daddy, who seemed supremely proud of Henry but a little slower in his own gait. Julian flew down the day I was going to make our pitch for NOIR to my men. I was excited and nervous. We all had big stakes: Henry's continued sobriety, my venturing out on my own, and the healing of our relationship.

"I always start with the name," I began. "NOIR. What does it conjure up? Black as the night that covers me? Or maybe black as in just a little naughty." With this last remark, Henry perked up, and I had his full attention. He and Griffin both nursed mugs of coffee. They look like the Bobbsey twins. Julian sipped his customary chardonnay. I continued.

"Henry, the location you picked out helps guide us. It's tucked out of the way. That informed me that this place should be a little risqué, very cozy, very sophisticated, and very expensive."

At this, Griffin perked up. "I like that part."

"I see the bar area and the restaurant as totally separate. People who are in the restaurant want intimacy mixed with good food. Creative food. I see black velvet banquettes so couples can sit as close together or as far apart as they want. I have found this fabulous black velvet fabric with a bold merlot stripe down the middle. This burgundy stripe also informs the color palette of the restaurant. I see black and burgundy, but I also have a little surprise.

"The pièce de résistance. To accentuate the cozy feel even further, I am proposing we cover the ceiling with voluminous fabric in this black-and-burgundy paisley print." I showed them the swatches I had in mind. "I have an example where Julian did this in a Boston restaurant. After the fabric, I found these black origami-like lacquered chandeliers." I placed photos in front of them. "I understand this may be out of your comfort zone. This is nothing like your other restaurants. But think about it just in its conceptual nature, Henry. NOIR is like no other. It needs to announce itself."

Julian finished his chardonnay. "Bravo," he said. His opinion on the presentation delighted me, but I was much more concerned about our clients. I gave them each a mock-up of my design. Then I backed away. It was up to them. I realized I hadn't taken a breath.

"How much over is this from the initial budget we gave Julian?" Griffin asked.

"About five thousand. And that's due to the fabric on the ceiling. It completes the look."

Julian interrupted. "Exactly. This is a solid proposal." He was defending me.

Henry grinned. He had a knack for breaking up tense situations. "I can see it. Griff?"

Griffin and I looked at each other like we were surveying the chessboard. Julian stood up and shook his head.

"For God sakes, you two. We are planning a restaurant, not a funeral. Henry, no wonder you drank with them around. Now, allow me to make a suggestion for you guys. I have a dear friend who offers a yoga class that will change your lives. You both should go tomorrow. I will make arrangements. Bailey, I give you permission to stay a few extra days." This was the extent of Julian's suggestions regarding the project.

That afternoon I was still walking around the space when Griffin came in.

"Can we sit a minute?" I could tell he was either going to reject or accept my proposal. His emotions were a mystery to me. Like his feelings.

"You think you can accomplish all this for just five thousand over the initial budget?"

"Yes. I always try to give worst-case scenarios," I said more confidently than I felt.

We engaged in a staring match and I suppose I won. He pulled something out of his pocket. It was half of Julian's design. He smiled. "Create something memorable."

"That is my intention." I realized my heart had been beating rapidly.

"So, you want to check out this yoga class that promises to change our lives this afternoon?" And we did. Many times. It would be one of Julian's finest suggestions for me. And one of his last.

※

Julian sent me to Atlanta to oversee the project. Henry had selected a challenging location for the new venture. It was on the verge of condemnation. I snapped pictures of the bare walls as workmen and exterminators arrived. This space was just begging for transformation.

These men showed up unadorned. They wore perspiration-stained T-shirts and painter pants, but each day when I entered with my arms full, they raced to get the door for me. I instructed them what to tear down to make way for my ideas. These workers erected walls and moldings. They erected bar areas. They erected booths. They erected. I created. I loved creating magic. The day we implemented my idea and hung the fabric from the ceiling and installed the chandeliers, I was giddy but focused, like sampling a foreign food for the first time. I stood from every vantage point to make sure it was draped properly. I love taking a space that looked down on its luck and then putting it back together into something preening with beauty.

One afternoon when I was reviewing my notes, I heard the door open. It was Henry. He just stood there. His appearance made me stop what I was doing.

He looked different. His green eyes were clear. His hair combed. His shirt tucked in. He seemed steady. Mature. I realized this place wasn't the only thing that had undergone transformation.

"Wow, this is really something." He sat down beside me in a booth.

"Are you pleased?"

"Very. I need to say some things to you." He seemed serious. He fidgeted with the sleeve on the paper cup he was holding. It made me nervous.

"Bailey, I'm really sorry about all the things I said to you during the intervention."

I stopped him. "You don't have to do this."

"Actually, I do."

"Is this part of the recovery handbook?"

"Yes. I am sorry. For the record, you are not a pale imitation. I was way out of line. I had no business saying those things to you. I am especially sorry for the remarks I made about you and Griffin. Maybe I'm jealous of you. This place exceeds all my expectations." He paused. "So, you're going out on your own after this?"

"That's the plan," I said.

"I want us all to be okay again."

"We're okay. Of course. I forgive you."

"You and Griffin?"

"We're fine."

"I'm barely sober. I can't get caught in the middle of something messy between you and Griff. Are you sure?" Henry asked.

"Sure. We're family."

"Does he know you're going out on your own?"

"If he doesn't, he hasn't been listening. Even Julian knows and I haven't even told him yet." I laughed.

"Thank you for your forgiveness." Then, "You are really something, little sister." We both smiled. It felt like something had been lifted from the chambers of my heart.

That night I regaled Daddy with the day's events. He seemed impressed. "Both my kids are so talented. You know, honey, if you wanted to stay at Henry and Griffin's you're welcome to rather than stay with your old daddy."

I almost laughed. I don't know whether Daddy was trying to be progressive or a healer. "There is no chance I would be staying with them. They have no booze." We chuckled.

The next morning, I went to BLANC for breakfast. Griffin sat down next to me. "I made some mango jam I want you to try." We looked at each other. I put my knife in the jar. "I can't believe you turned that mangy building into something so eye-catching."

"That's my job."

"Are you going out on your own? Will you be moving home?" Griffin asked. His questions had dropped an unexpected anchor through the surface of my heart. I didn't answer him right away.

"Yes. No to your second question." He looked at me as if he were waiting for a different answer. "However, I wouldn't be opposed to going to that yoga class later." After another moment, he nodded and just said, "Namaste."

The restaurant and opening came together better than I even imagined. NOIR oozed success. This ushered in a new level of fame for the boys. It marked the time I would leave Julian's nest and go out on my own. He was very supportive, even giving me smaller restaurants and university cafeterias. My men were proud of me. They were proud of my design for NOIR. We had survived and repaired our relationship. We were better together, always.

Chapter Ten

Over the next few years, our New York neighborhood earned the reputation of becoming the next SoHo. I had my doubts, but we had won the vintage lottery hands down.

I was on assignment for Elizabeth, who had been invited to a party and was looking for a dress appropriate for a 1960s theme. I suggested vintage Pucci. I was scouting out such an outfit when I saw a storefront being renovated for a new business. This was how I found my new job and my new life.

It was not uncommon for businesses to come and go, but it was uncommon for one of these establishments to catch my eye. It was a smallish building with large windows and a few workers inside. But that was not the thing that caught my attention. It was the name of the establishment. High above the doorframe and big window hung a giant question mark. What was it? Was it already having an identity crisis, or was it just looking for a name? I peeked inside. That's when I saw him. That's when my heart started beating just a little bit differently.

He wore black pants and a white shirt. He could've been a waiter in one of Henry and Griffin's restaurants.

I stepped over the threshold and hoped I would catch his attention, maybe even get the answer to my question—why the big fat question mark? He noticed me.

"Can I help you?" he asked in a decidedly English accent. He ran his fingers through his curly blond hair. He moved toward me. He took his time. With all the New Yorkers and their fast walking, I found it refreshing.

He extended his hand, but I ignored it and pointed to the sign that had drawn me to him in the first place.

"You like my sign?" he asked easily. In fact, I would describe his whole demeanor that way—very easy. Very natural. He had a boyish face, but he was not skinny or lanky. His blue eyes twinkled. He was of medium build. He was not as tall as Griffin, and his blond hair was freshly cut, unlike Griffin, who often wore his longish, which I attributed to the nonchalant quality he possessed. This man carried himself with great ease.

"Yes. Your sign." I nodded. "What are you opening up in my little neighborhood?"

"Your neighborhood, is it? But you're not from around here."

"No. But then neither are you. I'm from the South. Right outside of Atlanta."

"I'm from England. A town right outside of London." His attitude exuded patience. He smiled again. I felt the attraction. But I was not going to be deterred from my investigation.

"The sign?" I asked again.

"Oh yes, the sign," he said simply. He had charisma, but I guessed he could also be a little bit of a bad boy given the right circumstances. "I'm opening up a new restaurant. I am the chef and owner. I'm Elliott. Elliott Graemmer." He had me at restaurant. My head whirled in all kinds of directions. My heart tumbled. I tried to remain outwardly calm, but that was a very tall order because I found him so damn attractive.

I must've failed because he asked, "What's wrong?"

He had completely disarmed me. When I opened my mouth, my whole life just spilled out at his feet.

"It's just funny. I'm in the restaurant business myself." I handed him one of my newly printed business cards. "I design restaurants. I am rather good at it. It's also in my blood. My father owns a restaurant right outside Atlanta. My brother and his friend have opened up three restaurants in Atlanta that are pretty well-established. You may have heard of them."

"Your family or the restaurants?" That smile returned to his face. It was really hard to answer with my knees betraying me like this.

"Both. My brother is Henry Edgeworth, and his partner in the restaurant is Griffin Hardwick."

"Oh. The color-wheel guys. Everyone knows them." Without meaning to do so, he slapped me back into reality. Because that was what I wanted. I wanted people to say my name and it be identifiable with a restaurant whose vision I had single-handedly created.

I wanted my brother and Griffin to be as proud of me as I was of them at this very moment. Leave it to my brother and Griffin to bigfoot their way into me flirting with a good-looking man. Was that what I was doing? Flirting? It felt good but a little odd. I had never been with anyone other than Griffin. I had never even been attracted to anyone other than Griffin. The needle on my heart's compass had never budged away from him. Until now.

The man looked around and said, "I'd love to pick your brain. I would offer you something, but we don't have anything hooked up yet. There's a Starbucks around the corner." He shouted at the two men in the back of his building that he would be back and would bring them some coffee. I thought that was a kind gesture. And that is how we began.

We strolled into the Starbucks together. "What's your name?" he asked, placing my paper cup cappuccino in front of me. "Cappuccinos should never be served in paper. Does that make me a snob?"

"No, that makes you civilized. I'm Bailey Edgeworth."

"Nice to meet you, Bailey Edgeworth."

Our conversation was natural and effortless. I learned that his father, like mine, owned a restaurant when he was a little boy. "Pop hated the term 'chef.' He would've thought it was too pretentious. People are very impressed by a chef who graduated from Le Cordon Bleu."

I didn't know about other people, but I was certainly impressed. Even though he grew up miles away, across the pond, our life stories were very similar. His mother died when he was ten. "What brings you to New York? Why didn't you just stay in Atlanta and work in the family business?"

"I'll make it short and simple. I am not a cook. My father had a philosophy that women did not belong in his kitchen. I never learned to cook the way he or my brother do. I visualize and design for restaurants. After college, Julian Palmer offered me a job here in New York. I've worked for him for five years. Ironically, I spent a great deal of time back in Atlanta because he was working on my brother's and Griffin's restaurants. Working with him has been a great experience. I've overseen several solo projects over the last years. In addition to the boys' projects, I've built a solid reputation of my own."

"Julian is a pretty heavy hitter. So, you want to be the next Julian Palmer?"

"Not exactly. I just want to be me. Establish my own reputation, my brand. I don't want to be my brother's baby sister—or Julian's assistant." What I didn't say was I didn't want my life to be defined by commas. Hank Edgeworth's daughter, Henry's sister, Julian's assistant, and whatever the hell I was to Griffin. I wanted to be Bailey Edgeworth, visionary. But that's the thing about commas, sometimes you get to choose them. Other times they choose you.

For a few minutes, we kept company with our own thoughts, and I realized my initial question had gone unanswered. "Elliott, why the big fat question mark?"

"I could be suave and say to lure beautiful young women like yourself to come inside, or I could give you the real answer, the unsexy version, and say it is simply because I don't have a vision nor do I have a name for my restaurant. I could use someone like you."

Was he offering me a job? I hadn't looked around enough to even begin to offer him a vision.

"That's pretty good publicity. I don't even know what kind of food you specialize in." And that opened the door for another few hours of very easy conversation. He loved simple French food with a twist of American.

"Are you any good?" I asked. "The English aren't exactly known for turning out premier chefs."

"I don't like to brag, but yes, I think I could be, given the right atmosphere. But don't take my word for it. Let me cook for you sometime."

"Are you asking me out or offering me a job?" He threw his head back and laughed. He found me amusing.

"A job, maybe." He cocked his head. "But who knows? Why limit ourselves? Maybe we can help each other in our quest to make names for ourselves. Why don't you come by Tuesday in two weeks and bring your résumé? We can have a proper interview. By then I should have the coffee maker working and can prepare you a little something so you can sample my talent."

Oh, I had sampled some of his talent already. Night had completely taken over, and we walked together another block or two.

"Serendipity. It was nice to meet you, Bailey. See you Tuesday, and maybe we can work on the name."

I had completely forgotten my original task of looking for Elle's vintage dress. I might have landed my first account since leaving Julian. I was feeling more at home in my own skin and in New York. One chapter in my life was ending and a new one was just beginning.

Chapter Eleven

I rose bright and early the next morning, my purse brimming with a wad of cash and my only assignment to find Elle's dress. I also had a secret hope that in my quest to find something perfect for Elle, I would also stumble upon the perfect vision for Elliott's new restaurant.

Bringing cash to a deal also brought "flexibility" or, in Elle's line of work, a willingness to negotiate. And I loved to negotiate the price.

I found it in the third shop. It was crammed in the middle of the rack. It was an honest to God Pucci dress. It had flared sleeves and everything. It was the grooviest dress I'd ever seen. It was fifty-five dollars, and I quickly bargained my way down to thirty-five. Elle would look like a throwback to Goldie Hawn circa 1970. As I was leaving, I saw a vintage yellow quilted Chanel handbag with the gold-link strap. It would be perfect with the dress. The only problem was it was a hundred and twenty-five dollars. Too pricey for me, but not for my attorney friend Elizabeth.

On my way home, it began coming to me, the vision for Elliott's restaurant. I did not get the vibe from him that he was a vintage sort of guy, which would make buying things for him a little more challenging. I saw him as a modern art kind of guy. Very sleek. Very abstract. And because I did not know much about modern art—like, nothing—I took the subway up to the Guggenheim to further my education. Ideas for Elliott's restaurant ricocheted through my brain. I discovered I enjoyed looking at paintings. They were just another form of beauty.

The next morning, I heard muted laughter from the next room—Elle and an unfamiliar male voice. I smiled. Operation Pucci must've been a success. The next day, when she freely handed me a hundred-dollar bill and told me to do as I wanted, I was sure of it.

"I am going to marry that guy," Elle remarked over the cappuccino we were sharing. With our ragtag furniture, it seemed odd for us to have a high-end espresso machine. But this was just one benefit of being in the restaurant business. I always got my brother's and Griffin's castoffs.

"You seem pretty sure of yourself," I said, constantly amazed by the female species that I was technically a part of.

"I am, Bailey. Robbie is definitely going to come back for more of this."

I may not have been confident in the whole arena of womanhood, but I could hold my own in the vision department. And my vision was telling me, like a Canadian Mountie, Elle was most certainly going to get her man.

That night, I was sitting in my bed, tossing around ideas for the Englishman and what I saw for his new restaurant. I was really starting to get a vibe about him and his sensibilities when my phone rang. It was Griffin. It made me wonder if he had ESP and suspected I was thinking about a man other than him.

"How are you?" he asked in a very serious tone.

"I think I'm supposed to ask you that." A long silence seemed to stretch from Atlanta to New York and back. "I'm serious, Griffin. How are you doing with Henry?" Another pause stretched out between us like a contented yawn.

"To be honest, Bae, I'm relieved. I was always waiting for something to happen. Always on guard. Always worried what sort of trouble Henry would get into. I know it sounds horrible to say, but I just need to be out of the caretaking business."

For a moment, I thought he was directing his comment at me. I wanted to say something. My voice faltered. Unspoken words hung between us like an expectant noose. It made me sad that the secrets

Griffin had endured in his childhood, he was reliving with Henry. This was before I learned that many human beings live half their lives with secrets.

The next morning, I woke up refreshed, ready to do research for my upcoming interview with Elliott Graemmer. As if I had been struck by a mighty lightning bolt, I felt downright stupid. Grammar. The big question mark. I suddenly knew the title of his restaurant. I wondered if he knew he had done this or if it was just one of those magical things. The top line should be grawlixes—@%&#—and underneath it should be spelled out GRAEMMER. It seemed catchy. A winner.

I went to a new vintage store to see if I could find a knockoff of some of the modern art I had seen at the Guggenheim. I found another dress for Elle, and then I saw something else tucked behind a bunch of boxes. It was a painting. An abstract painting. I had the proprietor of the store pull it out for me so I could get a better look.

It almost looked like a 3-D painting of brightly colored ribbons waving gently in the breeze. One ribbon was the color of fresh shrimp, another ribbon sky blue, and several ribbons the color of cantaloupe. But the pièce de résistance was the celery color that bookended all the waving colors. I saw it almost immediately. A watery celery would be a perfect color for the walls in Elliott's restaurant. This picture could hang on a wall going to the restrooms. The colors just peeping out to bid you closer. I tried to breathe before I bargained. I didn't want the shopkeeper to see how badly I wanted it.

"How much for the dress and the painting together?" I asked.

"The dress is seventy-five. The painting I will give to you for two hundred. So two seventy-five."

"You don't even have a price tag on this painting. You should be able to give me a better price because I am buying two items." But for once in my life, I was at a disadvantage. I had no idea the value of such things.

"You have a good eye."

I hoped he didn't think that giving me a compliment would diminish my objective. "Remember, I have cash." In these places, cash was king. I wanted to appear confident. Confident enough to walk away.

"Okay. I will take some off the dress and this wonderful painting. I will give to you for two twenty-five."

I had not planned to spend that much. My inner voice told me to walk away. But I had made the fatal mistake of falling in love.

"Two hundred," I countered.

"Deal."

Part of me was delighted by my purchases. I had purchased a vintage Diane von Furstenberg wrap dress for Elle. And I had purchased a beautiful painting for a job I had not secured yet.

I propped the painting in my bedroom. Even against the dull white wall that was in desperate need of paint, the painting popped. If I did lose the job, I'd have to keep telling myself the painting was not a folly. A week or so later, all my worry proved to be in vain.

I had taken the liberty of sending over my portfolio ahead of time. I had it tabbed, as always. The first tab contained presentations that Julian and I had done together with me as the lead designer. The second section, the one I was most proud of, featured projects I had done independently. It would go a long way toward establishing myself as my own designer apart from Julian. Even separate from the boys. The third section was devoted to awards I had garnered. The fourth, which I thought held special appeal to prospective clients, was the uptick in business they would receive after an article had been written about me. The fifth held references. Along with Julian, I had references from many of the deans of colleges I had designed for. I had been sketching ideas and the placement of the restaurant's name in case Elliott hired me. I felt good. It was my goal to wean off all of the projects I had collaborated on with Julian until I had a portfolio that was completely mine.

Chapter Twelve

As I walked into his restaurant, I noticed that the big question mark sign was still hanging above the window. I would use this in my pitch to Elliott. I heard someone walking toward me. It was him.

He looked different. He was all cleaned up. He still had the little brown stubble that was either a characteristic of laziness or simply rugged good looks. He had on a pair of freshly starched khakis and a purple-and-white gingham shirt tucked into his trousers. It made an impression on me because many guys were wearing untucked shirts, and I simply hated it. I smiled back at him.

"I've been looking forward to seeing you again, Bailey," he said easily and extended his hand. We shook. If I could have nicknamed this restaurant, I would have called it "Chemistry" because, again, the chemistry between us could not be denied.

He motioned for me to sit down at one of the two sets of table and chairs. We were the only two people there.

"I've been reviewing your portfolio and wondering what incredible visions you would have for me today." I sat down, and we were very close to one another. I could smell him—a mixture of the outdoors and lavender. I felt instantly comfortable. "I see you brought your sketchbook," he commented.

"I never leave home without it," I said. I was anxious to show him my ideas. He had turned his own chair around and was straddling it. "Wait a minute," I said. "Before I begin, I thought you were going to give me a taste of what you cooked?"

"Who's to say I won't? All in good time, Ms. Edgeworth."

I opened my sketchbook and began with his own question mark and my idea about working his name into the title with all the symbols.

Before I could complete my idea, he threw out, "It almost implies the name of the restaurant is: Fuck Grammar." He chuckled. "As I was a poor grammar student, I happen to love that idea enormously."

"I just like all the punctuation marks et cetera playing off your name."

"I love it. Please continue," he offered.

And for the next three hours, I described to him the color of the walls, the textured fabrics for the chairs and banquettes, the silverware, and artwork. This had been my first real solo presentation. I felt in control. Energized. Alive. If he could pay me enough money, I knew this could work. That was how my vision worked. I could tell Elliott and I were very simpatico. But first, he had to prove himself to me. Could he follow up my perfect vision with cuisine to match? Or was he just another good-looking Englishman?

"I love it," he said and paused. "But you knew I would, didn't you?"

"I don't take anything for granted, Elliott. I liked it myself. And I hoped you would be able to see what I see."

"Julian said you were the best. Yes, I have spoken with him," he said as if answering my unasked question. "He actually said given the right set of circumstances, you may even surpass his reputation."

"I'm glad I didn't know that when I walked in," I said. But the "right set of circumstances" could be an elusive and intangible creature. It made me happy to hear that Julian's opinion matched my ambitions.

"You know, I'm still waiting to see if your food can match my brilliance," I said. I was afraid he might be a god-awful cook. Daddy, my brother, and Griffin had left big shoes for any other chef to fill. Would I be disappointed?

I looked at my watch and then outside. Night was creeping in on us. How did this happen again? When I was with Elliott, time just seemed to float away.

He glanced at the windows too. "I wish I could say I planned this. I am not that smooth of an operator. But I prepped a light supper, a little tasting menu. I hate the word, but: tapas."

"I absolutely detest that word. That word should go away, just like emojis."

He laughed. "You don't have strong opinions about anything, do you? I love that. Now let me see if I can pass your test. I know I have big shoes to fill." Had he been reading my mind? He excused himself and I heard the busyness of cooking going on.

"Do you want any help?" I asked, hoping he would turn me down.

"Something tells me you should stick to what you do best—the vision thing—and you should let me do what I do best: cooking."

After a few minutes, Elliott came toward me. He carried a drink in one hand and a plate of food in the other. "I hope this will become one of our signature drinks, Bailey. I call it the Maraschino Moscow Mule. It has lemon, citrine, and ginger beer mixed with Luxardo and topped with a whimsical maraschino cherry."

I took the drink from him, said "cheers," and took a sip. It was delicious. He had paired it with a plate of lightly battered oysters and tiny pasta with slices of ruby red grapefruit and celery. I loved the marriage of color and flavors.

Elliott seemed pleased that I was eating with such gusto.

"I should warn you," I said. "I'm not one of those girls who just picks at her food."

"I would be disappointed if you were." He nodded in appreciation and disappeared. I left one bite behind on the plate for good manners. Next came another drink and a delightful braised pork belly. The Bulleit bourbon spiced old-fashioned made a wonderful union with the barbecued braised pork. I was eating and drinking so fast on this course, I simply nodded my appreciation and satisfaction at him.

"I think I'm going to need a cab to get home. These drinks are tasty, but I can tell they're pretty potent!"

"I'm glad. I want you to enjoy yourself. Don't worry, I'll get you home. Safe and sound. That is the end of the alcohol portion of the program, I promise. Next comes dessert."

"And the long-awaited cappuccino you promised."

"Maybe. Maybe not." He gave a sly smile and disappeared. I didn't care how good a chef Elliott was, and admittedly these two dishes were simply delicious, but I doubted he could hold a candle to Griffin's cappuccino—and I wasn't sure I wanted him to.

Finally, darkness took possession of the day. He brought a cup and saucer brimming with steam along with a warm brownie topped with what he called "fig ragu" and brown sugar and maple syrup ice cream.

And that is the thing about food. Food, like life, can constantly take you by surprise. You have to be open to the possibilities. And that is the thing I loved about food the most. I have never really cared for figs. I thought they were slimy. I much preferred their cousin, the date. But what Elliott achieved with those figs was something otherworldly, especially matched with the ice cream. I loved the way all three flavors settled in my mouth.

I hoped he made his cappuccino with a hint of cinnamon. I thought that would be the perfect way to wash these flavors down. But it wasn't cinnamon. It wasn't even a cappuccino. It was hot tea. A nod to his homeland. It had an interesting flavor I was having a hard time identifying.

"It's green cardamom you're tasting," Elliott said. Even in my somewhat compromised state, I was impressed. Green cardamom is one of the rarest and most expensive spices. Paired with the tea, it was delicious, especially with the trace of fig ragu.

I was pleasantly surprised. I liked it. I was relieved it was not Griffin's cappuccino. But in looking at everything else he put before me, I wondered if my brother and Griffin could come up with such creativity in their kitchen.

While I nursed my tea, I watched Elliott. He enjoyed an appreciative audience. He had that in me. "Let's talk numbers," he said, almost dampening the mood.

He took a small piece of paper out of his shirt pocket. He slid it over to me. "This is what I propose: the first number is what I expect the renovations to cost. The second is your design fee with three installments as the job progresses."

"Oh, I see your game now. Get me drunk so I'll accept anything. Remember, Elliott, I have been trained by Julian to negotiate." I didn't want to start haggling this late at night with a tank full of booze.

"We don't need to decide anything tonight. Just tell me if I'm in the ballpark."

Poor Elliott looked so expectant. I couldn't imagine that he would offer anything that would be even close to what he really needed to match my vision. But when I looked at the piece of paper, I was pleasantly surprised. It exceeded my expectations.

I tried to maintain my composure and my own rule of thumb from shopping at my vintage stores. "I'll have to think about this, Elliott."

"I want you to. I want you to be happy with the price. Because, in the end, Bailey, I want you." And then he added, "I want your vision." I was not in any hurry to leave, but the delicious and unique tea had done very little to sober me up. I took my phone out and hit the Uber app.

"So, it's time for you to go?" It was a question. "I think I could talk to you all night long, Bailey. Can you come in the morning to discuss numbers? I'll make it worth your while and make you something yummy for brunch. Noon?"

Was there anything this man did not do and do brilliantly? I was willing to bet not. I accepted his offer of brunch and gathered up my things, left for the waiting car, and went home to sleep that night with renewed anticipation.

The new day started with the routine morning gymnastics in the bathroom for Reggie and Elle. I shook my head in wonder and awe. Along with my appreciation of vintage stores, I also had a secret love of vintage poets. This looked to me like a scene out of Longfellow's "The Children's Hour," about his amusement and love at watching his three daughters. In my version, Elle would be a stand-in for Longfellow's daughter Edith—Edith with golden hair—and Regina would be the laughing Allegra. That would leave me as grave Alice.

I handed Elle the Diane von Furstenberg wrap dress. She eagerly reached into the bag and pulled it out. "It will go perfectly with the new boots I just bought." She slid the dress over her head.

"Yes. I know."

"See, Elizabeth, it pays to live with a visionary," Reggie piped in now, dotting concealer under her eyes. "I can't wait to see what you come up with for me and my date Friday night."

"Speaking of which, you were out very late last night, Bailey," Elle said.

"It was a job interview for new restaurant. In fact, after you two quit hogging the bathroom, I need to get ready for a follow-up interview at noon."

"Is this a job interview or a date?" Elle eyed me suspiciously.

"I would like to hear the answer to that," Reggie added.

"This is just what happens in the restaurant business. I had to see if my incredible vision matched the Englishman's cooking. I am going back at noon for seconds." I smiled slyly. Elliott had awakened in me a "me" I liked.

"A nooner. Going back for seconds? I think our little Bailey girl is up to something," Reggie added.

"You said he was English. What's he like?" Elle asked.

"It's just a job interview. His name is Elliott. He is kind, and he does have a talent for cooking. I like him."

"Elliott the Englishman. I think I need to take you in hand and give you a makeover." Elle was adjusting her new dress.

I'd rather talk about makeup than about Elliott. "Besides, I haven't even accepted the job yet."

The girls exchanged looks. "But you will." Was it that obvious?

"Step aside. Let the master work. I need to get in your closet and find something that's going to play up the figure you keep hiding and accentuate your green eyes," Elle said.

"For the third time, this is just a job interview."

Elle shook her head. "Consider me to be helping you dress for success."

Both she and Reggie burst out laughing. "Maybe we're just keeping an eye on what you have cooking." Reggie walked out of the bathroom, suddenly leaving it very empty.

Chapter Thirteen

I wore the outfit Elle had picked out for me to meet Elliott.

He was sitting at one of the two tables when I walked in with my sketchbook. He showed no wear and tear from the prior evening. He looked refreshed. Handsome. He wore a darker pair of khakis and a brown-and-blue checked shirt. The blue in the shirt danced in complementary fashion with his eyes. He smiled as I approached him. A small arrangement of flowers punctuated the middle of the table. Fresh green hydrangeas mixed with some apricot-colored roses and a few sprigs of Queen Anne's lace.

"I didn't know if you would show or not." He got up to meet me.

"I make it a policy never to turn down free food." I shook his hand formally.

"There are no free lunches. I'm surprised Julian didn't tell you that."

"Touché." I quickly scanned the room to see if it held the same possibilities in the daylight that it had held the previous night. The sunlight added an extra dimension.

"I have French press coffee or Earl Grey tea. I find it a little difficult to totally abandon my English roots."

"By the way, nice flowers."

"I read somewhere that Henry Edgeworth named his first restaurant VERT because that was his little sister's favorite color. They're for you." I noticed a card attached.

"They're beautiful. I do love flowers. We love Queen Anne's lace in the South. It grows on the side of the road. I made Daddy keep a pair of shears in the car so we could pull over and cut them for his restaurant."

"I hoped you would approve. Now, tea or coffee?"

"I'll have what you're having."

He disappeared and brought a silver tray with a pot of hot water, a selection of teas, a sugar bowl, and a tray of scones. "An authentic English breakfast," I said.

We busied ourselves preparing our tea and plates. Elliott's scones were good, but my Southern brother could beat him every time.

After we finished and Elliott had removed the tray, our conversation picked up again.

"Do you know, I have never seen the entire space? Will you give me the grand tour, Elliott." It was my intent to stick strictly to business. Putting my attraction to Elliott aside, I was eager to see what possibilities this place offered.

We both stood up. He was about a head taller than I was.

"From your point of view," I went on. "I would like to hear about what brought you to this space and what you see. I want the full tour. I want to hear your impressions, good and bad."

"Wait a minute, I thought that was your job," he countered.

"A good visionary listens. Listening to you is essential because, ultimately, that will inform how I actually see the space transforming."

"You're quite something, Bailey Edgeworth. I don't think I have met too many people your age who have quite the same level of confidence."

"Really? How old do you think I am? And how old are you? You seem pretty confident."

"Oh no. I don't mean to be patronizing. I like it. I like it a lot. I know you worked a few years for Julian. So how old are you, about twenty-six?"

I would have to ask Elle, but I thought you really couldn't ask people their age during an interview. "I'm twenty-five. And you?"

"I'm twenty-eight. A young twenty-eight." He gave me a boyish grin, and I really couldn't argue with that. We seamlessly shifted back into a more businesslike mode. I was eager to see his space.

We walked around, and I nodded approvingly. The space was awash in potential. A blank canvas of possibilities. I could see the articles about Elliott. I could also envision the articles about me and how I partnered with this Englishman to create one of New York's finest dining establishments. But first things first.

"What do you see for the kitchen?"

"Not your job either?" he countered.

"No. I have lived with too many chefs, and I respect them too much to interfere with their kitchens. My job in the kitchen is purely aesthetic and to ease the workflow. What you choose to cook on, what knives you like, and your cookware—that's all you. Trust me, there's enough around here for me to do." I got quiet again, studying my surroundings and letting ideas percolate. He must've mistaken my silence for disapproval.

"You don't like the space? Do you think I've made a mistake?" Elliott asked.

"I didn't say that. I just need to focus." I walked deliberately, trying to commit to memory every nook and cranny. "Can I take some pictures?"

He nodded. I retrieved my phone and started snapping. I needed to think about how best to utilize this space. Like our previous meetings, the day just skipped away from us.

"You've done it to me again, Bailey. It is now getting to be suppertime. Do you expect me to cook you a third meal?"

"Are you offering?" I asked.

"I can take you out. There's nothing left in the kitchen to eat."

My brain switched off. I didn't want this to be a messy relationship where business was mixed with pleasure, and the lines got blurred. I had to keep my head when all about men were losing theirs, as Rudyard Kipling had said. "No. I can't stay for dinner. But why don't we sit down again and talk further about my design fee?"

"Okay then." Elliott seemed almost hurt. As if I had rebuked him.

"But I would be open to another cup of tea."

"I'll heat up the water now." While Elliott was away in the guerrilla-style kitchen that consisted of a hot plate, a kettle, a mini refrigerator, and a toaster oven, I made some preliminary notes.

When he returned with our tea, we began our negotiation. Elliott said, "Okay then, I'll just get right to it. I am prepared to offer you an extra fifty thousand dollars on top of the figure you have in your purse." Just who was this Elliott Graemmer, I wondered? Did he have that kind of discretionary money? I would definitely have to Google him when I got home.

"Here are my terms. I expect half up front, and I would like the other half in escrow upon completion of the job." I had learned a lot about negotiation from Julian. There were too many stories out there where good and talented designers had great vision but not so much finesse with money. I had seen many crash. I had only seen Julian lose money on one job the entire time I worked for him. While I didn't always concur with his vision, for example in my beloved restaurant VERT, I couldn't fault him on the way he handled financial transactions. He was the gold standard. No pun intended.

"Done. Here are my expectations. I want your exclusivity. I don't want you off on another job. I want you here, handling the situation so I can do what I do best, and that is plan the menu. I want us to be a team."

We shook hands, and he handed me a check, making our partnership official. To celebrate, Elliott put on a fresh pot of tea and brought in some scones. "Aren't you the least bit interested in what the card on the flowers says?"

I nodded and took the card. It read:

> Love of beauty is taste;
> The creation of beauty is art. —Ralph Waldo Emerson
> You create beauty and art, E.

He understood me. What I wanted to accomplish. We settled into comfortable small talk.

"You knew you were going to hire me all along?"

He nodded and grinned.

"Can I just ask you a personal question?" I asked.

"Go ahead. I have no secrets."

"What's your backstory, Elliott?"

He laughed out loud. "The short version is I've got some family support. My father was a chef. He was Queen Elizabeth's chef. Now he is a member of the House of Lords."

I had been rendered speechless. "So, Daddy is funding your little dream."

The expression on his face changed immediately. I could tell I had hit a nerve. A preemptive warning shot. "Don't make me sorry I hired you, Bailey. I thought you were different. I came to the United States because I wanted to make a name for myself. My name. My reputation. I thought you got that."

I did. After all, as I had often told Henry, what we become is the only thing we can truly take credit for. I was instantly sorry. "I do understand, Elliott. That's the reason I came to New York City too. I wanted to make my own reputation. Maybe we can help the other achieve our dreams." The tension evaporated into the late-night air. When I looked at my watch, I was astonished that it was two in the morning. And this became our nightly ritual. We could talk about anything. And everything. He would join my small and precious company of men. Without preamble, we unceremoniously crossed the threshold where business partners were becoming something much more.

The next morning, the girls ambushed me. "What's he like, Elliott the Englishman?"

"What do you mean?" I asked, ducking into the bathroom and away from their questions.

"You know what we mean." Elle blocked my admittance.

"It's not like that. I don't want to mix business with pleasure. Not yet." They seemed to be pacified, at least for the time being. It was never really about what, but who. I thought about it as I got ready. I wasn't entirely sure if my heart even belonged to me anymore. It had always belonged to Griffin. He was the owner, the proprietor, and the ruler. My heart may beat in my chest, but its gravitational pull tugged firmly toward Griffin. I had an image of Elliott and Griffin in this giant tug-of-war with my heart in the middle. Could I be devoted to Griffin and desire Elliott? In addition to my heart, would I lose myself in this imaginary tug-of-war?

Chapter Fourteen

Elliott was becoming a master of wooing. He brought me flowers weekly. And I noticed that with each arrangement, like his food, he always added something different and distinctive to make it special: an orchid with interesting shading, hybrid tulips, rare amaryllis, variegated succulents, and sometimes, cleverly placed English ivy to remind me of him. Many times, he would select a beautiful card sharing our mutual hopes and dreams and end by choosing a quote or line from one of my "favorite vintage poets," as he referred to Yeats, Browning, Shakespeare, and Keats. Our relationship bloomed as naturally as the flowers he selected. Was the terrain of my heart changing? I thought about both men. Griffin with some flimsy history and a single word: Bae. Whereas Elliott, with his romantic musings, was offering me flowers, beautiful notes, and a future awash in possibilities. Elliott understood the contours of my soul.

Elliott invited me to his apartment for a "simple" New Year's Eve supper. There was never anything simple about the way Elliott prepared a meal. But his invitation evoked feelings of apprehension and nervousness. I had never been to his apartment before, and something in me wondered if I was crossing over the threshold into new territory of our relationship. The restaurant would not open until April, and I didn't know if I could trust my own feelings to not go full force across the line. But I was also anxious to see what his apartment looked like. Would it reveal something new and different about this man that occupied such a central role in my life? I rang his doorbell at precisely 8 p.m. He greeted me at the door in a most casual manner, right down to his bare feet.

"Come in." While his feet conveyed an easy-going style, he spoke in a courtly demeanor. "You come bearing gifts." He looked delighted.

"Lower the bar," I said. "I wouldn't dare bring wine or champagne, lest it would conflict with what chef prepared, and I wouldn't want to incur chef's wrath!"

"Your punishment would be severe, Ms. Edgeworth, and I would show no mercy." We laughed. We embraced. I removed my coat, and he waved toward the rest of the apartment, indicating I could have a good look around while he finished up. My eyes landed on the small but familiar arrangement on the tiny table. The green hydrangeas, apricot-colored roses, and Queen Anne's lace brought a smile to my face.

"Feel free to poke around while I put the finishing touches on our supper." I liked that about him. No matter how grand the occasion or the meal he always referred to the meal at night as supper. It was very quaint.

His apartment was decidedly masculine. A big brown suede sofa weighed down the old and frayed Oriental rugs that ran throughout. Books on every subject were stacked high in a corner. It looked like an English country home or a Ralph Lauren ad. There were very few personal touches. No pictures of family and friends or travel adventures, except for the small sterling silver frame that housed a very old black-and-white picture I assumed was of his parents—with Her Majesty. Whether he knew it or not, his good breeding was on full display.

Supper would not disappoint. He had prepared plump lobster tails in a dill sauce, a citrus and Cointreau reduction compote, and roasted potatoes. For dessert, he served poached pears in Madeira with a pistachio and date ice cream. When he unveiled dessert he said, "something green for Bailey."

After dinner, we relaxed on the massive couch and settled into our usual comfortable conversation. As midnight approached, Elliott popped the cork on a bottle of champagne.

"I have something for you," I said.

"Oh, we've arrived at the gift-giving portion of the evening," he laughed. Because of the buzz that the restaurant had already generated, we had been invited to many social events, including art gallery openings. Perhaps it was on a night when better wine was served, and I had enjoyed it a little too much that I bid on and won a painting I thought would be perfect for Elliott's office.

"Bailey. I love it. You knew I would. It's not fair. I have to compete with your vision." He reached around the couch and produced a card and a very small box. The size of the box caused in me a surge of panic. "What?" he asked. "Did you think I would not get you something? What kind of total imbecile would I be to not want to acknowledge a holiday that celebrates beginnings?"

I read the card first. It began with a quote from Shelley: "Ah the dawn of the New Year! May we find inner peace, gentle spirit, God's grace, forgiveness, dreams, and prayers."

For a chef, he was a beautiful writer. Then he presented me with the box. I opened it gently and slowly. I was speechless. It was the beautiful coral and opal brooch I had spied and fallen in love with but deemed too expensive in my favorite vintage shop, The Sleepy Anarchist.

"How did you know? How did you know?" I repeated. I felt like a silly schoolgirl.

"You are not the only one who studies things. I know you go into that eclectic shop. I counted on them knowing you. They did, of course, because you are so memorable. They told me you had your heart set on this. I wanted to see you smile."

"But you hate vintage stores," I said.

"True. Maybe you could help me learn to like them."

"It's beautiful." We stood up and he carefully and deliberately attached the brooch to my collar. His eyes met mine and an unspoken question formed. I felt the electricity between us surge throughout my body. My heart started beating faster. He pulled me closer. He looked at me for a moment longer as if the question had been answered. We then shared our very first kiss.

Far, far away from the revelers at Times Square, far away from the chandeliered ballrooms strewn with confetti, far away from TV-lined restaurants muted to make way for noisemakers and the sound of corks popping, far away from the sounds of laughter, inebriation, and desire, we stood together, a new couple, on the threshold of falling in love. As the clock struck midnight, we kissed again, but my heart and head declared open warfare on each other. I had poured all my energies into my career and ambition. Suddenly I felt like I resided in two places, one belonging to my head and the other my heart. This damn tug-of-war. Griffin was comfort food. Elliott was like an exotic and exciting dish that Anthony Bourdain would have showcased. I was eager to sample.

"If it's your plan to leave, you better leave now before things get too much more out of hand," Elliott said. I was finding it very hard to choose. New love can be so intoxicating.

After a brief moment, I said, "Why don't we leave the decision to my Uber app . . . " My voice trailed off. Elliott brought out a playful side of me I liked. I pulled my phone out and hit the familiar app. And waited. I looked down. I saw the answer. "Two minutes away. Why do you live in such an upscale neighborhood that has so many Uber drivers?" I said, stepping away from him. From my own feelings. Relief flooded me like an engine when you floor the gas to make a hasty getaway.

"FU," he said.

I looked at him quizzically.

"Fuck Uber," he said and smiled. And we ended the night with laughter, like so many other nights. But the landscape of my heart was most definitely changing. Elliott made me smile. He made me laugh. Elliott made me forget work. For once, it was nice to see the tangible expression of a man's love: the flowers, his cards, and his beautiful notes. He made me feel loved. He made me feel desired. For the first time in my life, I felt like a real woman.

Chapter Fifteen

I consulted my expansive go-to file for architects, painters, and interior decorators. Walls were torn down. Walls were erected and painted. My original idea for the color of the walls, a watery celery, turned into a diluted honeydew. It was perfect. It made me think of the wonderful honeydew and mint sorbet that Griffin had concocted the night of prom.

People came. Workers went. Days turned into weeks. The weeks turned into months. Countless cups of hot tea and coffee and bottles of wine were consumed. My to-do lists grew, and then they shrunk. Elliott and I had only a few minor dustups since the original one about his family. We were both very busy. While we enjoyed our days together, we did not blur the lines between business and pleasure. I was proud of that. Proud of myself. I was learning a lot about myself and learning a lot about Elliott. I liked the people we were becoming.

It was a Friday. It seemed like the right time to hang the painting with its brand-new frame that I had bought so many months ago. Occasionally, I would bring in a bag with interesting things like the antique sterling silver salt cellars I had bought in a consignment store to introduce something vintage into the aesthetic. I liked the idea of having a sea of modern with one element from the past. But I'd been waiting to present him with the painting to see if all of my elements had come together as I imagined. They had. Next Friday would be the soft open. We were inviting a lot of our friends, so the restaurant could work out any kinks before the grand opening. I was lucky that Henry had agreed to come next week.

I had the workers hang the painting on the wall near the bathrooms. When I showed Elliott, he loved the painting and the placement.

"It's wonderful, Bailey." He looked at it proudly, even reverently. We smiled at each other and at the restaurant we were building together. I felt we were almost like proud parents.

"I think this calls for a little celebration. I have a cold bottle of champagne in the refrigerator." Elliott disappeared, and within a few minutes he was back with a good bottle and two glasses. As he fiddled with the cork, I looked at him and then the painting. Nighttime was staking its claim to the city, which seemed so typical for us.

For a man of means, he had a hard time opening it. I found his ineptness endearing. He finally poured the champagne into our glasses.

"To us. To our little restaurant. To achieving our dreams." We hadn't quite achieved our dreams, not yet anyway, but as usual, I nitpick.

We toasted with champagne. It was the good stuff. However, it seemed like an incomplete moment. Like it needed something else. A kiss perhaps. But I had been the picture of restraint since New Year's Eve with Elliott, and I was not going to let my guard down. Not yet. We both sat down and easily entered into our customary conversations.

As we chatted, we heard a loud noise in the back. Urgent footsteps came toward us. Then from the dark emerged a small-framed woman with short, jet-black hair dressed from head to toe in black. She carried a big red satchel. Elliott's demeanor changed immediately. In fact, the whole vibe of the restaurant changed. Was it just my imagination, or did the temperature inside get about thirty degrees cooler all at once?

Elliott rose to his feet. The expression of happiness drained from his face. It was replaced by one of serious dread.

"Jane. There's someone I want you to meet." She didn't seem the least bit interested, but she humored him. "Jane, this is Bailey."

I extended my hand to this little quirky-looking woman who was a good deal older than Elliott. She did not extend her hand back to me. But simply nodded and said hello.

"Come on, be nice, Lady Jane." The look on my face begged the question. Elliott did not make me wait. "Bailey, this is Jane. My wife."

I don't remember what niceties were exchanged with that woman. I am sure there was an attempt because, after all, I *am* Southern. All I know is that I gathered up my things in a most efficient manner, got myself home, and retrieved the nearest bottle of bourbon I could lay claim to. I got a glass and shut the door to my bedroom.

In the whole tenure of our relationship, Elliott had never mentioned a wife. We had talked about so many soul-bearing subjects that you would think he would have at least mentioned that he was married. Did he have children? What did I really know about Elliott? A tsunami of uncomfortable emotions coursed through my body like boiling blood. Anger. Confusion. Stupidity. Betrayal. Sadness. Every uncomfortable emotion crisscrossed feverishly through my body. I hated him. I hated myself. But I really loved the bourbon I was drinking. The phone rang. It was Griffin.

"Hey, Bae. It's me. Are you ready for your opening next week?" he asked.

I would've been ready about two hours ago, I wanted to say. "I guess so. I really wish you were coming." Right now, I needed Griffin more than my brother.

"I know. But I'll be there for the grand opening. The big shindig. Henry will be a good eye and audience for you."

"Yes. But he's not you." I sounded like an insecure schoolgirl, and I hated myself anew. There was a long pause between us.

"Hey, are you all right? Has that Englishman done something to hurt you?" I was supposed to be a grown-ass woman, and I needed to handle it myself. Griffin had told me he was out of the caretaking business. I knew that meant me too. I took a deep breath and pulled myself together.

"I'm fine. You know how it is. He has one vision. I have another. You know I nitpick. We just had a last-minute artistic difference of opinion." An unmentioned wife is a little more than an artistic difference, I kept thinking.

"If you're sure," Griffin responded. I gave him the best gift I could give him: ignorance of the situation.

"I am. It will all be ironed out when you get here."

"Okay. I just wanted to give you a heads up about your brother."

This scared me. I could tell that Griffin was not going to give me the gift of ignorance. "Oh Jesus. Is he back in rehab? The last few times I've seen him he was sober as a judge, what happened?"

Griffin laughed. "Nothing like that. Henry has been walking the straight and narrow. I just wanted to tell you myself. You're getting a new addition."

I was confused. "Are you and Henry opening up a new restaurant?" There had been some talk that they might add another restaurant to their color wheel. For the second time, Griffin laughed.

"No, Bailey. You are in for some big news," he said. I'd had enough of that for one night. "Now, you will have to act surprised when your brother tells you. I know you hate surprises. Henry is a daddy. He has a three-year-old son, and his name is Hank. Henry has been to court and was granted full custody. You will fall in love."

How much bourbon had I actually consumed tonight? "What the hell? What are you telling me?"

"I could see Henry telling you all this in a crowded restaurant. That would be just like him. But I think it is a good thing for him. A steadying thing. He's so different, Bae."

"You said 'court.' You said 'custody.' What the hell are you talking about?" I got the spare bottle of water I kept under my bedside table and took a big swig. I needed to sober up. Fast.

Griffin proceeded to tell me that back during my brother's checkered dating history, he had an affair with a waitress from Guatemala. She didn't stay around long. A few months ago, Henry got a call from DSS telling him that the woman had been in a fatal car wreck, leaving a son whose birth certificate listed Henry Edgeworth as the father.

"Is that it?"

"Just one more thing, I promise. Hank doesn't speak much English." This was too much information all at one time. For some reason, I just started laughing, and I couldn't stop. Griffin started laughing too. "I guess I can see how this would all be a little overwhelming. In trying to put it together to tell you, I must admit I did have to laugh. Especially imagining the way your brother might tell it. You wouldn't believe how he has cleaned his act up, and Henry had a whole lot to clean up. He is going to raise the boy by himself. You can already tell he's smitten. I am going to be looking for my own place so he can turn my room into Hank's. Bailey, I want your promise that you will be supportive. There is a thing called a second act. Forget what F. Scott Fitzgerald said. Your brother, my best friend, is entitled to his."

Hearing Griffin defend my brother, in its own way, was a thing of beauty. I knew then that Griffin hadn't gotten out of the caretaking business altogether. I had taken him at his word, because that's what he wanted me to do. We had that much honesty between us. Henry had a son and Elliott had a wife. That was fucking dandy a week before the biggest night of my life.

Chapter Sixteen

The week before the opening, things were definitely off kilter between Elliott and me. The introduction of Jane brought with it a whole lot of unforeseen trouble. She never moved around quietly. When she and Elliott had a conversation, it was never in whispered tones but always in raised voices. To say they were mercurial was an understatement. I now know what Paul McCartney felt like. Elliott and Jane were like the culinary equivalent of John Lennon and Yoko Ono to my Paul McCartney. Pots and pans were on the wall and the next moment on the floor. Besides feeling like a third wheel, I felt like a marriage counselor or a child trying to smooth things over between feuding parents.

Elliott made apologies. Over and over. I got the feeling he really didn't even like Jane. That conversation was for another day. The day of the opening, I felt at peace. I felt that whatever Elliott and I had created was good, and nothing Lady Jane could do would get in the way of our success. My brother came. He looked good. And happy.

The restaurant opening was teeming with people. Excited people. You had to almost slither through tables to speak to everyone. This is the way my daddy loved it. I wished he could have been there, and something in me wondered why he wasn't, although he did call and extend his congratulations.

I introduced Henry to Elliott. Elliott shook Henry's hand and then made his rounds like a triumphant victor. Henry and I stood at the front of the restaurant and watched the crowds interact. I loved every minute of it. I could tell my brother did too.

Henry handed me my drink of choice, a sidecar, while he nursed a tonic water with lime. That in itself would've elicited a joke from me, but I could detect a sea change in my brother, and I was willing to honor Griffin's request and be supportive.

"My little sister has done it. They are going to be talking about this restaurant for a long time. What you've done with the place is magical. I love the way the artwork complements the wall color. Did you select the artwork? The salt cellars were an unexpected touch." Little did Henry know that that was the highest compliment he could've bestowed.

"I can perform this magic for you anytime. I appreciate you coming."

"I wouldn't be anywhere else. That Englishman is a bit odd. He is very peculiar in the way he cooks, but you can't argue in that he knows what he's doing. He is talented. A word of advice: if he's going to make it, he needs to either hire a baker or go to Balthazar and invest in some of their interesting selections of breads."

I smiled. I knew my Southern brother would hit on the bread. Who knew that a Southern man could bake a scone better than an Englishman? But then again, my brother inherited the nitpicking gene just as I had.

The next morning when we were having breakfast together, Henry told me his news. There was no laughter or awkwardness. In fact, he spoke in tones of respect for the mother of his child and love for the son he had. The news brought tears I hadn't expected. My thoughts reflected on that wretched intervention. I felt gratitude that we had repaired our relationship. Henry had other news—news that Griffin had not shared with me. "I want you to talk to Dad with me and Griffin. He needs to retire. He's very forgetful. I think he needs to sell the big house and move into something smaller."

"I think Daddy would rather die than retire." But we often don't get a say-so in our own aging process.

The next week brought the official grand opening of our restaurant, Griffin's arrival, and Lady Jane's departure. Things had settled back down into a natural ebb and flow between Elliott and me. But underneath, I was still very angry at him.

We opened a bottle of champagne. "To tomorrow night. Here's hoping for a good night." We toasted, and then I gave him the present I had purchased before Jane arrived. "Bailey, you are going to spoil me." And then he looked at the sport coat and tried it on. It looked even better on him than in the box.

"What do you think?" I asked. He looked handsome.

"I think it clashes," he began. "I think there's too much of something." He pretended to remove a imaginary wedding ring. "I think it clashes with a wife. So if given the choice, I choose you and to get rid of the wife."

I hadn't prepared for this. But that's not to say I didn't welcome it. He took another sip of champagne and moved closer to me. He pulled me close and began slowly kissing me. I jerked away. I needed to hear the words. "What are you saying, Elliott?"

"I'm saying I choose you. I sent Lady Jane home. Back to England. We are going to get a divorce, American-style. She doesn't like it here, and I don't like it there. We settled things before she left. This seemed to be the right moment to tell you. I think you must know how I feel. You are the most amazing woman, Bailey. I'm saying I love you." He approached again, but this time, he kissed my cheek and brushed the hair out of my eyes. "I want you by my side when I open up my restaurant tomorrow night. But you should probably go home right now because I can't promise you I will be a perfect gentleman. You are driving me crazy. Driving me to drink." He went to the bar and poured himself a glass of Glenlivet—my brother's favorite, once upon a time. No man had ever said those words to me. Not even Griffin. Elliott saw me as a woman, not as a girl he needed to protect. Elliott saw me as an equal. That was more intoxicating than any drink I had ever had.

Griffin arrived in the afternoon. He was staying at a hotel in Midtown. When I offered to get him a room closer to me and the restaurant, he responded, "I will leave this Bohemian paradise you call your neighborhood to you. But I have an extra bed in case you want to crash." Griffin had logged too much time now in Buckhead, and it showed. Griffin's arrival made me nervous. More nervous than I wanted to admit. I needed him to be blown away by the restaurant. I wanted him to see me. See my talent. But I also wondered, had we moved on? Really moved on? I mean, did Griffin expect me to stay with him tonight? Did I want to stay with him? And what about Elliott?

Griffin picked me up, and we rode to the restaurant together. Our conversation mainly centered on the restaurant and how Henry was relishing his "second act." Again, I was grateful that the three of us had survived intact.

When we arrived at the restaurant, it was already in motion. The sound of happiness surrounded us. People everywhere were having a great time. I saw Elle and Reggie and their boyfriends, Robbie and David. A large and glorious arrangement of flowers greeted us as we approached the hostess stand. I learned they were sent by Griffin. I turned to him and smiled and noticed that they matched the walls. I was pleased. He stood at the mouth of the restaurant and just observed. Elliott came up and introductions were made.

"Thanks for the flowers, mate. What do you think about my restaurant?" Elliott was eager to hear Griffin's opinion. So was I.

"I think it looks great, man. You can really tell Bailey brought her A game. Every little detail. That is going to make this place really sizzle. You got all the details right, Bae." He turned to me and mouthed "fantastic."

"We know it looks good, but what do you think about the food?" Elliott shot back defensively. More defensively than he should have been.

"Haven't gotten that far, man."

"I reserved a table. It's . . . " But I couldn't find the open table I had reserved.

"My mistake," Elliott interjected. "I thought you had reserved that for us, Bailey. I gave it to someone else."

Something caught my eye. I looked down where the menus were stacked, and I saw a small arrangement of flowers—just what Elliott had given me on New Year's Eve. It was sweet. I smiled. Griffin's large arrangement made this one look paltry. And I instantly knew the real reason Elliott had taken it off the reserved table. He did not want to be dwarfed by Griffin's largesse.

"No worries. I can just eat at the bar. Bailey has told me what an outstanding chef you are, Elliott. I'm eager to sample the menu. Anything you would highly recommend?"

"Everything. Anything. Anything you want. It's on me."

I hated that Griffin was going to have to squeeze between people to sit at the bar, but he was low maintenance and made his way over. I was hoping that instead of having him order off the menu, Elliott had given it some thought and was going to have things sent to Griffin so he would be astonished like I was the first time Elliott cooked for me.

It was loud in the restaurant. The good kind of loud, when everything is working on all cylinders. Elliott clinked his glass of champagne with a knife. He wanted to make a speech.

"Welcome to Blank Graemmer. For those of you who hated grammar as much I did, the word should be evident. Thank you all for coming. If you will bear with me a moment, I would like to say a few words. This restaurant is a love letter for two people. A love letter to my father, who will always be the most excellent chef I know. Everything you eat tonight will be influenced by him. But this restaurant wasn't solely influenced by my father. It is also a love letter to my partner in crime, the woman who has been here day in and day out, sharing my hopes and dreams and . . . her love of vintage shopping with you. She has shared her enthusiasm and spirit and, last but never least, her unique and talented vision. My dearest friend and soul mate, Bailey Edgeworth. Cheers, everyone, and let me know if we can do anything to make your dining experience better." He leaned over with his glass and toasted me. I was somewhat taken aback by the public display of affection but touched that he expressed himself so eloquently. We parted so that we could mix and mingle with our guests. I headed for the bar to catch up with Griffin.

He handed me a sidecar. It tasted different from the week before. "Yummy. The bartender did something different," I said.

"Yes. He let me mix it for you. I have totally gone new-school on my sidecars. I've always made yours with bourbon, opting out of the usual brandy." I just smiled at him and clinked his glass of Saratoga water with mine. "To you, Bae."

I gulped the first one down, and the second one went down with equal ease.

"Go easy. Why are you acting so nervous? This place is amazing. Don't you want to eat something?"

Eat? My insides resembled the contents of the blender. Shaken. Stirred. In disarray.

I felt the tiniest bit of sweat creep into the palm of my hand and onto the back of my neck. My past and present were colliding. I was still so angry at Elliott, but I wanted Griffin to approve of him. I accepted another drink from the bartender, and Griffin took it away and asked for a glass of sparkling water. Designing restaurants was my gift; juggling two men in the same room clearly was not. I couldn't say who was winning the tug-of-war. Certainly not my heart. It felt like the rope was squarely around my neck, constricting airflow into my lungs. Feeling nauseous and hyperventilating, I willed myself to settle down. For the next hour, Griffin received and exchanged plates of food. Watching him eat soothed my nerves. "That boy knows what he's doing in the kitchen. I'll give him that."

"I will say, he is a different kind of chef than you and Henry are. You both seem to whip up whatever is around. Elliott is a little picky.

He wants a certain kind of ingredient and nothing else will do. He may spend a truckload of money on truffles or green cardamom, but from your samples, I think you can tell it's worth it. He's a bit of a perfectionist."

"I'll bet. I would hate to pay his bills. And did you get a look at his sport coat?"

"That came from an upscale consignment store," slipped out. I blamed it on that second sidecar. But Griffin said nothing. He was not going to spoil my night.

He met my roommates and liked them immediately. They exchanged looks with each other and then looked at me. Then at Griffin. I had no idea what they were trying to tell me. "Lady World," I said, which was their cue that I had no idea what they were thinking.

Elle had consumed just enough cocktails to answer honestly: "I'm glad we finally got to meet the famous brother last week and now the equally famous Griffin. Little Bailey here did not tell us you were so good-looking."

It was Reggie's turn. "She talks about you all the time. It's nice to see the missing puzzle pieces of Bailey's life. Elle is right, she talks about how talented you all are, but she never mentioned your handsome looks before."

I was getting embarrassed. "Y'all are drunk. I am cutting you off . . ."

"I think I like talking to these wonderful ladies who obviously have good taste," Griffin piped up. They were having fun at my expense, and I was having a blast. I loved having the people I loved enjoy each other.

When the crowds thinned out, and closing time approached, it was clear we had had a good night. Elliott seemed somewhat taken aback when I left with Griffin. I wanted to get Griffin's feedback. I needed his feedback. I figured there would be time and many chances for Elliott and me to sit down and replay the night's events. Elliott was quiet as he watched us leave together.

We passed the front desk and concierge station before taking the elevator to Griffin's room. I was exhausted. Last week after the soft open, I could've stayed awake all night on pure adrenaline. But tonight, with the grand opening, I had nothing left. The room did not boast two beds, just a king-size bed that was terribly inviting. I didn't care.

"In that big Mary Poppins satchel of yours, do you have something to sleep in?" Griffin asked. He had always mocked my big bags. He would have looked utterly confused if I announced my overstuffed satchel to be "on fleek."

I pulled out a half bottle of Fiji water, a can of LaCroix, a notebook, a decorator's binder of fabric samples I had forgotten to return, my wallet bulging with credit cards and cash, ChapStick, lipstick, lip gloss, several pens, a couple of knobs, mascara, Neosporin, my phone and charger, and, at the bottom of my bag, I fingered the shirt.

"Oh my. That really is Mary Poppins's bag," Griffin said, already removing his sport coat and shoes.

I pulled it out and went into the bathroom. I took all my clothes off and left them in a small pile on the floor. I put on the shirt. As I emerged from the bathroom, Griffin glanced at me. He resumed his task, then looked at me again. Did he recognize it? It had been such a long time.

"You're rocking the flannel, Bae." But he said nothing else. Neither did I. Crawling into the bed, I didn't tell him that I wore his shirt not only when I was cold or tired, I wore it when I was sad. I wore it when I was happy. I wore it when I needed something I couldn't quite define. I wore it when I needed to be close to home. The faded blue and green only made it softer. More precious. Sometimes I didn't need to wear it at all. I just needed to know it was there. It was my most treasured "vintage" item I owned. When I stretched out in the bed, it was as if Wynken, Blynken, and Nod had personally scooped me up in their wooden shoe. I wasn't sure I actually told Griffin how my vision for the walls went from a watery celery and turned into a diluted honeydew or whether I had traversed into sleep and was still talking.

I had no idea what time it was when I finally woke up. I had the distinct feeling morning had started without me. These "heavenly beds" certainly lived up to their billing.

When I was almost awake, I realized I was in the nook of Griffin's body, and his arms were wrapped loosely around me. Neither one of us had a notion to move. "You were tired," Griffin said, still not moving or shifting. "I could tell you looked thinner. You've been working too hard." Nothing was said for a while. Maybe Griffin thought he had chastised me because he added in my ear, "My God, you amaze me, Bae. Can you really comprehend what you pulled off last night? I am so impressed by what you've done. By what you've become. Your reputation is well deserved. You completely blew me away with your talent."

Maybe I was still worn out, because I felt tears roll down my face. I didn't want him to see. I didn't want Griffin to see my vulnerability. But it is very hard to hide such feelings. Still, we did not move even though the morning was trying to nudge us into action.

"I wanted you to be proud of me," I whispered.

"You didn't need to go to New York City and open up a restaurant with a shitty Englishman to do that. I am blown away by who you are." There was still no movement, just the sound of our breathing. Together. And quite easily, effortlessly really, we came together as we had done after their openings. Sweetly and passionately. Emotions tumbled out in mutual affection. I wish I had been wise enough to commit this to my well of memories.

Afterword, we stayed connected, our breathing labored before returning to normal. Still, we made no effort to disconnect.

"Now, will you come back to Atlanta where you belong?" Griffin mumbled in my ear like sweet nothings.

"No," I shrieked, turning my body to face him. "I didn't ask you and Henry to stop opening restaurants after VERT. I don't want to be a Johnny One-Note. Besides," I said, breezily, "I have three projects already starting. One Peruvian restaurant, an Indian restaurant, and the college cafeteria in Ohio."

I was feeling too good and too happy to fight with him. Needless to say, the mood was broken. Griffin untangled himself. "I'm going to order us a proper breakfast. That means French press coffee. Not the damn Earl Grey stuff he makes you drink."

I laughed. And I returned the lightness of the moment with my own rejoinder. "I guess we can check the box that says we've had 'concierge on the premises sex' now."

He laughed as I knew he would. "A concierge always makes sex better, Bae. I've dated girls who wouldn't dream of having sex unless there *was* a concierge on the premises." He laughed.

"You are such a Buckhead snob," I said, and part of me hated for the moment to end. "Before you leave, we should call Henry and see how the new daddy is. Can I take a hot bath before we have to check out?"

"That's a great idea. Take as long a bath as you want. You know, Bailey, you could take some of your own money and check into a hotel and get a decent night's sleep once in a while. Better than you spending money on outfitting that dandy Englishman."

"I could. But you don't always come with the room." I realized what I said and how it must sound. I quickly corrected myself, "I didn't mean . . . ," I said, lowering myself into the bubble bath.

"It's okay, I know what you meant," Griffin said and then stuck his head into the bathroom. "But it would've been okay if you had."

I didn't say anything. I wondered if we should've had a talk about our relationship. It would have been hard, and it could have ended us.

Chapter Seventeen

"So, little Bailey, which one did you go home with?" Elle eyed me suspiciously, letting it register that she knew I had on the same clothes this morning as the night before. Reggie poked her head out so she could hear the answer.

"I went back to the hotel with Griffin. That was my plan all along. I wanted to hear his feedback about the restaurant. He had two queen-size beds. I was completely exhausted. I crawled in bed and crashed." Well, some of it was true. "Besides, I have big news for you. My brother has full custody of his three-year-old son, Hank. We FaceTimed with him this morning before Griffin left." I had loved that. Griffin had never FaceTimed before, so I got to show him how. I couldn't tell them, but my heart was about to burst open.

"Are you trying to tell us that you have two good-looking guys, one a foreigner, and you didn't sleep with either of them? God, Bailey, you're hopeless!"

"Totally agree," Reggie added. "It's completely obvious that they are both crazy about you. Are you that oblivious?"

"No. I like Elliott a lot. Just so you know, we have been trying to keep our relationship very businesslike until the restaurant is up and going. So we'll see where things go. Speaking of which, I need to change and get down there or I'll be late."

"I think we all know where this is going," Elle said. It's hard to argue with a woman's intuition.

Thank God they had totally focused on Elliott, not Griffin. How could I possibly describe him? Paragraphs that began with ellipses followed by disconnected prepositional phrases and commas, peppered with air quotes, a truckload of exclamation points thrown in for good measure, and an end with question marks. I was grateful their attention had landed on Elliott.

I changed my clothes, ran a brush through my hair, brushed my teeth, grabbed my satchel, made a pit stop, and headed for the restaurant. I was anxious to see and talk to Elliott.

I put my satchel on a chair and approached Elliott. Immediately, I could tell something was very wrong. It was like a dark cloud had taken residence over him. "What's wrong?" I reached over to touch him.

He pulled away. "My back hurts. Where were you all night?"

"You know I stayed with Griffin. He had two beds. I totally crashed. I was exhausted. Maybe that's what's wrong with your back—your bed. I wanted to get Griffin's feedback. Remember? I told you that. By the way, he was just blown away by your cooking. And he doesn't give compliments out freely."

"Oh really? I thought he was blown away by your vision." I could tell he was in pain, but he was acting like a jealous husband.

"I think you know you were a big success. And I think you need to make an appointment with the doctor." I had almost started believing my own lies. But my small secret about Griffin paled in comparison to him obscuring that he had a wife. I considered us even.

"I sent Lady Jane home. I'm getting a divorce. What can I do?" he pleaded.

"You basically lied to me for months. I want to ask you some questions, but I will only ask once. Are there any more secrets? Children? Crazy aunts in the attic?"

"No. That's it. Just a bad back and a soon-to-be ex-wife. But when I told you I loved you, that was real. That was honest." But how was I to know that the ex-wife would be the easier thing to get rid of?

"I need some time to process this. When will your divorce be final?"

"Not long." He grabbed my hand, but I pulled it away.

"This is new for me. New terrain. I have never had a boyfriend and certainly not one who is married. We are not like you Europeans. Wives and girlfriends taking vacations together. We are pretty monogamous over here." I almost tripped over the word even as I said it. Monogamous.

"I'm counting on that, Bailey. It is nice to celebrate with you."

For the next few months, we were on a constant high. I moved on to other jobs. But at night, I returned to Elliott. The restaurant garnered countless good reviews. It got lots of attention, lots of traffic. The waiting list for a reservation grew. Ironically, I thought it might just be Elliott's restaurant that turned our little neighborhood into the "up-and-coming SoHo." We each were celebrated. Magazines came and did profiles on Elliott and his restaurant. I was always mentioned with my own culinary pedigree. We went to openings. We went to parties. We sipped the finest wine and champagne. We gave Uber a lot of business. These were heady times. But I had not yet returned to Elliott's apartment. My feelings were still in a state of flux.

When we weren't attending parties or grand openings, we were working. We both worked constantly. Success takes a lot of work. I had no idea just how much. Daddy, Henry, and Griffin all made it look easy. Elliott had become increasingly dependent on me. He would ask me to restock items I had originally ordered. I would leave my "day" jobs, the ones that were paying me, and then I would slip into the role of handler, counselor, problem-solver, or ego-booster to Elliott, who no longer paid me. I had never before been involved in the day-to-day operations of the restaurants I designed. It put a strain on me.

Elliott's back pain never seemed to abate. It was possible I was just a little too unrealistic. I wanted our "first time" to be when we were both excited, not worn out, drunk, or in pain. But there were always little displays of Elliott's love and affection. A lingering glance, an unexpected squeeze of my hand, a playful peck on the cheek as he passed by me, a gentle caress to chase away frowns that conveyed my worry, a single stolen kiss in the kitchen when we were alone, a loving shoulder massage. Sometimes he would just scoop me up into his arms and kiss me with a lovely reckless abandonment as if he couldn't possibly stand it for one minute longer; other times he would pick me up and we would leave the restaurant altogether and walk hand in hand in the neighborhood we called our second home, stopping in stores to browse like a normal couple, letting the sunlight warm our faces. Elliott was patient with me, never pushing me for more. He literally wore my anger down.

Token gifts appeared, like scented candles and soaps, and more extravagant gifts, like a much-wished-for strand of beads with interesting stones from The Sleepy Anarchist with Elliott's business card attached. On the back it read: "Always, E." That was his customary way of signing anything to me now, even when we were ordering something mundane like arugula. One time, he left me a handsome gray box, and inside was a beautiful flower pin that looked like it had diamonds as petals and a beautiful pink stone for the center (which I would learn was a pink sapphire). It looked to me like vintage Van Cleef & Arpels. The card:

Yes. It is real. Flowers of all kinds deserve to be real. So is my love. Always, E. PS: Your love of vintage has now proven costly! But please, don't worry: we had a good week.

And flowers, there were always flowers in beautiful vases with accompanying love letters to match, and a week never passed without there being something green, even if it was a simple green ribbon tied to my coffee mug or wineglass. His gifts and thoughtfulness always took me by surprise and always had the capacity to make my heart expand just a little bit more. It seemed the gravitational pull of my heart was changing its course.

I often thought the Victorian poets were onto something with this courting business. There was something to be said about longing, about wanting, about desiring, and, yes, about waiting for the right time and the right person.

Midafternoon was slowly becoming my favorite part of the day, before patrons started trickling in, before the cooking crew came to work, before some crisis could seize our attention. It was just us, at a small table, having a cup of tea and enjoying the precious moments we had together before they were stolen from us by the day's occupations. I felt like me. A mature me. The feeling was intoxicating.

"I was thinking of going home over the long Labor Day weekend," I said. We had already decided to close. I felt like I could steal away without missing a beat.

"Hmm, why don't you take the week before Labor Day off. Go see the other men in your life and then come back to me. I want us to spend Labor Day together. Spend the whole weekend in my apartment. We won't even have to leave. I'll cook for us."

I understood. Elliott must prefer planned sex. It was fine by me. It gave me something to look forward to.

I played along. "I don't want you cooking in the kitchen all the time."

"Who says anything about cooking in the kitchen at all?" He smiled and took my hand in his. Just the way he touched me was both tender and exciting.

"Touché." I was filled with nervousness. And I knew just who would help me with my dilemma.

❧

"Well I sure hope to hell you're not going to go to one of those vintage stores you like and buy some old granny nightgown," Elle said. Both she and Reggie were home alone on a rare night and I had told them about my Labor Day plans.

"She's right. This deserves a full-frontal assault in the department stores. Bloomingdale's and Saks Fifth Avenue, here we come.

We'll get you all fixed up," Reggie added, and my excitement faded quickly, thinking about my first bra purchasing experience and how long it might take for these girls to get me into proper attire.

"You think Elliott is the kind of guy that likes all that negligee stuff?" In my very limited experience, men did not seem to care too much. But I must've brought up a valid point because the girls looked at each other and seriously considered my question.

"Let's think about this a minute," Elle said. "Our Bailey makes a good point."

"Maybe not Elliott. But I bet someone like Griffin would really appreciate it," Reggie piped in authoritatively. I hope I concealed the big grin I was wearing on the inside. How wrong these poor girls were.

"Totally," Elle agreed. "Griffin would definitely be old-school. Elliott strikes me as a down-to-business person,"

"Are you saying that we don't have to shop at all?" I asked.

"No way. You're not getting out of our little shopping adventure that easily," Elle admonished.

"Why don't we go Sunday after I get out of church and hit Saks's lingerie department first?" Reggie proposed.

When Sunday came and the elevator doors opened to the lingerie department at Saks, I froze. Almost the entire enormous floor was dedicated to women's underthings. "Oh my Lord. This is like Lady World on steroids," I said in amazement. My eyes tried to take it all in.

"Are you looking at the merchandise, or your vision thing?" Reggie deduced.

"Sorry. Occupational hazard," I admitted. But my eyes had already landed on something definitely feminine.

"Let's pick out something red. How about red, Bailey?" Elle suggested.

"No. I don't like red. I don't feel good in red," I said, and Elle backed off.

But I was already walking toward the nightgown I had spied earlier. It was beautiful. It was long and silky and mint green. If you could touch something as inanimate as a nightgown lovingly, that is the way I touched it.

"I like this one," I said.

"For my *mother*," Elle exaggerated. "Not for you. You need something sexy."

"I want something long and flowy. I want something feminine and romantic. Like this." I pulled the nightgown off the rack in my size to get a better look.

"Did you hear that, Reggie? I think hell is freezing over, or is that our little Bailey growing into a woman?"

"I think it's pretty," Reggie said and hugged me. Then she slipped me a naughty black number.

Four hours later, I left Saks with enough bags and undergarments to get me through the next century. I was in complete shock at the price of what "barely nothing" and flimsy lace cost. Outside, I had agreed to take them to dinner for all their help. "Thank you, guys. You are the best friends ever." Elle gave me a high five, and Reggie gave me a hug, the kind of absorbing hug a mother would give a child, so tight you couldn't see where one person ended and the other began.

Chapter Eighteen

Two weeks later, a month before I was to go home, I received a call from Henry. Daddy was in the hospital after suffering a fall. He was disoriented. In addition to motor impairment on his left side, Daddy had been diagnosed with Alzheimer's.

"I'll come home immediately. Who's looking after little Hank and the restaurants?" I asked, although the answer seemed pretty clear to me.

"Griff." Getting out of the caretaking business altogether my ass, I thought. "Listen, Bailey, I need you to sit tight for a few days. They're running a bunch of tests. Let me see where we are in the next day or two, and you and I'll come up with a plan. Right now, I just need to keep Dad quiet and still."

It surprised me how much my brother sounded like an adult. Maybe Henry himself was in the caretaking business. Looking after the restaurants, looking after little Hank, and now looking after Daddy. Now that Daddy was in the hospital, we talked on the phone several times a week, and I was amazed constantly by Henry's efficiency in his efforts on Daddy's behalf. We talked about Daddy as if he were no longer there. It just seemed as if parts of his mind had already joined my mother.

"Listen, you have a plane ticket for next Friday," Henry said. I quickly told him I would be there a full two weeks.

"Okay, then. Thanks, Bailey. I need to get Dad settled into the rehab facility. I have contacted a realtor about putting the house on the market. The doctors all agree there's no way for him to ever return home. He'll be in a wheelchair now, Bailey. You need to get comfortable with that fact. It is a big change. But sometimes if I bring a sprig of lavender or say something to him, he will question me, and say something like, 'Now Henry, there is only one surefire way to ruin a good white sauce, and that is with too much salt.'" Henry stopped and laughed and allowed his heart to remember. "I think he has forgotten the term *béchamel*."

I suppose that is what new circumstances require. Our hearts to get comfortable with them so that we can begin to accept them. Like Henry and Hank. When I talked to Daddy myself that evening, his voice sounded a bit gravelly. I had to remind him that like Henry, I, too, was in the restaurant business.

"Well, Bailey Ann, that's good. But I hope you are not a chef. Women don't belong in the kitchen." I had to smile. The essence of the man was still holding firm and very much intact.

Daddy looked better than I thought he would. He almost looked like himself, just in a wheelchair. I expected a crippled old man with vacant eyes. I hugged him like there was no tomorrow, and who ever really knows about that anyway? The three of us and little Hank spent time with Daddy in the sunny courtyard. All my men. Henry had brought Hank's fire truck to keep him occupied. Daddy spoke to me first, and I thought it was because he had not seen me in a while. Then I realized it was because I was the most precious thing to him.

"Annie? Where's your wedding ring?" I looked at Henry and Griffin. He thought I was my mother. I could tell Henry did not know how I would react. But my brother had given me a wonderful education in how to deal with Daddy and "meeting him where he was," as the literature suggested.

"Silly me. I was washing dishes this morning and forgot to put my rings back on."

"I am always telling you that, Annie. That's just another reason women don't belong in the kitchen."

My brother saved the day. Henry produced our mother's wedding rings, which I barely recognized myself. "Here they are." Henry handed them to me. I tried to put them on my left hand, and they were too tight.

"I must be getting plump with all the good food you fix me. I'm going to try these on my right hand," I said and put them on more comfortably, and then I kissed my daddy's cheek.

"Well, honey, you've been wearing them on your right hand for as long as I've known you," Daddy said, and Henry nodded in remembrance. Griffin smiled and patted me on the back, recognizing that memories that were not a part of you require acceptance too.

Over the next weeks, the three of us began packing. We took my mother's clothes that my father had never dealt with and most of his clothes to Goodwill. Because they were all about the same size, Henry and Griffin each selected a sentimental sweater. The furniture was divided into three stacks: a stack for Henry, a stack for Griffin, and then another stack to be sold or consigned. They each agreed that if and when I gave up the vagabond lifestyle I was living, they would share the furniture with me. These were hard days. Emotional ones. But they were made considerably easier because we had each other. All the while, countless buyers came to see the house. The first week went by so quickly. Griffin had agreed to sleep at the house because without Daddy and his big presence, it got a little creepy at night.

Daddy adjusted to his new environment fairly easily. I knew that was a gift itself. I wondered if he would ever remember he had a daughter named Bailey or if I would just have to be content knowing he had his wife back. By the following Friday, everything was done. All that was left in the house was the big sofa and the bed I slept in.

Griffin and I were going to change and go to VERT to open up and have dinner before I left tomorrow. I was excited to return to my own identity. It was midafternoon, and Griffin and I were in the kitchen packing up the final cookware when there was a knock on the door.

When I opened the front door, a young couple with two small children stood before me. When they saw me, they turned to one another, and the man said to the woman, "I told you, honey, this is not a good idea. Excuse us. We have not contacted the realtor or anything." The man spoke almost apologetically.

"Do you want to see my dad's house?" I called to Griffin, "Can you take the children out to the backyard so they can run around?"

The woman gushed, "You must be Bailey. The daughter. We love the outside of the house." She stepped in and looked toward the back, "Is that your husband?"

"Oh no. That is my brother Henry's business partner, Griffin. We're busy cleaning up. Why don't you just take a look around and let me know if you have any questions?"

"He's one of the famous Color-Wheel Boys," she said to her husband, but her eyes were roaming appreciatively over Daddy's house. Henry and Griffin had grown a little weary of the term but, thankfully, never of their restaurants.

After a while, the couple completed their tour. I could tell they were in love with Daddy's house. I understood their feelings perfectly. "We would like to buy the house. We'll even pay your asking price. But here's the thing—" the man began, but his wife interrupted.

"What my husband is trying to say is, would it be possible to close a week from this Friday?" The woman explained, "We're renting a house, but we must be out next week. I would just hate for the children to have to bounce around like that."

It seemed like a reasonable request, and they were offering the full asking price. It just meant, for me, this could be the very last night I spent in this house. Ever.

I thought this family would love our house. They reminded me of another small family who had moved in so long ago. "Let me call my brother, and let's see what we can do," I said. I wasn't a wheeler-dealer but simply someone selling something precious to her. I wanted it in the right hands.

Luckily, Henry was happy to accommodate the couple. The woman squealed with gratitude and hugged me hard. She did the same with Griffin. "We will take good care of her." It was odd to me that she saw the house as a "her." With Daddy, Henry, and Griffin, I had always seen it as masculine.

"If I may make one tiny suggestion, I think your daughter should have my room. It has the best view of the backyard, and it will allow her imagination to roam until she finds herself." She hugged me again, and then we shook hands. After all, this was a deal. After they left, the realization hit me. This would, in fact, be the very last night I spent at home. Forever.

⚘

Around four-thirty, Griffin and I arrived at VERT. The place looked decidedly tired. It made me sad. Julian and I had agreed on so many things, but with this restaurant, my restaurant, we had a colossal conflict over competing visions. But he was established, and he won.

Griffin had disappeared to put on his work shirt, and I walked around viewing everything. I landed at the bar and sat down. I heard the familiar voice in my ear, "What will it be, ma'am, the usual?" I smiled at him as he placed a cocktail napkin before me.

My particular feelings for him had always been contained in one of those secret compartments in my heart. I always knew where they were. But with everything going on with Daddy and the house, it felt like they were seeping out everywhere.

"Try to make it like you don't own the joint and buy the liquor," I said and laughed.

The dinner crowd trickled in. People were peppered at the tables and comfortable booths. It was a subdued atmosphere. A very tame crowd. Griffin motioned for me to take a table, but I was fine at the bar. It allowed me to oversee everything going on. I loved this vantage point. What VERT lacked in buzz or crowds, it certainly made up for in food. The quality had not diminished one bit.

Around nine o'clock, Griffin came up to me and suggested we go home. He did not say "for the last time." But I noticed he grabbed a bottle of Perrier-Jouët Belle Epoque, one of their finest and my favorite champagne. I knew it was to toast our house.

While he washed the glasses, I went upstairs. I sat on the edge of my bed looking at it. It had taunted and teased me these last two weeks. I had not given in to it. I kept telling myself, "You are with Elliott now. This part of your life is over. Like the house." I blamed it on the house. But leaving this messy and easy, so very easy, thing I had with Griffin brought a sadness I had not expected. It brought with it a longing not so far removed from an ache. It was like a period at the end of a sentence. Or a paragraph. Or a chapter titled: Bailey, The Early Years. It was as simple as a recognition that my childhood was over. Maybe I needed one last grand gesture so the chapter would have a fitting ending. Proper punctuation. And then I could cleanly and clearly move on with giving my heart to Elliott.

I was completely settled in my feelings for Elliott. The emptiness of Daddy's bustling house, the end of my childhood, and my new nightgown all seemed to turn on me, wagging a wicked finger and teasing, "Why did you pack me in the first place?" I heard the care-free busyness of Griffin washing glasses and uncorking champagne. Maybe I was being presumptuous. Maybe he didn't even think about being with me like that anymore. He had certainly never expressed his feelings like Elliott. Or just maybe I wanted to put Elle's theory to the test and nothing more. I removed the nightgown from my suitcase. The price tags were still attached, reminding me of what some of our favorite things cost us.

"Hey, Bae, are you all right up there? You didn't get swallowed up by an empty box, did you?" Griffin's voice echoed in the now cavernous house.

"Be down in a minute. I'm just washing my face." *And any sin I may or may not commit tonight,* I thought. Part of the answer was that my heart wanted both things. I wanted to be faithful to Elliott. I needed to be with Griffin one last time. I'm sure no one else thinks about punctuation marks at times like this. No, a real girl would be putting on lipstick. A real girl would be shaving her legs. A real girl would be brushing her teeth. A real girl would be putting perfume in naughty places. Real girls would not be thinking about punctuation marks. They would be thinking about birthmarks or cellulite or loose skin.

I hadn't even tried on the nightgown since we left the store. I slipped it on and looked at myself in the bathroom mirror. Could I do this? Could I do this to Elliott? I walked around my bedroom, letting my body grow accustomed to its first real negligee. I thought maybe I would feel stupid and chicken out. But it only made me feel beautiful. There are housewarming gifts when you move in, but what is the equivalent when you move out? I needed this last thing before we left this place. I closed my eyes and saw Elliott's sweet face. It made me sad.

I walked downstairs and stood before Griffin in the nightgown I had selected first. Griffin looked at me as if I were the most beautifully marbled dry-aged beef. Or the key lime pie with the Macadamia nut crust that Henry makes. He smiled. He came so close to me that when he exhaled, his breath lightly kissed my nose. I tried to remember Elliott. But the years, the weight of memories bearing down on me, and everything that happened in this very kitchen were just too much. I stupidly told myself Elliott and I had not had sex yet, and so I could be faithful to both my past life and my future one.

"Bae."

I had taken us both by surprise. He poured the champagne into the two glasses and I let it tickle my nose. Griffin made a toast: "To this beautiful and kind house. She was good to us. She gave us our life's passions. She gave us a home." We toasted, we drank, we kissed, and then we turned off the lights and went upstairs. It had been eight years since the first time Griffin and I had been together, before anyone else.

As we were climbing the stairs, I realized that this moment was not a sentence at all. It wasn't a paragraph. No, this moment wasn't even a chapter. It was the end of the book. A book you read and when the words "The End" loom large, your heart tightens. And hurts.

Griffin removed his clothes. As I started to take off the nightgown, he moved closer to me. "No, leave it on." Dammit, Elle had been right. I would never understand men in the way Elle and Reggie did.

"Do you like it?" I asked.

"I do. I do indeed, Bae."

This was unlike any time before. We were gentle with each other. We touched more. We kissed more. We looked into each other's eyes more. The tears in my eyes reflected back to me with tears in Griffin's own eyes. It dawned on me. This was bittersweet sex.

In our sea of first times, this was a last time. The last time Griffin and I would ever have sex in this house. The last time we would ever have sex together. It was a house, but it was our home. It was the place that kept us moored to something and to each other. We came together because we wanted each other the way we had in San Francisco. It felt urgent, but it brought tenderness and laughter and sweet sleep. Much later, I turned to Griffin, and we began again, slowly and kindly committing to memory this last-time-in-this-place-we-call-home sex. Our tears were safe with each other.

On the way to the airport, Griffin and I were prisoners of our own thoughts. So much had happened over the course of the last three weeks. I had not talked to or thought of Elliott much.

"Do you mind taking a look at a place I'm thinking about buying? Hank needs his own room now, if for nothing else than for all the toys Henry buys him. I think it's past time to close up shop on two men and a baby."

I laughed. We pulled into the driveway, and before us stood a beautiful but small condo with a For Sale sign in front of it. Griffin fished the keys out and we walked to the front door. "Are you sure you don't already own the place?" I asked.

"Maybe. Take a look around," he said.

I loved the high ceilings. The natural light. I especially loved the old dentil molding throughout. It had a great layout and a wonderful living space with sturdy built-in cabinets. A small bedroom and bath stood off on one side, and the master bedroom and master bath stood on the other. He could have easily afforded something grander. This fit his frugal but very discerning taste. It perfectly suited him. We ended up in the kitchen. Naturally.

"What do you think?" he asked me. "I want you to give me your honest opinion. I've shown it to you before anyone else."

"I always do," I said. Once again, deep in my thoughts. There were so many things to like about it and I told him so.

"Will you decorate it for me, Bae?" I just looked at him for a minute. And then a minute more.

"Are you serious? You know I don't do this kind of thing." But then, I studied the kitchen a little more. "You could put a banquette in that corner over there like in Daddy's kitchen," I threw out.

"Yes. That's what I was thinking too," Griffin said. I realized, then, subtlety was not his strong suit. There was nothing casual about us just dropping by this condo and me having a look around. He wanted me to not necessarily recreate Daddy's house but to reimagine the vibe in Daddy's house. He knew I was the only one who could do that, and that's why he hadn't already moved in and asked an interior decorator to work some magic.

"I think I have your number, Griffin Hardwick."

"I figured you would, Bae."

"You can take the For Sale sign down for starters. You're not fooling anyone here." I grinned at him.

When we arrived at the airport, I took one long last look at Griffin. This time, I was wise enough to commit it to memory. I wanted to remember the last time I would ever be with Griffin Hardwick. We embraced. I heard his heart beat a little faster than it should have. As I left the car, I left the memories behind, knowing my past was full but my future of running a restaurant and romancing its owner was just beginning.

Chapter Nineteen

L abor Day weekend approached, and my excitement and my nervousness boiled over like an unwatched pot. The restaurant was going to be closed Thursday through Monday and would reopen on Tuesday. I was packing and washing clothes simultaneously. I wondered if it was bad form to pack the green nightgown I had already worn. This was exactly the kind of thing I would normally ask Reggie or Elle about, but I knew I couldn't reveal why I had already worn it. I loved the nightgown. It made me happy. So, I packed it.

I arrived at Elliott's apartment at six-thirty p.m. I had my large overnight bag and a painting I thought would be perfect for one of the walls in his apartment.

When Elliott opened the door, I was amazed. I was speechless. It was a completely different apartment than the one I had been to on New Year's Eve. He could see my surprise.

"Come in. Do you like it?" Elliott's apartment had been transformed. The things that were in it before were now gone. It had morphed from the quaint English country look into a modern, sleek New York apartment. I was in awe. It was perfect. I wondered if those had been Jane's things. Elliott was moving on from an old life too.

"Well, what do you think? I told the decorator she had to be done by today. You were coming, and I wanted to impress you."

"Mission accomplished. It's beautiful. It's fantastic. It is so you." I believe I handed my things to Elliott as I continued looking around. I had a case of astonishment. I loved everything about it. I wondered if I could push my own vision to these limits. I also secretly wondered if I could do this to Griffin's condo on the modest budget he had given me.

In truth, I was a little jealous. Jealous that someone else's talent had these nuances. Feelings of inadequacy flooded my being. Jealousy and inadequacy are not exactly the kind of feelings you want to have before having sex with the man you love for the first time.

The walls had been freshly painted in soothing warm beiges and grays. I walked over to his bedroom door. The artwork caught my attention first. It was a lovely painting of robust greens and blues. Nothing faint or bashful about these colors. The painting was hypnotic. The walls were obviously painted to complement the blue-green in the painting. Gone were the frayed Oriental rugs and the English chintz. The stitching and monogram of his white bedding coordinated perfectly with the colors in the room. Nothing in the apartment was coincidental. Every item was picked with purpose, with a grand plan. I liked that attention to detail. Elliott joined me in the doorway.

"I told her the bedroom must have shades of green for the woman I love."

I blushed. I had never had a man decorate his bedroom to please me.

In his bathroom hung monogrammed towels complementary to his bedding. The grays in the marble played nicely with everything else. I wanted to see the kitchen. Would this decorator have chosen marble countertops for his kitchen? Because marble, as beautiful as it looks, is not very practical for a kitchen used often. I would love to catch a mistake. But she was without error.

We strolled together to the kitchen. It had been gutted too. And instead of marble, she had chosen quartzite, which has the sleek look of marble but is less delicate and can tolerate stains from red wine to lemon juice. Damn her. The color was just right too: a bright mother-of-pearl. I noticed the red knobs on the stove, a built-in refrigerator and dishwasher. Everything in Elliott's apartment was state of the art, top of the line.

I was naïve. If Elliott had done all these major renovations, he must actually own his apartment. That caused me to rethink a few things. He lived in a very established neighborhood. I had known rent must be expensive here, but the fact that he owned it was another thing entirely. It made me wonder if this, too, came from "family support."

I also wondered where my little gift would find a home. I had thought it perfect for the apartment I visited on New Year's Eve. But now, his walls were crowded with impressive artwork.

"Now I'm wearing the color green for jealousy. The transformation is stunning."

"You like it? I wanted you to be happy here."

"What's not to like? With this kind of transformation, you should be in the before-and-after edition of *Architectural Digest*. Who did this?"

"Her name is Penny Prichard. She wants to meet you."

"*The* Penny Prichard? Why would she want to meet me?"

"She loved your vision for the restaurant. Absolutely loved it. That was the first thing she said when we met. So, of course, we talked all about you, and I mentioned your love of vintage and consignment shopping. She was impressed. She gets intimidated by those places. She would like you to take her shopping sometime if you're willing. Even if you're not, she wants to come by the restaurant and have a cup of coffee with you." Just what had Elliott told her? He must've read my mind. "She is as captivated by you as I am. It's not a hard job, baby."

He picked up my overnight bag. "There's enough room in my closet for you. I was specific about that requirement." I was once again impressed by the way Elliott expressed his feelings for me. I loved him for it.

"Are you ready for dinner and a cocktail?" He read my mind. He took my hand and gently seated me at the new glass-top pedestal table. Gone was the small mahogany table with barley-twist legs. I settled into my chair and watched him light candles, seemingly everywhere. He disappeared into the kitchen.

"A sidecar, my lady," he smiled. I had never known him to make one before. It was delicious. "I didn't know how to make it, so I called Griffin, and he walked me through his recipe. I know you are particularly keen on his version." I was touched.

"Very tasty. Right down to the sugar-rimmed glass." I recognized the glass. It was part of a twenty-four-piece set I had purchased in Queens at an estate sale two months ago.

He went back into the kitchen and got a bottle of champagne. "Don't rush your drink. But I think tonight is a celebration and calls for a little bubbly." He leaned over and kissed me, tasting the sidecar on my lips. "Not half bad. But I still prefer my scotch." He looked like he was working mightily. I wanted him to just sit down and enjoy. The perils of being a perfectionist chef . . .

He brought in the main course. Lamb chops, standing at attention, with the bones upright so they looked like parentheses. I wondered what the parentheses would contain if they could speak. He kissed me again as he placed the plate in front of me. "Before we eat, I would like to propose a toast." He opened the champagne, poured some into our glasses, and said, "It is better to travel happily than not at all." Robert Louis Stevenson, I recognized. "And I travel far happier on my life's journey with you by my side." We leaned toward each other and kissed again, this time a long, passionate kiss that almost rendered me dizzy. He sat down and produced a little box.

"A token of my love, my devotion, and my affection." He reached for my hand and kissed the inside of my wrist. With moves like this, I was going to have a hard time making it through the entire dinner. "Open it."

I completely loved and trusted Elliott. I knew where I stood with him because he always told me. I opened the box. It was a pair of beautiful earrings, round-cut diamonds with a small drop and then peridots shaped like teardrops. They were exquisite. I sat in his lap and kissed him tenderly at first, then passionately. He pulled back.

"Your favorite color. I thought about emeralds, but they seem too harsh and unfeminine for you." I loved him even more for thinking of me as feminine.

"They're perfect. To tell you the truth, I much prefer peridots to emeralds. How do you read my mind so easily?"

"Because I love you. Because you are my soul mate." For the first time, I understood that term. I finally revered its meaning as something important and treasured, not some phony tagline on a Hallmark greeting card.

His eyes, his hands teasing me, and the entirety of the evening I whispered, "I don't think I can make it to dessert."

"Fuck dessert. Why do you think I made something that could keep in the icebox overnight?"

We awkwardly got up from the table, not wanting to disengage even for a moment. Elliott bumped into tables and ottomans he was unacquainted with. His new furniture in an unaccustomed setting presented us with a challenge. We stopped momentarily to catch an expensive sculpture that bobbed in peril at the edge of the bookshelf we had so clumsily backed into.

We were both going to be black and blue from tonight—and not from any sexcapades. Maybe this is how feng shui came about in the first place.

We finally made it to the bedroom. I tugged at the buttons on my shirt, but Elliott stopped me. "Wait. Let me undress you. I have wanted to do this for so long." He moved my hand away. He began slowly, tenderly, and way too deliberately for my taste, removing my clothes. He peeled them away like one would remove the leaves from an artichoke.

"I have all sorts of lingerie for you to choose from," I said.

"Not tonight. I have been waiting a long time, and I want to see all of you."

Dammit. How had Elle done it? That made her two for two in the "knowing men" department.

Elliott had a muscular body—much more so than his loosely fitting clothes indicated. I found myself wanting to study him in the way he wanted to study me. We kissed, we gazed, we touched places that were once forbidden. Then, we gave into our bodies' desires. Time seemed suspended. Our breathing seemed suspended. We connected in a way that felt complete. When we were finished, my enthusiasm got the better of me.

"Best Thursday ever!" I said, trying to catch my breath. In some ways, this acrobatic adventure had left me with more adrenaline than I started with.

He laughed. "I may need a break before seconds."

"And I thought your best work was in the kitchen."

"Perfectionism, Ms. Edgeworth, in all things has its definite advantages." He scooted next to me and we embraced. All the adrenaline I thought I had evaporated, and we fell into a deep, sound sleep.

Sometime after midnight I threw on the black nightgown Reggie had selected and made my way into the kitchen. I was surprised at how hungry I was. I couldn't even remember what we had eaten or even if we had eaten.

The light in the galley kitchen was on, and Elliott was standing there eating a big piece of Bing cherry-rhubarb tart. He was stark naked. I didn't know which was more beautiful: the dessert or his frame under the perfect track lighting. I decided to have a bite of the former and seconds of the latter.

"Where are your forks?" I asked, staring at the ease with which he moved around without clothes.

"It's better with spoons," he said. He took one out of the tray, scooped up a bite, and then walked over to me, pressing his full body against mine and teasing me to open my mouth.

"I know what you're trying to do, Elliott. But I must tell you straightaway, nothing gets in the way of my eating, especially something tasty like that." He didn't move. He just laughed and continued to feed me the decadent dessert.

"You really are an original, Bailey. Most women I've met wouldn't admit to wanting dessert. Here, let me get a plate. Let's do it properly and heat it up. I love the nightgown, by the way—my dessert for later on."

"You're even a perfectionist about dessert after midnight," I said waiting for him to plate me a piece.

"We aren't heathens. No matter what the hour, proper presentation is key. Would you like some tea or coffee?" It was my turn to laugh. You would think it was eight o'clock at night rather than one o'clock in the morning the way Elliott maneuvered around in the kitchen in full chef mode. I noticed he had already cleaned up our dinner dishes. "Just how long have you been up? We could eat off the floor it's so clean."

"Not long. I don't sleep a lot unless I take an Ambien or something. I've always had a lot of energy."

"Yes, I see that. I think I'm the beneficiary of that."

"I didn't hear any complaints a few hours ago," he said, setting the beautiful dessert, complete with a scoop of mint and basil sorbet, in front of me.

"Now that I see all this, I would love some coffee." I figured if he wasn't going to worry about the time, neither was I.

"I thought you might say that. I'll have some decaf French press for you in just a minute." How had he read my mind again?

The sorbet was delicious. It was a perfect companion for the rhubarb. He brought in the coffee, and I reached for some cream. Elliott shook his head.

"What?" I asked, taking a rather large bite and letting the cherry juice roll down the corner of my mouth. He simply got up and kissed it away. This is what had gotten me into trouble in the first place.

"What are those rings you're wearing?"

"They are my mother's wedding rings." He took my hand and kissed it.

"It looks like you're married. I'm entertaining my fondest fantasy that the someone is me."

"My fondest fantasy is that you're not married!"

"Touché. And you're just as clever at two in the morning as you are at two in the afternoon. Soon Bailey. Very soon. Lady Jane is being her usual bratty self. But she has no choice. This is not the time to talk about exes." My thoughts exactly. We talked until about four in the morning before working off our dessert in a most delightful fashion and then falling back asleep.

I woke to the sounds of rain. I remembered it had rained the first night I had sex with Griffin too. I had no idea what time it was. Hearing the rain, sleeping in this wonderful bed, next to the man I loved, put me into a coma of happiness. Except Elliott was missing. I heard footsteps.

"Good afternoon, Sleeping Beauty. Brunch in bed." He held a tray bearing the most incredible smells that teased me just enough to open my eyelids.

"What time is it anyway? And where's my nightgown?" I asked, trying to get oriented to a day that had started without me.

"It's about twelve-thirty Friday afternoon. And your nightgown is on the floor where it belongs." He grinned and put the tray next to me in bed. I smelled the aroma of good, strong coffee.

I surveyed the tray of food: beautifully poached eggs, the thinnest and most exquisite smoked salmon atop a perfectly toasted piece of brioche, a side of honeydew and cantaloupe melon balls rolling around on a saucer like tiny marbles. I propped myself up in bed, and then I hesitated. I looked down at my bare breasts and then the poached eggs. I hadn't quite gotten comfortable with the whole eating naked concept that Elliott seemed quite at home with. He must've observed my bashful behavior because he dashed to his closet and fetched the most luxurious terrycloth robe I had ever seen. I tied it around my waist and adjusted myself to enjoy the delicious breakfast Elliott had prepared.

"I bet you find me a bit repressed," I offered in the way of an apology.

"After last night, I find nothing repressed about you, Bailey. And I find your ways entirely endearing."

I leaned over and kissed him, briefly worrying about my morning breath. I retreated behind the tray and started with a bite of honeydew.

"You always start with green. I must tell you, Ms. Edgeworth, I have big plans for you," he started as I was taking a bite of the salmon and egg. It tasted as good as it looked. It was free of heavy hollandaise sauce. I liked that. Good chefs may add a simple light drizzle of sauce while a mediocre one will just drown the poor eggs in lumpy, tasteless hollandaise.

"What are these big plans?" I managed between bites.

"Nothing you can't handle, I promise. I figured we could spend the afternoon pretty much doing what we've been doing, but tonight, I would like to go out and try some of the newest and hottest restaurants to see if there is any serious competition."

The idea sounded splendid to me. "Really? Like normal people? I've been really wanting to go to Conrad's 20/20. But those reservations are hard to get—kind of like our restaurant."

"Really, now? Maybe that is why I made reservations for seven o'clock. I thought we could have cocktails at Stevie's Lounge beforehand."

"How do you do that? How did you know I would want to try that restaurant out? And how did you get reservations?"

"Because I know and love you, and I saw you reading the review and sticking it in that big bag of yours. I just figured you might want to check it out."

I smiled, finishing up the last bite of food on my plate. I heard that Julian had done the interior for Conrad's as his final project before retiring. I was very interested to see what he had done.

Elliott removed the tray, and I let him unbelt the bathrobe and extract payment for such a fine meal.

Afterward, we stayed intertwined and connected. We glided from one topic of conversation into another as was customary for us. I loved the smell of him: fresh jasmine. It made me think of Daddy and how he, too, never bore the smells of his kitchen. Elliott and I touched each other frequently. Right in the middle of a sentence, he would imprison me in a huge bear hug.

I thought we had exhausted topics of conversation. I thought we had exhausted all of the words in the English vocabulary. I thought we had even exhausted each other. But each time, there was a thrill and a newness to each topic and body part we had yet to discover about each other. He was tender, yet strong. He was funny, charming, and insecure. He was a perfectionist but was open enough to show his weaknesses. In many ways, he was the yin to my yang. Where I looked at the big picture in a restaurant and wanted to articulate the "vibe," Elliott started with the smallest detail, expanded out, and then returned to that tiny detail. I was easygoing, and Elliott could be temperamental. He was late, and I was punctual. I was serious and introverted, and Elliott tended to be whimsical and extroverted. Our particular quirks laced together to form a beautiful pattern.

When we finally got out of bed, he walked me to the bathroom. "There is a basket of soaps and lotions that Elle said you fancied on one of your shopping trips. I hope you like the selection."

"Thank you, Elliott." I looked at all the offerings. I noticed Jo Malone English Pear & Freesia perfume and lotion. I thought about my first Jo Malone fragrance. Nutmeg & Ginger. From Griffin. There was some Kurkdjian's Amyris perfume and lotion I had discovered with Elle, and lastly, a bottle of Tom Ford perfume and soap in Portofino. My mind went to Italy, to the painting I had given that Christmas, and to the person who had always wanted to go there. One of these things would have been more than enough—and expensive. The whole sampling was certainly pricey. I was definitely into high-quality smells. Propped up in the very back of the basket was a book, *Sonnets from the Portuguese* by Elizabeth Barrett Browning.

"How do I love thee, let me count the ways . . . " he began. I went over and kissed him.

"And here I thought you were going to join me in this big bathtub."

"No, thanks. I'm a shower and body talc kind of a guy. But there's some Chanel No. 5 perfume tucked underneath in case you want to go old-school."

"I think I'm good. You thought of everything." I was decidedly new-school in my scents.

"That was the general idea. Let me draw your bath." I was already regretting going out tonight. This easy intimacy with Elliott felt good and right.

I wore an LBD—as Reggie referred to half the dresses in her wardrobe. I smelled and looked feminine. I felt pretty. I allowed Elliott to zip me up. "You smell as good as you taste," he said as he nibbled on my shoulder.

"I think it just smells like English pear. I don't think it tastes like one," I said.

Elliott selected the sport coat I had given him. He looked put together in a very offhand kind of way. He looked handsome, like the English gentleman he was. We stopped for cocktails first. I had a sidecar, and Elliott got his usual glass of Macallan scotch. We paid our bill and ducked out so as not to be late to our seven o'clock reservation. That was one thing Elliott was prompt about. Being on time is a must for a crowded popular restaurant. Elliott believed this strongly and penalized repeat customers who were habitually late.

When we arrived at Conrad's 20/20, the place was already buzzing. A statuesque hostess showed us to our table. A flower arrangement of poppies, succulents, and orchids in deep jewel tones stood in the center. That's what made Elliott a perfectionist. He knew the flowers he would normally choose would clash with the deep color palette and décor here. He had come here first, surveyed the landscape, and then chosen the flowers for our table. He was about to explain when I put a finger to his lips. With Elliott, I felt like a proper couple. There was no reason to hide or sneak around.

"I just figured it out," I said. "I think they're beautiful."

"I'm glad." We kissed and sat down. Throughout dinner we enjoyed the occasional kiss and holding hands across the table. But I hadn't gotten completely comfortable with public displays of affection.

Elliott and I were easily recognized with Elliott's blond good looks and my long hair—plus we had distinctive accents. His was British, mine was Southern. Almost immediately, a scotch and sidecar arrived followed by an amuse-bouche prepared by the chef just for us.

The owner came over. The chef came over. Many people I did not even know came over. Plates of food came and went at a dizzying pace. If Elliott and I had wanted an intimate, quiet evening, this was certainly not it. Many of the people stopping by our table were fellow patrons wanting a reservation at our place.

Then Julian strolled over. "The chef here is excellent but no match for you, Elliott. You are the best. As for you, young lady, I think the student just may have surpassed her teacher. Your abilities and your patience to search the internet serve you well. But you will never enjoy my reputation because you are far too nice. It's good to see her smiling. You bring out the best in her," Julian said, winking at Elliott.

"Forgive me, but I was trying to learn from the master. What about my brother?" I said.

"Henry is good. The second best. Elliott is a natural. You were always so serious, Bailey. I found it utterly charming and challenging. You were my best student. You two represent the pinnacle. I am so glad you found each other. Elliott, show the girl a little fun."

"I'll do my best. But she is a little stubborn taskmaster." And we all laughed.

At the end of the evening, there was no check. Compliments of Lucius Conrad. As we were sipping our drinks, we nibbled on the assortment of sweets they brought to our table. We quietly reflected on the evening, our eyes and hands meeting briefly from time to time. We then simply shook our heads in agreement. Julian had been right. Conrad's was no match for us. We clearly had something special. We walked hand in hand outside to our waiting car and went home to take Julian's advice and have some fun.

⚘

It was a little after nine o'clock the next morning when I woke up. Elliott was still asleep. He looked so peaceful. His face was relaxed, his body in repose. I noticed the bottle of Ambien, and I was glad he was able to finally sleep. It was a wonderful thing to behold. I quietly groped around, found the bathrobe, and made my way to the kitchen.

There wasn't much I could do around Elliott's kitchen. I didn't want to mess it up. I made some French press coffee and took a piece of leftover brioche to his Magimix toaster. I was the sister of a Michelin star chef, and this was the best I could do. I retrieved some marmalade and cream from the refrigerator and decided to eat my breakfast in the living room. It was the room we had spent the least amount of time in, and it was the one that intrigued me the most.

Penny Prichard had done an amazing job creating this color palette. The walls were painted a dove gray. The rest of the color palette was done in cozy beiges and warm pinks and silvers to conjure up the feeling of mother-of-pearl. Even the bound rug had a nice texture to it and was tone on tone in colors of the dove gray and mother-of-pearl family. The artwork perfectly complemented the cream sofa and the sheared-lamb rug. Gone for good was the heavy, masculine feel of the place. This was a place I could've designed for me. I loved the introduction of the apricot color and the touches of blue and green thrown in for good measure in the three plump pillows on the sofa—adding a certain uniqueness and whimsy. I couldn't help but wonder: what if the colors of the pillows were recreated in the rug and simple apricot-colored pillows piped in blue or green were placed on the sofa? What dimension would that add? How would that change the vibe in here? I found myself taking pictures of the rug and the artwork and the mix of colors. I curled up on the sofa. Before I started my research, I checked my texts.

Three were from Reggie, all wanting to know how things were going, ending with her signature word—*hugs*.

Four texts from Elle. The first one asked: "How was it?" and was accompanied with three winking emojis. Elle never met an emoji she didn't want to use. The second one read: "How did you like all your lotions and potions?" The third one said: "You can thank me later." And the last one simply: "That Elliott is a sweetie. How did he like the green nightgown?" with another set of brightly colored emojis.

My mind lingered on her last question before I responded: "Love everything. Including the lotions and potions. How about coming to the restaurant Thursday night for a proper conversation and thank you? We haven't worked our way to the green one yet." I also sent one to Reggie with a similar invitation for Thursday night.

I had a text from Henry with a picture of Hank and Daddy. It made me smile. The last one was from Griffin. "Are you okay? Any ideas for the place yet?" I considered his questions but only briefly. In the doorway, wearing nothing but a smile, was my Elliott. My heart lifted. And they say Americans are uninhibited.

"Well hello, young miss. Have you seen my girlfriend? She is young, beautiful, and frisky."

I had to laugh. I didn't see myself as any of those things. I was twenty-six years old, I didn't feel so beautiful, and this was the most continual sex I had ever had in my life. I had been too serious in my life until now. I had been so focused on my career and achieving my life's ambition, but I didn't tell Elliott that.

"I haven't seen anyone matching that description around here," I played along.

He walked over to me and grabbed my hand. "Well, then, you'll just have to do."

Afterward, we lay side by side. Elliott's stomach made a loud rumble.

"I was thinking we could switch it up today. Maybe go out for lunch and go into some of those favorite shops you frequent, and you can explain to me again why they are so wonderful, stop in at the market, and then I could whip us up something simple like a tuna Nicoise salad for supper. Maybe eat in the living room?"

Had he noticed that I had eaten my breakfast in the living room, and how had he read my mind again so completely? I was already hungry for his "simple" salad.

Our day was a full one—and an interesting one. For the first time, I noticed the painstaking way in which Elliott selected the food he prepared. He looked at all of the ahi tuna before announcing his selection for the butcher to cut. It was thick and blood red.

"Just got it in this morning," Bucky, the butcher, announced as he wrapped it up and gave it to us. We then walked over to the selection of olives. Elliott sampled several black olives before he made his choice. He smelled and felt each and every tomato before several made the cut and went into his grocery bag. Cheese, eggs, and lettuce were next. He refused to buy the green beans. They were limp and not suitable to be mixed with the other ingredients. He also grabbed a lemon for good measure. At checkout, our bill seemed extravagant. The three of us, Reggie, Elle, and I, had eaten a meal together for much less. I knew now why he was gone most mornings for so long. He was meticulous. He wanted to approve of the ingredients he was cooking and preparing. That's what made Elliott the best.

At home, a symphony of sounds came from his kitchen. Boiling eggs, searing tuna, slicing tomatoes, cheese, and lettuce. He was busy slicing lemons, opening jars of capers, and measuring out olive oil to dress the salad. Once again, he did this in his bare feet. I enjoyed the image. He looked so casual, and yet there was nothing casual about the way he prepared anything.

As we ate and drank another delicious meal, we settled again into relaxed conversation. I noticed that even at night without natural light, this room held a gleaming elegance. It was a bit formal, which I liked, but it was a room you could feel quite naturally at home in.

Later on, we were tender with each other, slow with each other. Our kisses seemed important. So were our touches. Our eyes held each other's. They expressed our love and devotion. I was happy. Our being together felt like the essence of contentment.

Monday morning, as I gathered my things, I felt the pull of sadness. Being sad about going home caught me by surprise. As I gathered my toothbrush, I wondered what toiletries, if any, I could take home. Elliott noticed my hesitation.

"I wanted to ask you this all weekend. But I would never want to rush you, Bailey. But this place, this apartment, I did for you. I would really like for you to move in with me."

I didn't answer him. I hesitated. While I declined a formal change of residence immediately, there was a definite shift in where I spent most of my time. Elliott had single-handedly lifted the cloak of seriousness and sadness I often wore and replaced it with a colorful swing coat full of fun.

Chapter Twenty

A utumn arrived in her customary fashion in New York. The lush colors receded from the trees. The happy blues disappeared from the skyline. Even the cheerful colors in the planters on Park Avenue became more muted. Life was beginning to grow smaller and shrivel up. But not inside me. Life and love, like the essence of hope, exploded within me.

Elliott and I attended the 40 Under 40 awards gala at the Waldorf Astoria. I procured my first long dress for the occasion at Bloomingdale's. Henry and Griffin sent congratulatory flowers.

Elliott and I were becoming quite the "It Couple," especially in the culinary world of New York City. I was even introduced to Danny Meyer and David Bouley. I told David his restaurant, in my opinion, was the perfect union of sumptuous food and incredible atmosphere. I told him I had had my most memorable meal at his restaurant. They were both surprisingly approachable. We extended invitations to each of them.

While I spent more nights at Elliott's place than at my own, some things did not change. On Thursdays, like clockwork, Reggie, Elle, and I would get together at the restaurant at our usual table that Elliott reserved for us, and we would catch up, eat, and laugh. Every piece of my life was finally in order. My professional life was going well, my personal life with Elliott was off the charts, and finally, thanks to these two wonderful women, I had secured a comfortable place of my own in Lady World.

❦

The indefatigable Penny Prichard was a force of nature. We met the first time for coffee at a Midtown restaurant close to a client.

She arrived a few minutes late, weighed down by a tote on each arm and several notebooks poking their heads out of her purse. She was not what I had pictured at all. I pictured her with her hair in a clever blonde bob freshly done at Bergdorf. I pictured her in red heels. Instead, besides smothered in all her professional wares, her dark hair had been blown around by the winds, and she wore black pants and a loose gray, comfortable-looking sweater. She schlepped in. I loved her immediately, although she talked a mile a minute.

"Oh, honey, sorry I'm late. A client delayed me. We were discussing the differences between the color beige and café au lait. Give me a break. Waiter? I could eat something. Could you eat something?"

After the initial whirlwind of her arrival, we settled into a relaxed conversation.

"I am so glad we could get together, Bailey. I've been intrigued by you from the moment I met Elliott and saw the restaurant. My curiosity was heightened, I must tell you, after I heard that man talk about you. I have never been jealous over a woman in my life. To have a man speak so openly about his affection for you must feel incredible. I was going through a pretty shitty divorce, so it just made me want to be around you both." Now I was intrigued about what Elliott had told Penny about me.

"The feeling was entirely mutual. After I saw Elliott's apartment, I was incredibly jealous of you, Penny. It was so impressive. I really want to pick your brain."

"I would like to pick yours too. Elliott gave me a tour of the restaurant. The things I found most interesting he said you purchased at some thrift store. Sorry, I guess you call them vintage stores. But I was impressed by your keen eye. I would like to go with you sometime so you can show me the ins and outs of how you look for things. I know it's an art. I just don't have it. But some of my clients were really hit hard by the recent recession. And loathe as I am to use this word, they want me to decorate on a budget. By the way, nice earrings. Please tell me those didn't come from some junk store."

I laughed out loud and couldn't help myself. I didn't think the woman had taken a breath since she sat down. "No, Elliott gave me these. I think he has the same feeling for thrift stores you do!"

"Well, thank God for that—he doesn't scavenge through trash like you do. The earrings are absolutely exquisite."

She had made the term "budget" sound positively dreary. She said it the way she said the word "thrift"—with put-upon disdain. I decided we could help each other. I discussed my idea about getting a rug in the colors of the pillows that were at Elliott's place for Griffin's apartment, and she provided names of her vendors after I gave the promise that this was the only condo I was decorating and that it was in Atlanta. Her conversation, like her hair, went in a million directions. But we exchanged cell phone numbers and made plans to have dinner at Elliott's restaurant a week from then.

Elliott and I settled into a routine. While we did not make love every night, when we did, we made it count. Even with the rigors of the day, the staff dustups, the ordering of ingredients, and replacement of things—and now the extra night out to attend functions— we still walked hand in hand, still preferred each other's company to a room full of people, and still liked to end the evening intertwined in bed. Sometimes our sex was mind-blowing, but sometimes, just as often, when we got a night off, our sleep was mind-blowing. We would wake each morning to discover the familiarity of each other's sleeping positions. Elliott still chose to walk around the apartment with no clothes on, and I continued to grope around for the bathrobe.

Quite frequently, I would look up in the restaurant to see him standing there. It was still a lovely novelty to me. He would always smile at me across the room as if to say, "You—yes you, Bailey Edge-worth—are the prettiest woman in here, and you are going home with me tonight." I would smile back, and we would always make our way to the middle of the room just to be near each other.

After a lifetime of feeling not at home in the world, I felt at home with Elliott. He grounded me. He made me feel mature. And always, he made me feel like a woman. He still had his back pain, and he had nights where sleep refused his entry, but he would give in and finally take some pills. Many nights, I was the one up late ordering things for Griffin's condo. I would often wake in the morning with my pen in one hand and my computer in the other. Griffin groused occasionally about all the boxes that arrived.

"Are you sure you're staying in my budget?" he complained.

Fall collapsed into the holidays. I would go home the three weeks before Christmas, which would allow Elliott to go home too.

"Darling, as much as I hate it, why don't you spend Christmas in Atlanta with the other men in your life? I think New Year's Eve is much more romantic anyway, don't you? I dread going to England like a mother! I'll have to listen to Pop's criticism that I only have one successful restaurant. If that isn't bad enough, I have to deal with Lady Jane and finalizing the end of this disastrous marriage. It will be perfectly horrid. The thing that will keep me going is you. Coming home to the beginning of another new year and celebrating with the love of my life. You just might get me through this week of a perfect shit storm."

"Well, Merry Christmas to you, too, Scrooge!" I laughed.

"If it makes you feel any better, I've already been shopping for you," Elliott said, shifting his mood.

"Does shopping equate to buying?" I asked.

"You will just have to wait and see what Santa left behind for you. And then you can determine if you have been naughty or nice," he said with a little twinkle in his eye.

"Well that just begs the question—does Santa want me to be naughty or nice?" I walked into his arms.

"It would help his feelings tremendously if you were very, very naughty."

"Then I will just have to be very bad." We lingered in bed. It didn't even matter that he was crossing the pond and I was boarding a plane to Atlanta.

Chapter Twenty-One

Henry picked me up at the airport. As we merged into traffic, Henry said, "Griff has already moved into his office. I guess you will stay with Hank and me. Unless you want to snuggle with Griff on that office couch." This was the first time since Henry had gotten sober that I had heard him make a joke.

"Henry," I warned.

"Sorry. No questions."

"It's the Englishman."

"Oh. Didn't know things were that serious." Henry then changed the topic to Hank, Daddy, and Christmas. I knew on some level he had a point. Griffin and I had never been under the same roof for three weeks without some sort of horizontal hijinks occurring.

I remembered the first time we were alone together in Griffin's office. It was a Tuesday or Wednesday. VERT had just opened. I brought in the paper and the magazine that contained its reviews. I handed them over to Griffin, thinking he might want to read it alone.

"No. Please stay. I want to read them with you before anyone else." He handed me the magazine.

"Are you sure?" I asked. When he nodded, I turned to the review and read the headlines aloud, "VERT Blooms." I smiled at him, our eyes exchanging stored-up emotions. That was enough. Griffin nodded and closed the magazine. We then collided seamlessly as always. Words and clothing fell away.

Before fame was anointed, before articles were written exclaiming success, before nicknames were born, before congratulations were bestowed, and before the first honor awarded, it was just this.

Just now. Just us. I remember now, it was a Tuesday. Somewhere I heard the sound of champagne corks popping, but neither one of us made an effort to move.

"I think your adoring public wants you."

"They can wait. I sign their checks." We had laughed and began again. Enjoying these moments, punctuated with joy and kisses. Our clothes lay on the floor in a puddle of togetherness. Only later did we untangle and get dressed. Celebratory sex. Those memories followed me like shadows on a sunny day. It made me smile even now. I just hoped Henry couldn't read my mind.

Griffin greeted us at the door. "Welcome to Brown Box Land." He gestured to the sea of cardboard decorating the landscape of his condo. I embraced him, and then we kissed as spouses reuniting at the end of the day.

"You're so welcome." I surveyed all the boxes. I studied the rooms and remembered the pictures Griffin had sent me. It was remarkable how much of Daddy's furniture he'd chosen to keep. It made me smile.

"Love what you've done with the place."

"I can't help it. I love your mother's and daddy's things."

"How much of this furniture are you married to?" I said and was instantly sorry. I noticed my little girl bed tempted me in the second bedroom. It would have to go in storage. I had ordered a cool daybed that would allow this room to be a spare bedroom and an office for Griffin.

"You're the visionary. Henry and I flipped. I am going to work tonight, and he is going to help you, but I can stay a little while."

"No, I want you to be surprised. But it is cocktail hour. Why don't you make yourself useful and fix me a drink?" I was already on the threshold of his bedroom studying. For me, opening the boxes and remembering the contents was like Christmas Day and birthdays all rolled into one.

"One step ahead of you." He disappeared. As I walked around his bedroom, he returned and handed me the glass.

"I put the shaker in the freezer. Don't get all drunk, now, and pass out in my bed."

With this statement, none of us dared make eye contact. Henry looked like his eyes were permanently glued to the floor. I tried to look up like I was reimagining his room rather than imagining what Griffin had just said. And Griffin moved out of the room as if it had suddenly gone up in flames. A moment passed.

"I guess I will leave you to it," Griffin said. For once, my brother kept his mouth shut.

When we were alone, I asked, "Now, would you help your delicate little sister open boxes?"

"I never had one of those. But I will be happy to help out." We both laughed and got to work. I told Henry of my plans to bump out a wall into the living room to make a little bar area so Griffin could do what he loves best. The crew would return the next day to finish up.

"Did you hear the news that we got tattoos?" Henry asked.

"Have you and Griffin gone crazy?" This shocked me.

"Nope. After getting Hank, and with Dad's illness, I decided to ink our initials right here." He patted his heart. Obviously Henry was very proud of his decision.

"Well, that begs the question. What did Griffin get? And where?" It seemed like such a departure from the Griffin I knew.

"Can't say. I am sworn to secrecy."

"I wouldn't dare get a tattoo."

"Never say never, little sister."

※

I had spent the day supervising the workers and finishing up last-minute details before returning to Henry's utterly charming house. The quintessential picture of domesticity—without a wife. Although to hear Griffin tell it, that was an easily fixable problem. The women might come and go, but Henry's talent remained constant.

After taking my shower, I decided to pay Griffin a visit at VERT.

"Hey barkeep, fix me a drink, and don't be parsimonious with the bourbon." He turned around and smiled.

"When have I ever?" he responded. Just like that, we had reestablished our footing. Whatever awkwardness stood between us yesterday was clearly gone today.

Alex, the hostess, came up and brushed against Griffin's side. She was stunningly gorgeous. It piqued my curiosity. There was something familiar about their touching. The way she patted him was playful. It was the kind of gesture reserved for spouses who navigate around each other in the kitchen.

And then there was their exchanged glances. It made me wonder what was going on between them. For just a moment, I observed them, forgetting to breathe or blink. I downed my drink and asked for another. Had he inked her name in a naughty place?

"Go easy, girl. You know I'm going to like your design. Maybe you better have something to eat." He handed me a menu. As I checked out the offerings, my gaze wandered and I noticed the people drizzling in. My second home looked even more tired than the last time I was here. But when my scallops came, what she lacked in atmosphere, she made up for in cuisine. The cooking still dazzled.

The next morning, in our rattiest clothes, Griffin, Henry, and I started painting. I made us all stop mid-stroke if colors were too muted or too dark. I took the paint myself to watch it be remixed. It gave Henry a chance to check on Hank and Daddy, and Griffin time to make a food run for us. That was the upside of having three restaurants. It didn't matter if your home kitchen was indisposed.

Once the color suited me, we painted again. We adapted to our roles without fanfare. We made progress. We made mistakes. We corrected them, and then we made progress again. At the end of every day, we were weary, sweaty, and happy. Days passed without Elliott ever checking in. Day after day, stroke after stroke, I observed that through this process, we were also healing. We were better. Together. We were a cord of three strands not easily broken.

On the night before the great unveiling and after performing a little Christmas magic of my own at Griffin's condo, my eyes landed on the painting of Italy that I had given Griffin so many years ago. It made me sad to think it was hanging all alone on the wall by itself, and my heart clenched at the thought that Griffin had not yet been to Italy. Then I strolled into the kitchen and into the living room and let myself twirl around with unbridled joy at the beauty I had created. I joined the boys at Henry's house. Tomorrow was Christmas Eve. Tomorrow Griffin would get to move back into his condo, and with any luck, he would approve of the magic I worked.

Griffin greeted me at the door with a glass of wine. During the last few weeks, I had almost grown accustomed to my sober surroundings. I had also gotten to know young Hank and it calmed my soul and my nervousness about Griffin's condo.

"I've been working on something I want to try out on you." Before Henry could introduce his creation, little Hank asked, "Are you going to make them the fig and arugula pizza, Daddy?" Hearing a three-year-old utter the words "fig and arugula pizza" made me chuckle, but it also made me proud. The next generation of chefs was already starting.

Great chefs never stopped learning or trying things that sounded peculiar to the rest of us. I had long stopped challenging Henry's ideas. My motto for his or Elliott's creation was "bring it on." With the right amount of fig, prosciutto, Gorgonzola, arugula, and extra virgin olive oil, it was incredible. My men were happy, but I was nervous, hoping I had transformed Griffin's condo into something he would like to call home. Would he share it with Alex?

The workmen were finished the morning of Christmas Eve. I'd told them there was a Christmas bonus in it for them if they were to finish before noon. I was lucky that they were eager to get some extra Christmas money. The three of us headed over to Griffin's that evening. Nighttime was beginning to throw her starry cape over the city. I made the boys stand outside while I did a quick walk-through, turning on lights, fluffing pillows, and straightening the new mono-grammed towels in Griffin's bathroom.

I opened the door and announced, "Welcome home, Griffin!" Henry and Griffin barely made it into the living room before they started exchanging conspiratorial looks. "What?" It made me anxious.

"Oh my God, Bae. I don't even know what to say," Griffin said.

If I didn't know any better, I would swear that Griffin was near tears. Even Henry looked impressed. "Do you like it?" As my first home-decorating gig, I was desperate to know. "You are my guinea pig, before anyone else, Griffin." He was having a hard time taking it all in, especially with the giant Christmas tree standing at attention in the corner of the living room.

"You did all this with the budget I gave you? I love the paint-ing above the fireplace. And the rug." He put his arm around my shoulder and left it there before bestowing a gentle kiss, forgetting Henry was there. I kissed him back. Not out of habit but because I was so happy.

"About the budget: I came in with twenty-three whole dollars to spare. But I think it would be a good gesture to pay Al a bonus for coming in under budget and on time. You never know when you'll need him on another restaurant." This was common practice for me in New York. I had built up a loyal arsenal of contractors and workers this way.

He whispered in my ear, "Already done." I smiled, and we made our way to the bedroom door. I stepped inside so Henry and Griffin could enter. "Don't worry. We'll come back to the Christmas tree."

"That's a lot of pillows, Bailey," Henry said. "But I would kill for that bathroom."

"The pillows do complement the painting on the wall. But the painting is a little high, don't you think?" Griffin said.

"There's a method to my madness. Christmas isn't here just yet." It was easy to be playful with him. The kitchen and patio were last.

I had chosen a distressed green color for the cabinets. It was warmer than I would've liked, but it played nicely with the grays and browns and didn't interrupt the flow. Both men's eyes landed on the banquette. I had almost duplicated my father's kitchen. It wasn't lost on either man, who each had logged countless hours in that kitchen, sparking and cultivating their own life ambitions. For a moment, I was overcome with my own emotion. I opened the built-in refrigerator door in game-show style to reveal Griffin's favorite water and a bottle of champagne.

"This calls for champagne, Bae." Griffin reached in and grabbed the green bottle—Perrier-Jouët—and a bottle of sparkling cider. I wondered if he remembered that the last time we drank this champagne was in a kitchen that looked just like this. It was the first time I ever wore the green nightgown. And the last. We had closed up Daddy's house that night. It was the last time Griffin and I had been together.

I opened the French doors to the patio. Luckily for me, Atlanta was having a mild winter, and I had placed a plate of cheese and crackers next to a white poinsettia. Griffin popped the champagne.

"Well, Griff, this is definitely a home," Henry said as Griffin passed me a flute of champagne.

"To Griffin's new home. Be happy," I said.

"To Bae and her unique and perfect style." He leaned over and touched his champagne glass to mine. The three of us stood together letting the celebratory nature mingle with the champagne before returning inside to the roaring fire in the living room.

"You kids gonna be okay? Somebody needs to get down to the shop and earn a living," Henry said as he put down his glass of sparkling cider. I hated for him to leave. It was a perfect Christmas Eve night in Atlanta. The cares of the day were falling by the wayside. "I was just going to go out to the market to get tuna steaks and check out my new kitchen," Griffin said.

"Not tonight. I want that kitchen pristine until tomorrow," I admonished. "I just want you to sit back and enjoy and let me tell you about the tree." He nodded. And I walked Henry to the door. "Let me send something over," Henry offered. "It's on the house."

"Yeah. Mine," Griffin said but made no motion to go anywhere.

"I don't think I've ever seen Griff this happy or content. You did an amazing job, Bailey. But are you sure you want to stay here tonight? With Griffin?"

This time I didn't scold Henry. I could see his concern. And he was right. Three weeks of sweat, of stubble, of being under the same roof and not hearing from Elliott, it could lead to us unwrapping things that had nothing to do with Christmas gifts. I returned to Griffin. To be honest, there was not an EpiPen strong enough to curtail the particular reaction I had to Griffin. We were too busy enjoying Griffin's new place and each other's company.

"I don't know what I will ever do to thank you, Bae," Griffin said touching my hand. "Now tell me about this Christmas tree." He grabbed my hand, and we walked over to what I knew was his very first Christmas tree. I had always wanted to do this for him. He touched the old-fashioned potato masher I had gotten Daddy at Williams-Sonoma, which hung on the tree. He also pointed to Rudolph with a silver cocktail shaker in its hand, an ornament that I had given him so many Christmases ago. Right beside it was a Santa Claus sitting in an easy chair with a martini glass that I had given Griffin in college. We smiled at each other. The unique ornaments combined with the lifetime of memories we shared made for a potent cocktail. He kissed me. Luckily for me, he was curious about the tree.

"You know there's no mistletoe above us, right?" I asked as we moved back to the sofa.

"I could've sworn there was mistletoe. It must be some of the magic you were talking about," he laughed. "How did you get this tree with all the lights and the decorations?"

"You see, you live in Buckhead. Anything can be bought and delivered in Buckhead. I selected the tree, and they delivered it, strung the lights, and added some new ornaments I picked out. I added the rest that you had in storage. But damn, those pesky Buckhead elves know how to charge." We both laughed. Christmas really did bring out the lighter side in me. Griffin continued to stare at the tree.

"There's a package back here. Did the elves leave this here too?"

"No. That's from me."

"Bae. No. You've done way too much."

"Open it and I'll tell you about it, and then you can tell me what your favorite things are. I'm liable to get a complex if the only thing you like is the Christmas tree." He walked back over to the sofa and opened the gift. It was a perfect companion painting to the one of Portofino I had given him so many years ago. It was one of those things I bought without asking the price. I had it reframed to go on the wall with its mate.

He studied the picture and the frame and then looked up at me and said the exact same thing he had said when I gave him the painting so many years before. "Bae." I leaned over and kissed him and whispered, "Do you like it? That is why Portofino is mounted so high. So its companion can go underneath."

"I love it. But I think I will take this one to my office."

I stared at him. "Well, think again, Buster. I bought this one to complement your other painting. Not to be separated." I got up and made him follow me into his bedroom.

"Now, go over to the side of the bed where you sleep."

"Okay. But I'm just a little afraid of you right now."

"I'm good with that. But just look." I hung the painting on the hook underneath Portofino. I had experimented with the paintings each way this afternoon before deciding which should be on top.

"See how well they go together, mounted on top of each other? This hardly cost anything. And yet it anchors this wall so well. Besides, from where you sleep, they will be the first thing you see in the morning and the last thing you see at night, so you can think of Italy each and every morning and night and go to bed happy."

For a moment, Griffin didn't say anything. Perhaps I had truly scared him. But then a smile spread across his face and he nodded. "I don't know what to say. They do look good together. They look good alone, but they make a striking pair. You're right."

"Well, that's good for starters. And I like it when you're just a little bit scared of me."

The doorbell rang. It was our food. As we sat at the bar area and ate, I explained to Griffin how I designed the bar to be the perfect area to create his bespoke cocktails. I grabbed our champagne, but I also grabbed a bottle of Sausalito's finest for a little Christmas cheer and a couple of my mother's wine glasses.

"I saw what you were doing with the bar area right away. I love it. I see now what you do. You pay attention. It's very individual. I think you have surpassed Julian."

"That was always my intent. To marry the basic truths of a person with some of their hidden whimsy and uniqueness. While I do enjoy your flattery, I want to know what your favorite things are."

"I love exactly where we are. I love this bar area, but I love the living room. The rug, the pillows, and the painting over the fireplace is the best. But you can't kid me. I know this did not come under budget."

I weighed my answer. "You'd be surprised. There are a bunch of shops off Canal Street that have great distressed furniture. Some of those places have back rooms with remnants of fabric that I was able to repurpose. Sometimes even bolts at great deals. Let's just say, with a little magic, I did what I wanted to do." I didn't want to tell him that one of these places was called The Dump—and that its name was richly deserved.

"I'm glad I didn't know what you were doing. That scares me for you. You could've gotten yourself killed. Unless you're still packing Henry's Swiss Army knife. God, I pictured those back rooms selling nothing but pot."

"Oh, they do. I bought so much merchandise in one shop they threw in a bag of pot for free! I never leave home without my switch-blade," I laughed, but Griffin looked horrified.

"Shit, Bae. Don't take unnecessary risks. What did you do with the pot?"

"I didn't smoke it. I still prefer eighty proof. I gave it to Elliott. He appreciated it."

After dinner, we returned to the living room and restocked the fire.

"Would you like some hot chocolate? I have some cherries. I'm sure you noticed I have your mother's china."

"No!" I almost shrieked. Could the long reach of memories stretch across the years and ensnare me once again? I was afraid to take a chance. "I am very content."

"Yes. This is nice."

I agreed. Something occurred to me. "Why haven't you been to Italy yet? You have the money. You'd better go now before you have a little Hank of your own."

"I've been so busy, and there are a lot of places in Italy I would like to see. I've been researching it. I want to go to Rome, Venice, and Florence, to the small villages around Tuscany and the vineyards of Umbria. I just don't want to be gone from the restaurants for two or three weeks."

"The world won't stop if Griffin Hardwick takes a holiday, you know."

"I know. Changing subjects, though, are you really okay, Bae? You seem to be working too much. Maybe you and Elliott should hire some extra help."

"I'm fine. And I have been working several jobs. But this one is ending." I motioned to Griffin's condo.

"Would you tell me if something was wrong? You're too thin."

I just looked at him. "Perfect for New York. I don't need rescuing, Griffin, I promise. I can take care of myself." Then I added, "Please don't worry, Griffin. You're out of the caretaking business, remember?"

"People who say they don't need rescuing are usually the ones who do. That is chapter seven, page twenty-eight of the caretakers' handbook." Griffin backed off. "You win, Bae. Oh, I love the distressed color in the kitchen and my bathroom. But Henry's right. There are a lot of pillows." I wondered if in a parallel universe there were another Bailey and Griffin christening every room in this condo and complaining about the number of pillows on the bed.

Chapter Twenty-Two

During the night, I got up to get a glass of water. I found Griffin as I left him, staring into the fire and then staring at the Christmas tree. It made my heart swell. I went up behind him and whispered in his ear, "You know, Santa won't visit little boys until they are tucked safely into their beds."

"This is the first time in my life I've had a real Christmas tree. Thank you for doing this for me, Bae." His hand grabbed mine. Words tiptoed away much like the elves themselves. We lingered, enjoying his tree. Finally, he got up and moved to the threshold of his bedroom. His eyes landed on the painting. He smiled again.

"I've changed my mind. The pictures of Portofino are my favorite. You're right. They do really balance each other out. They look good together. I guess we do need to get to bed. The wake-up call for Hank will be mighty early." He disappeared into his bedroom.

I found myself taking a leisurely stroll around the condo I created. My thoughts, however, lingered on those paintings. No one would ever know they had been separated.

Before turning out all the lights, I thought about Griffin's first Christmas tree. The thought of his childhood without them still haunted me. It made such an impression that I had never forgotten. I had known almost from the beginning that it would be the tree that captured his attention. It was beautiful. Listening is the most rudimentary form of love. It's true in business, but it's at its truest and best when applied to the human heart.

Chapter Twenty-Three

I heard a knock at my door. "Bae, get up. Henry just called." God it was early. "C'mon, rise and shine. I made coffee."

"Holy shit. We never did this when we were children." But I got out of bed, threw on some clothes, and splashed water on my face before going to see Christmas through a child's eyes.

"Can I come down now? Did Santa Claus come?" Hank poked his head through the banister. He was almost four, and he looked like an Edgeworth, but his olive coloring was that of his mother.

I tried to adopt the carefree feeling of the holiday. Being carefree was about as difficult for me as wearing a dress that required a slip. "I'm not sure, Hank. Have you been a good little boy?"

He looked at me with the most somber brown eyes. My eyes. "Yes ma'am," he said. My heart did somersaults and grew just like the Grinch's. He came downstairs and threw himself into Griffin's arms. Then Hank gave me a big hug. Clearly, there was a great affinity between the men and the new boy in their life.

Henry had done a wonderful job selecting Santa gifts. But what a four-year-old chooses to care about is anyone's guess.

After Hank had successfully waged his assault on what Santa had left for him, we turned to opening grown-up gifts. I knew Hank would not like the gift I gave him. But in time, I hoped he would appreciate that I had found a rare set of nesting dolls made to look like chefs in various colors and nationalities. I found them when I was out one day with Penny. While Hank liked the way they neatly sat inside one another, both Henry and Griffin were mesmerized. If I had given them to either man, I would've hit a home run.

I gave Henry a pair of mother-of-pearl cufflinks that I found at an estate sale. They had a wonderful patina to them, and their uniqueness had come with a price. Henry had started wearing French-cuff shirts soon after he opened NOIR. He felt the upscale atmosphere demanded more formal attire.

"Wow, Bailey, I don't have anything like these." He got up and hugged me and kissed me on the cheek.

Only Griffin and I remained. I insisted on going last.

Griffin opened Henry's present first. I found it incredibly thoughtful. Henry gave Griffin a beautifully engraved sterling silver shaker and jigger. On the shaker was etched out in block letters "Griff," what Henry always called him. On the jigger were Griffin's initials: GEH—Griffin Eugene Hardwick. Griffin was touched. He was more emotional and sensitive than any of us.

Henry and Hank gave me a beautiful silk scarf and a silk blouse. The blouse was white and tailored and would go with everything in my closet.

From the looks of Griffin's present, he was giving me a painting too. Eagerly I tugged at the paper. It was a framed article about me in *New York Magazine*, about being a visionary and being named 40 Under 40. Now I was the one who was touched.

"You're always lording your big accomplishment over us. I figured if you had it framed, you could just point to it in your office and save yourself a lot of conversation."

He and Henry had earned some major prestigious awards. That wasn't the real reason at all. He was proud of me and couldn't say it. And then, out loud, I said, "This would be truly great if I actually had an office of my own. I haven't made it like you two big shots. Not yet anyway. But I'm working on it. You know I love it. You knew I would."

He nodded in false modesty.

After Griffin and I collected our gifts, we all went back to Griffin's to get ready for Christmas lunch. As per our usual, it was served around two-thirty.

Watching Griffin and Henry in the kitchen was like watching synchronized swimmers. They did things in tandem. Seamless. Like a well-oiled machine or a lovely old married couple. I would never be unmoved seeing them together. Henry had gone by and picked up Daddy, and I watched my father play with his grandson whom he thought was Henry. Little Hank had folded into "my men" as effortlessly as Henry blended egg and sugar for one of his decadent cakes. Occasionally, Daddy would reach out and grab my right hand, squeeze it, and bring it to his lips.

"Love you, Annie." I knew the moment the words left his lips they were meant for my mother, but they landed on my heart just the same. In some ways, Alzheimer's had given me a glimpse of a father I wished I had known. A glimpse of my mother too. I let my hand linger until he let go.

"Love you too," I said, having no idea what terms of endearment my parents exchanged with each other. We both watched Henry and Griffin cooking.

"Guess what they call Henry down at the restaurant," I said.

Henry looked up, not knowing what was going to come out of my mouth.

"They call your son 'eye candy,'" I said, as Henry mouthed the word "thanks."

"You're kidding me," Daddy said. But that's what he said about most everything these days. With the scourge of Alzheimer's, words were becoming an endangered species. Now it was pretty much only that and "I love you."

"Eye candy means that Henry is something sweet to the eyes." I was on a roll. Daddy and Griffin laughed, and Henry just looked at me and said, "payback."

To finish off our Christmas dinner, Henry had prepared an exquisite espresso layer cake with a Bing cherry and fig reduction in Grand Marnier. Obviously, Henry had gotten the memo that figs were back in vogue. I thought of Elliott. He would've chosen Courvoisier, which would've been an interesting choice. Henry opted for something basic to cook with, but in his drink, he could be finicky, like Elliott. Christmas was already fading into memory when Henry, Hank, and Daddy left.

As Henry was leaving, he hugged me. "So, little sister. Did you get to see Griff's tattoo?"

"Nope. I was good."

"That surprises me. Too bad." Henry's eyes held a twinkle that piqued my curiosity.

I hugged Henry and Hank and gave Daddy an extra hug for good measure. I reflected on the limits of Daddy's memory. Did it truly matter if it was a Wednesday or Thursday? Did it even matter who the president was? My father had a deep recognition of what love was and who he loved. Wasn't that the most important thing to know as we navigated this crazy world?

After they left, Griffin greeted me with a dishtowel. Unfortunately for me, Griffin did not adhere to the same philosophy as my father, that a woman's place is not in the kitchen. I helped Griffin wash up the many dirty dishes and put my mother's china away until next year, reflecting on the day. We talked about the meal, about his condo and what a hit it was, about how well it functioned for entertaining. I was just about to ask Griffin about this mysterious tattoo when my phone rang.

It was Elliott. He sounded discombobulated.

"Elliott, what's the matter?" I said.

"It's just god-awful," Elliott began.

"Start at the beginning. Tell me what's wrong. Let me help," I said.

"What an unbelievable shit storm. This new and fancy stove is on the blink, and we need a new one."

"What about the warranty?" I asked.

"Fuck. Not you too. I've been so busy I never filled out the paperwork. I'm going to have to buy a new one. I don't have any money. With paying Lady Jane off, her attorney fees, my attorney fees, and the money I had to pay Penny for redoing my apartment, I'm wiped out." I took my glass of wine and went into the bedroom and closed the door.

"I'll be back in a few days and we'll sort it out. I have a little money in savings. But not enough."

"I need money now."

"Not this very second. Let me work on it. Maybe I can fly home tomorrow. Just calm down. We'll figure this out."

"And my back has been cramping like a mother. Fuck Bailey, I need more than your piddly little savings."

His tone and his comments jolted me. "Elliott, you should just take some of your medicine and call it a day. I'll call you in the morning."

"I just need to talk to you right now, baby." For the next forty-five minutes, until my battery died, I listened to him rant about his dad, his wretched wife, his bad back, and his bad luck. All the while, I drained my wine glass dry.

It was close to midnight when I got off the phone, and when I opened my door, I noticed Griffin had already gone to bed. I decided to open up another bottle of wine and get on my computer to see if I could fly back the next day.

I woke up hungover. Griffin met me with a cup of coffee. "Thought you might need this. It sounded like the rest of your night didn't go so well. Maybe you need some toast and eggs."

I proceeded to tell him about the stove and all of Elliott's troubles.

"Elliott has a wife?" That was the one fact that Griffin seized on.

"*Had* a wife. They're divorced now. That's part of the problem."

He disappeared into his bedroom before reemerging, saying, "Come sit with me while I fix you some breakfast."

When he placed the plate of food in front of me, he also put a check by my plate. It was made out to me. It was for the amount of the stove.

"I can't take this, Griffin." Then the realization hit me, and I almost stood upright. "No. This is your Italy money. I can't take your Italy money."

"That boy is a great cook. He needs a great stove. It's made out to you. Call it a belated Christmas present. Or your design fee—unless you've blown way past that. And no, it is not my Italy money." He tried to laugh.

"You're a damn liar, Griffin Hardwick." We both knew the truth. He opened up the palm of my hand and let the check rest gently before he carefully closed my hand. We just stared at each other for a few minutes. It was the most intimate moment we had had during these three weeks. Tears filled my eyes.

"No tears. We're all good here. Really. What do you want to do today? Want to join me at VERT?"

I sat back down and took a bite of eggs. My emotions felt like the eggs: scrambled. "I can't. I'm flying home this afternoon late. Can you drop me off at the airport?" I hated to ask. His generosity seemed more than enough. And there it was. The reason Griffin didn't go to Italy. Me.

Griffin took me to the airport. I didn't trust my emotions to speak. We were quiet except for the occasional exchange about Henry and Hank. The silence was deafening. My thoughts bled out onto the floorboard. Unspoken conversations darted back and forth between us, bypassing our lips but hitting my heart. Physically, I felt like I was having some sort of attack. When we pulled up to the curb, Griffin put the car in park. My heart was having a hard time maneuvering itself out of the car. It was as if it knew when I left it would break into a thousand irretrievable pieces. I wondered what Griffin, my Rubik's Cube of emotion, was thinking. Finally, I managed to extricate myself. When I was almost out of the car, Griffin leaned over and grabbed my hand.

"Wait," he said. I turned around, wanting to hear something, anything.

"Yes?" Was all I could muster. A moment passed. And then another.

"Hey, Bae," he paused. "Call me and let me know you got back safe and sound." That was it. Nothing more. I nodded and escaped inside. I turned around not sure where I wanted to go. Griffin's car was still parked. Options flew around in my head. I closed my eyes sending up a silent prayer. After another moment I looked out. Griffin was gone.

⚘

Once I landed in New York, I headed back to my apartment. I told myself it was late. That I needed to do laundry. That I needed to start work on the exciting new project I had just landed for Gabriel Modare, the Brazilian businessman who wanted to get into the restaurant business. He was handsome, rich, and ambitious, and he wanted my talent. When doing a project, I could count on one hand the number of times a client boasted that money was no object. But if I had been honest with myself, neither work nor laundry was the real reason I needed to be alone. I needed to let my feelings calm down, to be in repose before seeing Elliott. I took the coward's way out and texted Griffin, not trusting myself with any other contact. He texted me back just as formally and stilted. Only distance proved a salve.

I would never be like most girls. I still got excited about someone's used material that I got for a deal and could repurpose. I still thought about the words between the commas and the prepositional phrases that define us. Only one man and his generosity could bring me to tears. Griffin Hardwick, one of the Color-Wheel Boys, reluctant but not completely reformed caregiver, but more than anything, the unselfish benefactor of Bailey Edgeworth.

Chapter Twenty-Four

Elliott texted that he was in bed with his back so I spent the night at my apartment instead. It had been three weeks but I used my time to be productive. I called Gabriel Modare, and we agreed to meet at his new space. I wanted to hear his ideas and get the vibe before I started working and made it rain Brazilian money. I'd had several back-to-back projects since Elliott's restaurant opened a year ago, but this was by far the most ambitious.

He had jotted his ideas on a heavy piece of stationery that bore his initials embossed at the top. The paper was folded in half neatly, and his notes followed suit.

"I love your idea to call it Ipanema, Bailey. I have so many fond memories of that beach. But I love wood. Is there any way we can incorporate different styles and textures?"

"That's what this meeting is about. I want to hear about the things that make you happy and then incorporate those into the aesthetic of the restaurant. Do you like dark or light wood? What about wooden masks and artifacts?" I asked, making my own notes on his piece of paper. A perfect smile crossed his flawless face. I could see he had taken full advantage of the plastic surgeons that Brazil boasted.

"You have done your homework. Yes, I am a collector. I wouldn't be opposed to loaning the restaurant a few of my pieces."

It was my turn to smile. "That would be ideal. Your restaurant should be a reflection of you. Never the designer. Why don't you shoot me some pictures of some of your pieces, and we'll save that to the end—the pièce de résistance."

Along with his notes, he also gave me a check for my retainer. Nothing made it real like a client parting with his money.

I went back to the apartment to find both Reggie and Elle in the midst of coming and going. Elle stuck out her hand to show me the humongous diamond perched atop her ring finger.

"Wowza! Congratulations. We need to celebrate. That is some serious artillery," I said. Both girls laughed.

"I love your expressions, Bailey," Reggie said. Elle proceeded to tell us it would be a June wedding in Martha's Vineyard at the Agricultural Hall. My mind conjured up rustic, but when she showed me some pictures with Oriental rugs and chandeliers, my imagination recalibrated.

"Please help me with the vision, Bailey. In addition to being a bridesmaid." I sat down. Her request stunned me. In all the years of thinking about commas and prepositional phrases in relation to my name, it never occurred to me that "bridesmaid" would be a part of that. Life, like interesting food, holds delicious surprises.

"So. What did Griffin think of his condo?" Reggie asked.

"He loved it. It made him so happy."

"How ever did he show his thanks?" Elle asked.

I looked at both girls and shook my head. "He's practically like a brother. Did you forget about Elliott?"

"'Practically' is not related. Somebody is going to snatch him up. But Elliott is a great guy too." Both of them hugged me and left to celebrate New Year's with their guys. I needed to get to Elliott, but my mind kept coming back to willowy Alex.

I headed toward Midtown to Elliott's place. I still rang the doorbell.

He looked awful when he greeted me at the door.

"Bailey, you are a sight for sore eyes," he said as he embraced me. He had on jeans but no shirt. He kissed me on the cheek as though we had not been apart for more than three weeks. "I'm so glad you're back."

"No offense, but you look horrible. What's the matter?" I noticed that his apartment was dark. The drapes were drawn, and there was only one lamp on.

"Not the welcome home you imagined, huh? I'm sorry, sweetie. My back is killing me. I just took some pain meds and a muscle relaxer. Would you be too disappointed if we just did takeout tonight? I really need to take a nap." He kissed me again as an apology.

"No worries. Just be careful which muscle gets relaxed. We have been apart for three weeks, you know." I grinned.

"There's the clever girl I love. Thanks, love, for letting me take a nap. Then you can tell me if sex with a free man is better than with a married one!" Elliott disappeared into the darkened bedroom. I put my stuff down on the floor, and then I ordered Chinese from around the corner. I decided to do some work. I wanted to find some interesting pieces for Ipanema. I texted Penny. I had seen a cool wooden surfboard with her in an upscale outdoor store.

Penny replied, "I'll be back in the office by the middle of next week. It is New Year's Eve, honey. Take the night off with that cute fella of yours."

To Griffin I sent: "I appreciate your check."

But the text to Griffin sounded very businesslike and so serious. I quickly sent a second one. "What are you doing for New Year's Eve? Thank you for letting me stay with you over Christmas."

I wasn't really happy with the tone of the text, but I hit Send anyway. His reply was equally stilted.

"I'm working. Obviously like you are. You're welcome to stay at my place anytime."

I wanted to call Griffin. I wanted to hear his voice. I waited a full ten minutes before I sent him yet another text: "I certainly wish I had one of your sidecars to ring in the New Year!"

His response came back: "Bae, they are yours anytime."

I smiled. It was so easy to right the ship with Griffin. The door-bell rang, and I turned my attention to Chinese takeout and waiting for my Englishman to get up so we could celebrate the New Year.

While eating alone, I allowed my eyes to wander around and put my own spin on an *Architectural Digest* before and after. Only this time, it was his versus his. Which condo was the best? The condo that Penny decorated for Elliott or the one I designed for Griffin? I pondered it, but only for a moment. Yes, I would have to agree that Elliott's was grander, but in terms of matching the style to the man, I think I won hands down. I had captured the essence of Griffin and even explored a side that only a few of us saw. It brought me contentment and happiness as I tiptoed into a brand-new year.

Elliott was still asleep when the ball dropped, and the sound of fireworks exploded in the distance. I watched him sleep peacefully, free from pain and worry. I kissed his cheek before turning the lights out and going to bed myself.

The next morning, I felt the gentle nudge next to me. He looked remarkably wide awake. And so handsome.

"Good morning, my love," he said. So sweet. So dear. He smoth-ered me in kisses. He touched every inch of my body. "This separation damn near killed me. I don't like being apart. I've missed you des-perately." And with that, the words, along with our clothes, fell away.

Afterward, we lay together. Neither of us was in a hurry for anything except for each other. "I love you so much, Bailey. You are the most important thing in the world to me. And by the way, Happy New Year, baby." He reached under the bed and handed me a beautifully wrapped present. I put it on the nightstand next to me.

"Later." I turned back to Elliott to make up for lost time. After we finished, we did not linger.

"My God, you're going to wear me out. I haven't eaten anything in two days. Let me go whip up a breakfast for us."

"I didn't hear you complaining a little while ago. It's like you're on Viagra or something." I watched him walk away from me. I had missed watching his naked form.

"I assure you, no Viagra. Just heavy-duty pain meds. I didn't hear you complaining either."

"I never will." I got up and retrieved the robe from its hook. The closet seemed barer somehow, like it was waiting for my things.

As I crossed the living room, I nodded at how lovely it was in the daytime. I smelled the coffee brewing. I followed my nose into the kitchen, noticing there were no flowers.

"Oh sweetie. I was supposed to pick up your flowers yesterday. But with all the commotion over this business with Jane and the stove and this fucking back pain . . . "

"Elliott. We're here together. That's the most important thing. Besides, maybe you should cut back on the flowers a little bit." I remembered the check. I had deposited it in my account and written one to Elliott as Griffin suggested.

"Are you saying I can't buy my baby flowers?" His question had a bite to it.

"Of course not. Just cut back on buying your baby flowers."

"Stop being so bossy, Bailey!" He grimaced as he handed me a cup of coffee.

I felt reprimanded and nodded in an effort to back off before I went to my bags, which were still in the hallway. "I am also enterprising and resourceful!" I handed him the check. "I expect to be thanked properly." I leaned over and kissed his cheek.

"My God, Bailey. You are full of surprises. I knew you had saved some money, but wow!" It amazed me that he thought I had that kind of money. I was grateful he wasn't more curious. "Yes, you will be thanked properly and often."

Even Elliott's scrambled eggs with tarragon were perfect. We settled into easy conversation. With frequent touches. Frequent gazes.

Frequent I love yous folded into conversation as effortlessly as "pass the brioche." We ate our breakfast heartily, not bashful to show our large appetites for food or each other.

We both cleaned our plates, happy to be together and in a food coma. We settled onto the couch with our coffee.

"Would you like to open your New Year's present now?" He went into the bedroom to retrieve it. As was our custom, Elliott handed me his card first.

> My love,
>
> And so, we begin a new year. And we begin it together. That is enough for me. Your love is gracious and plenty. Your spirit sparks my life's ambition. You will always have my heart. I will always be the luckiest person in the room with you by my side.
>
> "I am certain of nothing but the holiness of the Heart's affections and the truth of the Imagination." —John Keats
>
> My heart and your imagination.
>
> Yours,
> E

He leaned over and kissed me and handed me the blue box. I just looked at him in amazement. I opened it to find a strand of intertwined sea pearls with a heavy gold clasp.

"Elliott, they are exquisite. I don't know what to say." I had become so rattled about finances. We were living precariously it seemed.

"Now, my love, I expect to be thanked often and properly," he smiled. He saw my frown.

"Please don't fret. I bought and paid for them a long time ago. You were wearing that purple dress, and I thought it needed something."

"If you're sure." I held them up against my bare skin.

"They're almost as pretty as you are," Elliott said as he kissed me.

I went to my bag to retrieve his gift. It was an antique shaving kit that I thought would be perfect in his bathroom. I loved that it was authentically English, like my Elliott.

He opened it. "Very nice." I could tell he was underwhelmed, and it was clear that he was much more impressed with the check. Then a big smile crossed his face and he began delivering on the promise to thank me properly and often.

Chapter Twenty-Five

After the holidays ended, the new stove was installed and the warranty papers were executed and mailed in, and the restaurant returned to normal. As did Elliott. He returned to the cooking virtuoso I remembered. Even his specials of the day were crisp and nuanced. We had some turnover, but all the new hires seemed even better, and our sous chef Rex had improved to the point that he was becoming an impressive backup to Elliott. My heart settled down. I tried to keep my worry at bay.

Elliott and I returned to our normal selves. Our better selves. He returned to being light and playful with me. Chasing away my cares, allowing laughter in like sunlight and catching me in a tight embrace to "squeeze out the fret," as he put it. We even returned to going out occasionally, finding our names or our picture on *Page Six*. Sometimes I wore the sea pearl necklace, but I always wore my favorite piece of jewelry—the peridot and diamond earrings.

After years of being barren, my world was suddenly populated with women. Penny and I saw each other several times a week. Elliott had recently hired a new waitress named Leah who seemed to brighten the place up just with her smile. She proved to be a godsend.

I saw Elle and Reggie every Thursday night for our weekly dinner date, even though we technically still lived together. We spent so many nights with our boyfriends. Elle, Reggie, and I were in full-tilt wedding planning mode. I was even getting excited about the wedding, sharing my ideas with the girls as if I were a wedding planner. Elle seemed impressed with my ideas. My vision.

"I see the wedding planner I hired was a waste of money. Who knew I could just go with you, Bailey? I didn't know how serious you would take my wedding," Elle said.

"Hello. Have you met me? You know I take my job kind of seriously." It was such an understatement that we all laughed. I could see soft lavender-colored napkins with sprigs of lavender tucked into each napkin at every place. I knew we could find a calligrapher to match the ink to the place cards. Elle was overjoyed.

The question hovered around again. Was it finally time to move in with Elliott? Reggie, Elle, and I discussed it. I spent most nights with Elliott, but there was the occasional night when he was having back pain that I liked having my own apartment. I liked my freedom. I decided to table my own decision until Reggie flew the coop.

My schedule was taking shape. Elle's wedding was in June. I would take a week off from my business around Labor Day when things were slow to go home and check on all my men. Elliott didn't like it. He didn't want to be apart that long, but he relented after I explained I needed to see my father. And I agreed to move in with him when our lease ran out in September. After Labor Day, my calendar was marked for the grand opening of Ipanema with Gabriel.

Two weeks after Valentine's Day, Elliott sank into a deep well. It seemed to me a potent mixture of wretched back pain and wicked moods. Rex managed the kitchen duties in Elliott's absence. Reluctantly, I turned down several promising job offers so I could be at the restaurant in the late afternoon. I finished up at Ipanema then headed to Elliott's restaurant to get ready to oversee the dinner crowd. It was hard to do the thing that came so effortlessly to both Henry and Elliott—small talk. I summoned those skills from long-ago Saturday nights with Daddy at the restaurant when we glided together from patron to patron. I would send complimentary appetizers to tables I recognized and to those I didn't in hopes of return business. I learned that sending complimentary items over with a smile turned out to be a happy substitute for small talk.

I neglected my own business to keep Elliott's afloat. I reasoned that the restaurant was just an extension of our relationship. After years of putting my career and my vision front and center, I decided to close my eyes and live a little. Instead of accepting high-profile gigs that would bring attention, accolades, and hopefully sizable paychecks, I took on smaller assignments. They were mainly cafeterias or private dining halls at liberal arts colleges or smaller restaurants that required only day trips. Going into each dining hall, I deliberately sought out the lonely table where I imagined I would be sitting.

I would introduce something beautiful and unexpected into these cafeterias that many viewed as utilitarian. My reputation did not suffer, but it did not soar or overtake Julian's, which had always been my goal. Like the potentially awkward conversation I never had with Griffin, I chose to keep moving. Eyes wide shut.

When I would get to Elliott's, I would often find him asleep in the darkened bedroom, a plate of leftover food next to a bottle of scotch, an empty glass, and a bottle of pills. Sometimes, he would be waiting for me on the couch with glassy eyes. He would be cranky and hungry, and he would expect me to fix him something to eat. Then he would retreat to the darkened bedroom. I often lingered, making notes on the night at the restaurant, and conducted internet shopping sprees for Ipanema and a smaller Peruvian restaurant, Aztec, that had just hired me. On scraps of paper, I jotted down wedding ideas for Elle. I threw my anger, unspoken conversations with Elliott, and my lack of control into the lonely atmosphere and then picked up my pen. I often fell asleep with the pen still in my hand.

The days were the hardest for me. I had no idea how to run a restaurant. While Rex had mastered cooking similarly to Elliott, he could not match him in the day-to-day selection and purchasing of food items. No one could. Elliott was meticulous. I went to the market and called Henry several times a day asking about fish, lamb, or some spice. I would call Griffin for any suggestions on wines and cocktails. I even picked his brain for the new trend in "bespoke cocktails." Both were kind not to pry too much as to why I was so involved in the day-to-day of the restaurant. I marveled at the way Elliott, Henry, and Griffin made this look easy. Well into the sixth week of Elliott being sick, Leah came into Elliott's office, which I now occupied.

"I'm just getting here. Thought I'd check in. Wow, you look like you could use a coffee or something."

I looked up at her. I knew I looked a mess. My appearance had been the first thing to go—along with about fifteen pounds. My favorite Chloé blouse was hanging, rather than draping, off my shoulders. Even my hair had begun falling out.

I felt like I was in left-brain living hell. Paying bills, making payroll, and ordering supplies were all mundane but necessary things I was ill-equipped to do.

"If you could make a decent cappuccino, I'd give you a raise right on the spot."

"Then you haven't tasted my cappuccinos. I make the best. And by the way, if you're doing payroll, it's Lea without an *H*. I haven't wanted to bother you." She smiled. My mind was already churning.

"I have to warn you, Lea without an *H*, I have had the best cappuccino, so you have some stiff competition." I looked up at her. I smiled for the first time in about a month, thinking of the cappuccinos that Griffin always made for me.

When she returned with the piping-hot drink, it was the best thing I had tasted in months. It was frothy and beautiful, and she garnished it with a chocolate *G* for Graemmer.

"What do you think? Do I get my raise?" she asked.

"You surprised me. I have a job offer for you. I would like you to help me in the office with all these bills and restaurant orders for a few hours every morning. I'll give you a raise plus an extra day off. When Elliott returns, we can keep doing our thing to allow him some free time to do what he loves best: creating memorable dishes. Deal?" We shook hands and forged a budding friendship. I couldn't wait to tell Griffin he better up his game!

Lea and I were settling in to tackle the bills when the door opened. It was Elliott. He was back. But he didn't look happy.

"What the hell, Bailey? I just got a call from the bank, and we are a month and a half behind on the mortgage. I got a call from the market that truffles that were supposed to be picked up last week didn't get picked up. Now they've gone bad, so they canceled our order for this week, but we still got billed for them. Just what the fuck are you doing? I'll never be able to get another loan if you completely trash my credit."

"I'm sorry. I'm really sorry. I'm trying to do the best I can to run your restaurant. I can pay the mortgage right now, and I will go down to the market and pick up the truffles," I said. His sudden barrage flustered me.

"I just wired the mortgage money for next month, which costs an additional twenty-five dollars, which pissed me off. And I went by the market to straighten things out with Bucky."

"What can I do to make things better?" I said.

"Nothing. You're a disaster at this, aren't you? You should probably stick to the vision thing. I know this is not your forte. See you later." When I looked up I noticed Lea had disappeared.

Rattled from my encounter with Elliott, I left him to his restaurant. After returning several work emails and phone calls, I decided to change it up and go up Madison Avenue. I found a pair of stunning lamps for the Brazilian place at a small shop. I saw a captivating picture in a gallery window I thought would be perfect in the bar area of Ipanema. They were getting ready to close and didn't have time for me. I took a picture of it anyway, intending to come back another time. Right next to the gallery, I found myself face-to-face with a bridal shop.

I found a beautiful silk charmeuse dress cut on the bias. It would be perfect for a wedding dress for Elle or even a bridesmaid's dress. I inquired about the colors and availability. I took a quick picture of it and sent it to Elle with the address and texted: "Playing hooky before the dinner crowd. Can you get off work for a little bit and try this on? Thinking about it for your dress or bridesmaids. It comes in a soft lavender-dove color."

Her text came back immediately, complete with emojis and exclamation points: "Getting taxi. Be there in ten." She breezed in the door ten minutes later looking expectant.

"What do you think? Did the picture do it justice?" I held up the dress for inspection, along with the color swatches turned to the soft lavender.

"I absolutely love it! But I love this one too." She spied my second-favorite dress, another slip dress with a beautiful organza overlay.

"Try them all on," I urged her. "I texted Reggie, and she'll be here in five minutes." Elle had already disappeared to try on a dress. It was a snooty kind of store, but they offered you champagne as you tried on dresses. I was almost giddy watching Elle try on all those dresses. They all looked perfect for her. I texted Elliott and told him I was running late.

He replied back: "It's okay, darling. Sorry. Take your time. I have things under control. XO." I was relieved more than anything to see that Elliott had returned to his old self. I settled into the couch, waited for Reggie, and accepted another glass of champagne in antic-ipation of Elle modeling the next selection. I needed a little buzz.

"I don't like this one as much as the other one. Bailey, why don't you try on the one you like for the bridesmaids, and I'll wait for Reggie to try on my favorite so she can vote," Elle shouted from the back. In a few minutes, Reggie breezed in.

"Am I too late to the party?" Someone handed Reggie a glass of champagne. I stepped toward her in a gown holding a ring of swatch samples.

"Wow, Bailey. You look like a bride," Reggie said, looking at me with pride.

I walked over to her and held the color swatch up to her red hair. "I think this would be a great color for you, Reggie," I said and clinked her glass in a toast. "Can't wait for you to see the main event." I sat on the sofa next to Reggie waiting for Elle to appear.

"Well?" Elle asked with uncharacteristic modesty. She looked breathtaking.

"Come here and turn around." I waited. She walked like she was practicing the real thing. "Picture this. I know you want a bouquet of white peonies and orchids. What if we do your hair up and tuck in some flowers from the bouquets to add a little interest from the back?"

"Love it!" Elle exclaimed. "I say we're done, girls!" We were all a little tipsy but a lot happy. My phone vibrated. It was Gabriel.

"Gabriel, did you like the picture of the lamps and the painting?"

He reminded me that price was no object before asking me if I was tipsy.

"Maybe." I said hanging up. I would've never admitted this in my younger days.

"Oh my God, was that Gabriel Modare? He's your client? You're going to be famous. He's in the paper all the time," Elle said. I laughed.

"Gabriel attracts publicity about as easily as he attracts tall, leggy blonde models. I will work on getting an invite for you," I said before we parted ways with plans to recap on Thursday night as usual.

I strolled into the restaurant, and almost immediately, Elliott imprisoned me in a big hug.

"I'm sorry, miss, we just stopped serving supper." And then he kissed me. I was still a little shaken from this afternoon. His behavior had completely changed. I noticed the man he had been talking to. He was well dressed in a casual way.

"Bailey, you remember Collier Sloan. Collier this is Bailey, my muse."

The man gave me a friendly grin, but I had no idea who he was. Blame it on the champagne. I thought maybe he was one of Elliott's rich neighbors or a fellow restaurant owner. I was drunk enough to be chatty.

"How have you been, Collier?" I asked. Elliott still had not released me from his embrace.

"It is not often I am in the company of a muse. May I?" He took out his phone and took a picture of us. He was the famous editor of the society page—*Page Six*. Three days later, our picture would find its way into his column: "The Genius and His Muse—The Magic Returns." That same day, I walked into the store on Madison next to the bridal shop and negotiated a good deal on the painting they were unwilling to sell to me before the article was written. Being a muse to a famous chef had its privileges.

Chapter Twenty-Six

That weekend was the beginning of March, a bipolar month of frigid days mixed with equally lovely days. Elliott woke me early with breakfast in bed. It was as colorful as it was delicious. He nibbled on my toes and ears as I tried to eat. Then he removed the tray from the bed, removed my nightgown, and proceeded to make love to me as if he were trying to earn a Michelin star.

"Happy, darling? It is so good to see you smiling again."

"I am happy. Do you have enough in you for seconds?" I asked. He did. He tried even harder, earning another Michelin star in my book.

"I hate to do this to you, but I don't think I can make it to Elizabeth's wedding. This back pain is so unpredictable. I need to be able to lie down. You don't mind going alone, do you?" he said as he took another pain pill. "Weddings are for women anyway. Besides, you're going to be way too busy to miss me." It stunned me.

✿❋

I broke the news a few days later. "By the way, Elle, Elliott isn't going to be able to make it to your wedding." This piece of news landed as I had expected. And dreaded.

"Honey, what's wrong?" Reggie asked, taking my hand in hers. "You can tell us. Even Dave noticed you're spending more time at our apartment than Elliott's. I thought you guys were supposed to be moving in together. Are you fighting?"

"Everything's fine. Just fine. You know Elliott has a bad back. It's just easier for him sometimes to sleep alone."

"Sometimes, Bailey, you are the Rubik's Cube of emotion. Speaking of wrong, have you taken a decent look at yourself in the mirror lately? Why are you laughing? Has someone else referred to you that way? You're way too thin," Elle said.

"You can never be too thin, my dears. And actually, no. It's just amusing," I deflected, remembering how I'd referred to Griffin that way from time to time.

"He must be good in bed. If he's more private than you," Elle said.

"He is," I smiled. It was true of either man. My friends exchanged purposeful looks but said nothing. I didn't know which was more frightening: them giving me a piece of their minds or staying stone silent.

The next week, as the weather grew nicer, Elliott slid into a deep abyss of pain and anguish. I reluctantly engaged Lea. She had prepared what looked like a notebook for debriefing a head of state. One page was devoted to paying the bills—if they were drafted or if we needed to write a check and what day the bill was due or the draft occurred. The second page was a list of our vendors and what we bought from each, on which days, with little notes ("Never buy tuna from Nick. He always tells you it's fresh. He lies.") The next page was devoted to Elliott's bank accounts and their numbers. The fourth and last page was a list of Elliott's passwords for his various accounts. His passwords were complicated logarithms even a genius hacker in Silicon Valley couldn't have breached.

He had given all this to Lea one afternoon when I was out on an appointment. It surprised me that he trusted her more than me. When I asked him about it, he said, "I can't have you messing with the books. I love you, but you can't do this. I can't afford to lose my sterling credit score in case I need to borrow money for the restaurant." It really didn't matter. I was just glad this time I was ready. Or Lea was. But this time, a week stretched into two, and after that, into a whole month. The whole time, I expected Elliott to come bounding into the restaurant as he had before. But Elliott appeared to subsist on a steady diet of pain pills, muscle relaxers, and scotch, while I existed on an equally steady diet of worry and fret with the occasional sprinkling of mind-blowing meals and sex, wondering when or if Elliott would return. This life had become increasingly unpredictable. My new normal.

Chapter Twenty-Seven

O ne afternoon, Lea and I were working on the bills and placing orders when she said, "Take a break. Rex is making you a dish he's been working on. Come have your lunch out in the restaurant like a real person. We need to put some meat on your bones. No offense, but someone as skinny as you is bad for business." Lea always said things in such a good-natured way that it was hard to take offense.

"That might be nice." I sat at a small table in the sun. Lea joined me, carrying a plate.

"This is a lobster and basil cake on mushroom risotto with sautéed spinach."

"Sounds good." I found myself relaxing and engaging in conversation with Lea.

"So, how long have you had a thing for cooking types?" she asked.

"You mean Elliott?"

"Griffin too." Was it that obvious? Did I talk about Griffin too much around her?

"That was back in my impetuous youth. We're just friends now. But he's probably my best friend."

"I get that," she said and told me of a reckless marriage in her early twenties and how she had settled down with a nice guy now. I hoped so. Someone with Lea's spirit deserved a great guy. Just then my cell buzzed. The familiar voice greeted me.

"Well, hello you. Speak of the devil. Lea and I were just talking about you."

"Just checking in. I hope you girls are ready to chuck New York and head down South." Hearing his voice soothed me like a good cup of his homemade soup.

"Stop. I'm not coming home, and you're not poaching Lea, but I will see you around Labor Day." I didn't know it would be even sooner than that.

⁂

I applied makeup the next morning the way Elle had taught me. I was meeting Gabriel at his restaurant. I was very excited but also nervous. I had spent obscene amounts of his money, and I wanted him to be blown away. I got there first and used my key. I turned the lights on and then I used the dimmer switch. Gabriel walked in. He didn't say a word. He just stared at the walls. It made me anxious. "I was thinking—"

He placed his tanned index finger to my lips to silence me. He was content to take it all in. I never knew if these money types were just interested in a vanity project or if they cared about the details. Clearly Gabriel fell into the latter category. He uttered one word, but it was the right one.

"Ipanema." That perfect smile appeared. "You captured my fondest childhood memory. This blue is almost exactly the color of the waters off Ipanema beach."

"I told them I wanted a paint color in the shade of Ipanema blue. Technically it's a little darker than the water, but I wanted all your dazzling woodwork to pop."

"Bailey, this is it. If I ever wanted you to come to Brazil and do a restaurant there for me, would you?"

"If you fly me, pay me, and feed me, of course I will go to Brazil." This brought hearty laughter.

"If I preferred petite, blonde, confident, opinionated, ambitious women, you would be just my type."

"Gee, Gabriel, if I preferred handsome playboys, you would be mine." We both laughed and agreed to meet in a few weeks. Being raised by men, I decided, had prepared me to navigate what was mostly a man's world. It had been lonely. It had been hard. But maybe it had been necessary.

Chapter Twenty-Eight

The weather was perfect for Elle's June nuptials. Walking around the Agricultural Hall in my tennis shoes and khakis, I was beginning to like the role of wedding planner better than my role as bridesmaid, which required a long dress and heels. The hall looked magical, more like a ballroom than a barn. Venessa White, the actual wedding planner, had done a spectacular job bringing my vision to life. There were chandeliers, countless strings of white lights, nicely weighted linens, and coordinating flower arrangements in lavender, green, and white for each table. I went around to each table and tucked sprigs of lavender, goldenrod, and juniper berries into each napkin.

"You are certainly a perfectionist," Venessa said as she put place cards on the tables.

"The same thing could be said of you. Besides, Elle is one of my best friends. I want her day to be perfect." I finished, took a few pictures, and went off to begin my second shift as a bridesmaid.

As I was waiting to walk down the aisle, I adjusted my bra and looked out upon the crowd. That's when I saw him. I didn't expect him to be here. Elle didn't tell me she was inviting Griffin. I would recognize him anywhere. The gray suit he wore on special occasions and those bracelets he had started wearing that were conspicuous despite the jacket. I wondered if he was wearing the one I bought him in SoHo. It was called Serenity. I had bought us each one but had lost mine. The instant I saw him, my heart leapt. It caught me off guard. Over the last year, I thought my heart had become too heavy for such carefree gymnastics. I was so distracted that I almost forgot it was my turn to walk.

161

As I went down the aisle and neared where he sat at the end of the row, I caught his attention and he turned to watch me. It rattled me. I saw his eyebrows shoot up; his mouth flew open in disbelief and he whispered, "Bae?" I forced myself to smile while not tripping over my dress. Under Reggie and Elle's instruction, I had been plucked, highlighted, uplifted, and Spanxed, and made-over until I didn't recognize myself.

I barely remember the ceremony. I vaguely heard Elle's soft voice as she exchanged her vows with Robbie. I vaguely remember hearing the exchange of rings and the pronouncement, their hearty kiss and the applause that followed. I just wanted to get to him.

"You clean up nicely, Bae."

I embraced and kissed him with a familiarity and an ardor reserved for devoted couples who have been reunited. "You're here," I said, finally releasing him and gaining my composure.

"I am indeed. I could say I'm your plus one or I could say Elle asked me to come up with her own bespoke cocktail, which I did, or I could say Elle invited me, which she also did. I don't think she wanted you to be alone." He seemed pleased that he could surprise me.

"You knew all this time you were coming and didn't tell me?" I said and swatted him. "So what's your bespoke cocktail for Elle?"

"I came up with two. Wedded Bliss, which is pink, for Elle. Dirty Bridegroom for Robbie." He was clearly tickled with himself. "The Dirty Bridegroom is pretty tame. Be careful with Wedded Bliss. It will knock you straight under the table," he laughed, and I did too. It felt good.

We walked inside the hall to find our places. We were at the table with Reggie and David.

"Wow, this is incredible! Who did all this?" Griffin asked.

"She is incredible, and you're sitting right next to her. It was Bailey," Reggie said and squeezed my hand.

"You did this, Bae? I'm impressed." He reached under the table and squeezed my knee.

"We want to see pictures of your place," Reggie said.

"All these nights when Bailey was on her computer, we thought she was surfing porn," David interjected, and Reggie gave him a stern look. We all laughed. "She was shopping for your condo."

"I'm lucky to have her." Griffin smiled at me. A dangerous alchemy of once-dormant emotions, free-flowing cocktails, and the ambiance of a wedding caused strange feelings to swirl inside me. I took a deep breath. Was it the cocktails or the atmosphere that were causing me to become increasingly unsteady?

The crowd was thinning. Finally, as Robbie and Elle were leaving, she threw her bouquet, but instead of finding Reggie, it landed right in my arms. I panicked and tossed it promptly to Reggie. She and David retreated to their hotel. This left Griffin and me and my belly full of Wedded Bliss cocktails.

"I'm going for a nightcap at a place I want to check out in Aquinnah. Care to join?" Griffin inquired. My vocabulary had collapsed. The word "no" had fallen out entirely.

We floated out of the reception and into a waiting car. We drove on winding roads for what seemed like forever, and yet time seemed suspended. We passed the lighthouse.

"What is your plan—to dump me in some deserted landfill or something?" I asked, not really caring where we were going.

"Or something." Griffin looked over at me and smiled. He brushed a strand of hair away from my face. The car turned onto a gravel driveway. It looked like a home, but it was a restaurant. There were few cars parked out front. We walked into a sparsely decorated space tastefully decorated but, oh, the view. The back was entirely windows overlooking the water. The full moon had taken over the cloudless sky. The image perfectly reflected in the water. I noticed an occasional ripple. It was as if the water and the moon were in a clandestine conversation. It was breathtaking.

We were seated at the best table. Upon our arrival, a sidecar and a snifter of cognac were delivered to us.

"Since when did you start drinking cognac?"

"You are a fine one to talk. I'm toasting the happy couple."

"I count on your sobriety." But I toasted with him anyway. We ordered nothing and yet plates of food arrived without question. I switched to a decaf cappuccino, and with my first sip, I shook my head.

"Really? I'm glad there are some things I can do better for you than anyone else," Griffin said as a tray of desserts arrived along with a plate of colorful sorbets. I looked at the green one, tasted it first, and found it drizzled in nostalgia. A petite woman with black hair pulled back in a tight bun brought a small plate of chocolate truffles over.

"I heard a rumor you were here. What do you think of the new sorbets? The watermelon and basil is my favorite." She leaned over and kissed Griffin in a familiar way. "Let me guess, this vision of loveliness in lavender has to be the very original Bailey." She met my eyes with the same familiarity as she kissed Griffin. I realized they knew each other well.

"I love your place, Elaine. You are right, it's the most remote point on the island but well worth the drive. And yes, this is Bailey." We chatted a little longer as we sampled each of her delightful sorbets. Was I afraid Griffin was going to introduce me to Elaine as something more than a fellow restaurateur? She gave Griffin a key and said it opened the back door and the room upstairs.

When she left, Griffin and I were imprisoned by our own thoughts. From time to time he looked at me and touched my hand.

"Are you sorry it's me here with you and not Elliott?" And then he asked, "Are you sorry it wasn't you getting married?" I shook my head. That had not even occurred to me. My mind was elsewhere, bouncing from the incomparable view to the empty table next to us.

I looked at that table, and I wondered if in a parallel universe there was another Bailey and Griffin sitting at that table. Would they be exchanging romantic musings and touching in a relaxed sort of way? Would happy conversations be stacked up like dinner plates on a Saturday night in one of Henry and Griffin's kitchens? Would they be free to express their innermost desires?

We got up, and Griffin used the key to unlock the door to the outside. We stood together in silence, listening to the water's movements, to the cicadas and the occasional breeze.

"Happy?" he asked.

I gave the question some serious thought. "This place is magical, Griffin," I said, deflecting. I followed him up the stairs, which led to a bedroom. It was designed as cleanly as the restaurant below— minimum fuss with maximum attention to the view.

I walked past the bed, suspended in time. Suspended in this moment, in this place, in this room. Suspended from any fallout that may happen here. Suspended in memories too numerous to count. I felt him behind me. Felt his breath on my neck. I turned around to face him. We kissed. Finally. Deep and full-bodied like the best red wine in the house. We kissed again. I heard and felt him breathing. We smiled at each other as we often did in these moments. A lifetime of collective shared memories. He looked into my eyes and kissed me again. He traced my lips with his finger, as if committing me to memory. I wanted to be with him again. I wanted to feel happy again. As I stood in the doorway of the bathroom, I watched Griffin unknot his tie, take off his jacket, and unbutton his shirt. I closed the bathroom door to begin my own undoing. Unaccustomed to the Spanx, it took me longer than usual.

When I opened the door, wrapped in a towel, Griffin was already under the sheets. I leaned against the door frame. He looked at me for a moment and then looked away. I felt something shift. "Griffin?" He looked at me again and shook his head.

"I can't do this, Bailey. It's too late. I don't want to complicate your life. No."

If that word had tumbled out of my vocabulary, it seemed to have found its way into Griffin's. My life with Elliott was very complicated, and this could only complicate it more. But this moment, being with Griffin, seemed natural, seamless, and easy.

"Why? For old time's sake?" I said it lightly, not knowing how to respond. This was the first time Griffin had ever turned me down. I was starting to feel a surge of panic and hurt, something I was unaccustomed to. I wondered if I had not had to wrangle out of that wretched girdle would we, like our counterparts in the alternate universe, be exchanging intimacies and musings about the wedding or the spectacular view from my room? I silently cursed the notion of Spanx interruptus sex.

"We're too old. You've moved on with Elliott. And I have Alex," he said. I looked at him wounded. My anger rising.

"So we're just going to move on with the vowels in our life?" I injected these words with forced lightheartedness.

"Huh?" he asked. Not even my conversation was working anymore.

"Alex, Elliott—A, E." I hadn't realized he and Alex were that serious. "You're rejecting me?"

"Yes, I think it's for the best. I'm with Alex. You're with Elliott." I was standing there nearly bare in front of him. Trembling, I grabbed his T-shirt and went back into the bathroom.

"You okay?" he had the nerve to ask. I would never be okay. In that moment, I realized I had never fully accepted that Griffin and I would never be together again. I wanted him to choose me. I loved Elliott, but my heart's compass had never freed itself from the gravitational pull of Griffin. But Elliott chose me, and Griffin rejected me. I began to cry.

Looking into the mirror, I saw my tears mixed with mascara, staining my face in the universal symbol of rejection and unrequited love. I turned the water on until I pulled myself together and could breathe again. I cleaned my face, threw on his T-shirt, and opened the door as if the whole of my being had not just been dismantled.

I walked over to the bed. He leaned over and pecked my cheek goodnight, like well-acquainted friends. It pissed me off.

When I was certain nothing else was going to happen, I pulled back the sheets. That's when I noticed it. It was so un-Griffin-like. I studied it. It was soft and unobtrusive. He made no attempt to move my hand from his hipbone.

"You have a tattoo?" My voice was so calm it fooled even me. "Henry told me about his tattoo when we were painting your condo. Why would you even get a tattoo? When have you ever listened to Henry about such things?"

"It seemed like a good idea. To get something important to me."

"What does your tattoo even mean to you?" I traced the letters like braille, B-R-E-A-T-H-E. Breathe.

"It's essential. To my existence. To my soul," he said in a nonchalant fashion. I continued studying and tracing the letters. When I got to the last "E," which was coincidentally nearing his southern regions, he pulled my hand away. "No, Bae." He was gentle but firm. I wrapped his arms around me like warm covers. I hated myself for wanting him. But my desire to be with him exceeded the anger I felt toward him. I closed my eyes, committing this moment to memory. Touching his body for the last time, feeling his breath kiss my shoulder blades, and inhaling the smells that belonged to him and him alone. I carefully placed it in my brimming treasure chest with all the other memories I had of him in the hidden compartment of my heart. .

An unexpected melancholy settled into my bones. I thought about my secrets. I thought about our secrets. I thought about the mantra that had become Griffin's tattoo. Then something landed so gently I was unaware of what it truly meant. Every third letter of the permanent ink spelled my name: Bae.

Chapter Twenty-Nine

When I returned from Martha's Vineyard, my emotions were in shambles. I felt like some vital organ had just been removed. Elliott wasn't feeling well, so I went back to my apartment. I kept replaying Griffin's refusal. Maybe it was me that needed "the talk." I was angry, but maybe it was all a misunderstanding. The anger would help me move on with Elliott. Luckily, Reggie and David were home, and so I posed it as just a generic question.

"How do you have 'the talk' with a guy?"

"If this is about you moving in with Elliott, I always thought it would come down to a 'who,' rather than of 'when.'" I waited for her to continue. She added, "I would just ask him if this is leading somewhere."

I looked at David, who looked increasingly uncomfortable at the subject matter. He nodded and said, "Try not to be too serious, Bailey. Just don't ask him if it's leading to marriage." I managed to laugh.

Sometime after midnight, I worked up my nerve with a little liquid courage to call Griffin.

"Hey, it's me." Casual start.

"Um, are you okay, Bae?

"Yes. Are you still at the shop?"

"No. Can I call you in the morning? It's just not a good time right now." Before I had a chance to answer, he hung up. It took me a second to figure it out. Griffin was with Alex. They were together in Griffin's bedroom that I decorated. Maybe his tattoo was some inside joke he had with her.

Without even having the conversation, I got my answer. Griffin had moved on. All this time I had been his casual. I kept looking at the phone as if some cruel mistake had occurred. Besides work, my life had been defined by these men. Griffin was who I called before anyone else.

I hardly slept. I could almost hear the wind blowing through the hole in my heart. The next morning, I was leaving to take the train to a university in Upstate New York that I was working on when my phone rang.

"Hey, Bae. What were you calling about last night?" I tried to gather my thoughts. Gathering up the contents of my portfolio had been a lot easier.

"Nothing important. It doesn't matter anymore. I still can't believe you got a tattoo."

He laughed. "Think about Julian and our yoga class." On the train, I remembered Julian convincing Griffin and me that we were much too serious and needed to attend this pranayama breathing class which would "change our lives." How had we let him talk us into that? We were a curious threesome, Henry, Griffin, and I. Henry was the genius, the virtuoso in the kitchen. You would expect him to be the serious one, but much like Elliott, he could be silly, whimsical, and fun-loving. But Griffin, not quite as talented as Henry, took trying and working at his talent very seriously. Like me. I lived in my head with my ideas, dreams, and visions.

The class had started promptly at five-thirty in an upscale studio on West Paces Ferry. Griffin and I went the first time at Julian's suggestion. When I was in Atlanta putting NOIR together, we attended more frequently. The instructor was not your granola yoga type. Her class was quite an operation. She folded blankets, accordion style, to open up our spines so we could get maximum air into our lungs. "Belly breathing," she called it.

"And don't be afraid if you just fall asleep," she had said.

"Don't count on it. I'm much too inhibited to fall asleep with a bunch of strangers breathing on me," I whispered to Griffin. He laughed. We went to the class many times together. "I don't know about changing our lives, but I'm glad I did it with you," Griffin said to me one night when we were putting away our blankets. The instructor approached us.

"You're Griffin Hardwick, one of the Color-Wheel Boys. You own those restaurants. Can't wait for the new one to open." Was she flirting with him?

"That's right. Tell me next time you're coming and I'll whip up a pranayama cocktail," he smiled. He then offered, "This is Bailey. Bailey Edgeworth, Henry's sister."

After yoga we enjoyed our time together, sometimes going for a small bite before we went to work. Sometimes we even discussed the sutras the instructor read. Sometimes we said profound things. Sometimes we made wicked comments. Sometimes we laughed, not sounding serious at all. Sometimes we lingered even after the bill was paid, drinking bad coffee. Sometimes we just exchanged glances, saying nothing. Sometimes we walked closer than we should have. Sometimes we were mistaken for a couple deeply in love. It was one of those happy times I took completely for granted. Looking back on it now, maybe had it gone slightly different, it could have been life-altering. But now it was simply a tattoo on a body that I could no longer lay claim to.

After that conversation with Griffin, we talked less and less. It was hard, being rejected. The ease we had once had with each other was gone.

One day, surveying my closet, I realized it was becoming barren. Most of my things had migrated to Elliott's closet. I supposed it was my turn to move out next.

Elliott had returned to fine form, getting up early, going to the market, and cooking with renewed panache. I decided to postpone a trip home. Henry assured me Daddy was fine. My heart needed a break. Elliott was being kind, responsive, and reassuring of his feelings. I appreciated him. It was lovely knowing where I stood with a man.

Chapter Thirty

Autumn ushered in an eagerness I had not anticipated. Elliott had returned to being an undisputed maestro in the kitchen. Right before Elle's wedding, Aztec, the Peruvian restaurant, had opened with stellar reviews. I was very excited for Luis Pompeo. He had worked tirelessly as both the owner and chef. He was about to earn his American citizenship, and I wanted to be present for him for that. It made me think of Elliott and how excited he had been.

I was spending much of my time putting the finishing touches on Ipanema. Luckily for me, Elliott and I were in such a good place he wasn't even jealous of Gabriel. I was very proud of my work, but each day that passed, I was becoming more and more content with our relationship.

The day before Ipanema was to open, Gabriel and I hung his exquisite mask collection. It was one of those things that requires trial and error. We played around with it, made mistakes, and tried different configurations before settling on our final arrangement that showcased each of the masks in his collection. I knew it was worth the extra time and thought. This was the kind of thing that food critics loved to take pictures of to feature in their reviews. He opened a bottle of his preferred champagne, and we toasted to our collaboration. It was the quiet before the storm. Opening night was wall-to-wall beautiful people and the who's who of Gabriel's celebrity friends. Photographers snapped countless pictures. Good reviews and notices followed. We all benefited. Gabriel gave me an exquisite wooden box from Brazil that had belonged to his grandmother. After I initially refused, Gabriel said, "You can. And you must." I was quite touched.

And then I got the call. The one I had been dreaming about from the beginning. *Architectural Digest* wanted to do an article on me. Talk about dreams coming true. I told Elliott first. He insisted on taking me shopping.

"This is a big deal for you, Bailey. National exposure. I want you to look as beautiful on the pages of the magazine as I see you each and every single day." I told the girls next, and they agreed with Elliott.

"You can tell that man loves you and is proud of you. I happen to agree with him. You cannot wear your scavenging clothes for a photo shoot. I bet your brother and Griffin are over the moon."

The girls were surprised that I hadn't told them yet. When I did, my men were predictably excited and sent flowers. Griffin texted.

"Make sure you put the flowers in the pictures and say they came from your brother and me who own three little establishments down in Atlanta."

"No can do, Griffin." I said with forced lightheartedness. It made me so sad.

As cavalier as I could be by text, I understood that my feelings wouldn't be so clear-cut when I saw him in person.

Elliott infused even shopping with fun. We chose a salmon-colored dress that would stand out and a green one. I ended up wearing the salmon one for the shoot. I also wore my favorite diamond and peridot earrings. I probably wore them too often, but what's the sense of having something you love and not enjoying it?

With the popularity of Elliott's restaurant, Aztec, and the über-popular Ipanema—thanks in part to the handsome publicity hog Gabriel—I was the culinary "it" girl. I didn't even have to know how to make toast to earn the honor. The photo shoot was done in Elliott's restaurant, but it also featured pictures from all the other venues, including some of the college cafeterias I was most proud of. Talk about free advertising.

It was just like my dream all those years ago when I was walking around Daddy's restaurant answering questions. My dream had come true. Except instead of Griffin, Elliott stood on the sidelines beaming and mouthing, "I love you." In many ways, this was far better than my daydream. Griffin would never be caught dead saying that for a magazine. Because even in my daydream, he wore a bemused expression. The only thing Griffin might mouth was "come home." But now I was on a roll.

There was brief mention of my culinary lineage and the Color-Wheel Boys and my background in working with the illustrious Julian Palmer, but for the most part, it was just about me and my unique aesthetic. The prepositional phrases and commas weren't in relation to anyone but me.

Afterward, Elliott retired to rest his back. I was alone when I toasted myself with Perrier-Jouët. Old habits die hard. I wanted to call Griffin to tell him about my day and to hear him say, "Bae, I'm so proud." But I had to protect my heart. It was in that moment I realized even when our dearest dreams come true, they are often accompanied by the slightest hint of sadness and regret.

Chapter Thirty-One

My misgivings about formally moving in with Elliott were misplaced. Besides the fact I'd be getting a tony address, the man I had fallen in love with returned with renewed ardor. He always made breakfast early before he left for the market, and when I entered the restaurant, he would greet and kiss me as if we had been separated for days. Whatever malady and wicked mood had befallen him in the summer had left him as suddenly as it had taken up residence.

There was a time Henry could not pass up a scotch bottle without emptying its contents into his stomach. He made bad decisions, slept with the wrong women, racked up a ton of legal bills, and put the onus of running three restaurants on Griffin. But out of that had come Hank and a new maturity. Geniuses like Henry and Elliott battled demons that the rest of us couldn't even imagine. I was proud of Elliott's rebound. There was talk about expansion of the restaurant and even a second. Honors and awards found him as easily as return patrons.

Just like that, the holidays loomed. I had not seen Griffin since that fiasco in Martha's Vineyard. I was so happy. Elliott was in fine form. Was it too much to ask to spend Christmas in New York? I approached Henry about the possibility of coming in January.

"What's going on with you?" Henry inquired.

"Nothing. It's just I've never spent a Christmas in New York before. What's another two weeks? I promise I'll fly down the first week in January."

"You haven't seen Daddy since last Christmas. Whatever's going on with you, fix it, Bailey. I want to talk to you about something you might like."

"You piqued my interest. There's nothing to fix. But I'll see you in January. I promise."

✴

The holidays lifted everyone's moods. Elle was happily married, and Reggie had recently gotten engaged. Any sisterly concern they had for me seemed to have abated. Elle and Reggie shared the difficulties of juggling family Christmases and get-togethers. I was happy that I did not share those issues, since my family resided in Atlanta. And just like that, my heart interrupted those settled thoughts in a know-it-all fashion and reminded me of Elliott. That night, with no evidence of internal commotion, Elliott and I decided to spend Christmas and New Year's together in the city.

A week before Christmas, Elliott and Lea met me at the door of the restaurant late one afternoon. Elliott's eyes were dancing with mischief. He handed me a fat envelope before saying, "I think those shops you frequent have been missing your presence. Take the rest of the day off. That's an order." Lea nodded.

It was true. Since I had moved in with Elliott, I had not had a lot of extra time for shopping. I popped in all my regular haunts. I texted both Reggie and Elle to see if they wanted to meet for a drink. I had found each of them a unique necklace at The Sleepy Anarchist. They gave me a discount for buying two, for having cash, and because they had missed me. I also bought Elliott presents and stopped at a little shop on Madison Avenue that did nothing except wrap presents in exquisite paper and ribbons. It was decked out in upscale holiday merriment. Presentation.

"It looks like somebody has already gotten her Christmas bonus," Reggie said, looking at the packages that circled my feet.

"Two are for you. I took the liberty of ordering cocktails," I said, watching them exchange glances. I wasn't the sharpest member of

Lady World, but I knew something was afoot. "Any news you can share, Elle?"

"October brought us a premature Halloween treat. I'm going to have a baby in July."

"That's wonderful news! I'm so excited for you. Of course, you are going to let me 'vision' the nursery?" We laughed.

"Bailey, I must say cohabitation agrees with you," Elle said.

"It does indeed."

We whispered. We planned. We joined the rest of the world in joy overdrive.

I arrived home late in the evening. Even as I was turning the key, I could tell something was different. When I opened the door to the apartment, I encountered a winter wonderland. It was enchanting. There was a Christmas tree, complete with countless white lights. Cedar wreaths dressed the windows. The tree was anchored by an array of colorful and beautifully wrapped presents. My first thought was that this was the work of the shop on Madison Avenue. I stepped closer and noticed Elliott standing next to me grinning and wearing a sport coat.

"Are we expecting company?"

"Just the lady of the house. Are you surprised? Do you like it?" he asked. It reminded me of my childhood.

"What's not to like? Yes, I'm surprised. You look nice." He took my arm, wrapped it around his waist, and embraced me and kissed me as if mistletoe dangled above our heads. We sat by the Christmas tree, and I added my presents to his. Later on, instead of presents, we merrily unwrapped each other.

On Christmas Day, Elliott prepared a Christmas goose with cranberry and currant reduction and a decadent English trifle for dessert. I called Henry. All my men were gathered at Henry's for a feast. I talked to Daddy first, telling him I loved him, and then Griffin and I spoke. It was awkward. I wished both he and Alex a merry one before turning my full attention to this wonderful Englishman. We opened presents, drank champagne, kissed often, and touched even more. It made for a very merry Christmas memory.

The day after Christmas, I went out to get something I had been waiting to go on after-Christmas sale. When I returned, I noticed the bedroom door was closed. It reminded me of when he was down with his back. Or worse. My heart instantly seized.

"Elliott?" I walked over to the bedroom door and knocked.

"Coming. I have saved the best present for last." He emerged from the bedroom in a suit and a new tie that I'd given him for Christmas. I hadn't bought him a New Year's present. He looked so handsome. But he also looked nervous. "Sit down."

"Okay. Are we going out?" I hadn't been aware of any plans. It was like he hadn't heard me. Now I was getting nervous. He sat down next to me on the couch.

"Bailey, I don't say this often enough. You changed my life. My heart beats differently when you're in the room. You are my soul mate. You are my partner. Your opinion means the most to me in the world. I love you with everything I have." He paused. I noticed little beads of sweat gathered on his forehead, and it just made him a little bit more endearing. He then lowered himself to one knee.

"New Year's has been special for us. I would like this to be another beginning. Just for us. Not only a new year but a new life together. I want you to be more than my lover and partner. I would like very much, Bailey Edgeworth, for you to do me the enormous honor of becoming my wife." He waited and sweated. "I have already made an appointment on the twenty-seventh at the courthouse to get our marriage license, so we will have everything ready if you say yes. Because I haven't seen your bridesmaid's dress from Elle's wedding, I thought maybe you could use that as a substitute. We could get married at the courthouse. Or if you want, I have been googling some all-night chapels. I just want you to be my wife. I don't care where."

At that moment, Elliott fumbled around in his pocket. In the whole time I had known him, he had never fumbled with anything. Not with words, not with objects, not even his self-confidence. But he was unsure of himself and unsure of my answer. He finally produced a box and opened it to reveal a beautiful peridot with diamonds on each side and a diamond band to match it. It touched me that he had put so much thought into his proposal.

I cupped his beautiful face in my hands and uttered a single word: "Yes."

Before I knew it, it was New Year's Eve. Because I loved it and it made me feel pretty, I put on the dress from Elle's wedding, without the aid of Spanx, my beautiful earrings to match my engagement ring, and my heaviest coat, and I took the hand of the man who was about to become my husband. The ceremony at the courthouse was brief but no less sacred.

We found a diner near the courthouse, which served breakfast all day long. I ordered scrambled eggs, greasy hash browns, and white toast with packets of jelly. A perfect wedding meal. It gave birth to the inkling of an idea in my brain. As we left, the sound of fireworks exploded in the distance celebrating us, our love, our hopes and dreams, our marriage.

Chapter Thirty-Two

It happened so fast. It was romantic, magical, spontaneous, and impetuous. So not me. Clearly not. But it was done, and I had married the man I loved. It wasn't until the next day that I thought: "Holy shit—I eloped without my girls or my men."

I called Henry to give him my nuptial news. "Geez, Bailey. Are you pregnant?"

"No, Henry. I'm happy." I waited.

"Well, okay then." To say his enthusiasm was muted would've been an understatement. Maybe his loyalty was divided. But I was his sister. "Listen," he added. "You're going to have to deliver the news to Griffin yourself."

"Can't you tell him for me?"

"Shit, Bailey. He deserves to hear from you," Henry said, deflecting my question.

And then there were the girls. "What? You get a purse or a pair shoes on impulse," Elle said.

"Not a husband," Reggie added. They eventually came around and embraced me, Elliott, and our quickie marriage.

For weeks I called Griffin without success. His message, "This is Griffin. You know what to do," had become the most annoying words in the English language.

I even had a hard time talking to Henry. When I finally got in touch with him a few weeks later, it was not pretty. "Things are fucked up pretty badly here. I told you to get things straight with Griffin. He's a mess. He gets drunk. I sober him up. Repeat. It is all I can do to maintain my own sobriety and not to drink myself. It's a shit show. I think under the circumstances you should postpone your trip home until I can get things sorted out down here. I have no idea how long that will be. It's a mess," Henry added again for emphasis. Most of the time, both men refused to talk to me, and it left me reeling. So, it turned out my marriage was the life-shattering event that caused Griffin to get drunk. But what about Alex?

Guilt, worry, and something I couldn't put a name on took up residence inside me. Elisabeth Kübler-Ross's five stages of grief bounced around, and with each bounce, the grief multiplied. I was angry. This was supposed to be the happiest time of my life, and Griffin was robbing me of it. He was the one who turned me down. Then I would become sad. What if history repeated itself and he ended up like his parents? For the first time, I felt truly isolated, forsaken by my men. Utterly alone. Had my impetuous marriage done something to the three of us that was beyond repair? Had I caused the three of us to permanently break apart? Then I would be angry because I didn't want to take ownership for the whole bloody schism. For weeks I couldn't sleep or eat. My hair and patience grew thin. The girls noticed. They listened. Their loyalty seemed divided too.

After fourteen weeks of this silent treatment, I couldn't sleep. One night around two in the morning, I got up and took my phone into the kitchen. It had been over three months. Almost a full season. If he wasn't going to return my calls, I was just going to have to wake him up in the middle of the night. Finally, the phone stopped ringing.

"Hello?" The voice was strained, but it was Alex. Not Griffin.

"Hi, Alex. I need to talk to Griffin."

"Yeah. He can't come to the phone right now." She paused. "Um, Bailey, I'll try to get him to call you when he sobers up." She hung up.

I thought about the conversation he and I never had about "us." I was frightened for him.

A few days later, I was about to leave the apartment, embarking on my first big-time, legitimate, "put my name on the map" job opportunity since working on Ipanema. My phone buzzed. It was Griffin.

"Hello," I said, reminding myself to have restraint in this conversation.

"I know you know."

"Back at you." I had gotten married. Griffin had become a drunk. "Are you okay?" I heard myself ask.

"I don't know. I need time, Bae." And then he said, "Can I still call you that?"

"Of course. That's my name."

"Your husband won't mind?" He almost choked the word out.

"Wait just a minute. You're the one who broke my heart. You refused me." I was shaking.

"I didn't marry Alex. It's not like that. You know that."

"How? When I called, you were sleeping with Alex. In the bedroom I decorated." Our words retreated. But neither one of us made any motion to end the conversation.

"Griffin . . . What about us? Are we ever going to be okay?" Silence covered us like a scratchy blanket. He didn't answer. We just sat there. In an odd way, we were at least together. I feared if I hung up, I would sever our relationship for good. So, I held the phone to my ear, cradling our fragile connection.

"There will never be an 'us.' Not anymore." More silence.

Finally, I said, "I hate this. What chapter is this in your caregiver's book?"

"Chapter Forty-Three. Relapse," he said. "Or regret." We sank deeper into silence. A thousand thoughts darted between us, but no words landed on our lips. My heart broke again even as it was bursting.

"I'm so sorry, Griffin," and I hung up the phone without letting him hear me cry. I shed tears for Griffin before anyone else.

My anger fell away. My happiness fell away. All that was left was unresolved longing and sadness I couldn't quench or bear.

Chapter Thirty-Three

The brutal winter yielded a warmer than normal spring. April ushered in sprouting daffodils and sun worshipers in Central Park.

Elliott and I established our own contours of marriage. Something that started so haphazardly looked like a well-thought-out decision. I loved him. His reputation did not dwarf mine, but rather we were on equal footing. I loved that about Elliott. We made a great team. A true partnership.

However, the interactions with my men recalibrated. Griffin and I no longer spoke or texted. Even when Henry and I spoke, it was superficial and usually about Daddy. The easy rhythm we once shared had been forfeited. Both the girls and Henry told me to be patient. I hated it. I showed restraint out of love for Henry. I realized that my desire for Griffin to heal was greater than my need to offer up a lame apology. Yet, when I heard his name, the air grew thin, and all the pathways around my heart constricted. I still found it hard to breathe.

It reminded me of when the boys left for college. While I was so bereft in the wake of their absence, I found myself. As undone as I was about Griffin, my once-hibernating career returned in robust fashion.

As was his habit, Elliott greeted me at the door and ushered me into his office.

"Hello, wife." He kissed me. This was always a signal that he was in a good mood or feeling frisky.

"Shall I lock the door?"

"No need. Something has come to my attention." He sounded grave. "Something is lacking in our marriage." It immediately put me on guard. I feared that it was something on my part. "Relax, my very serious wife. I think you'll like this. Do you realize we never took a proper honeymoon?" He smiled. I relaxed. "Settle down. Nothing grand. Neither one of us can be away from work that long. But what about a long weekend in the Hamptons? I have already rented a cottage. The last week of April is supposed to be magnificent."

"Can we afford this?"

"Now, Bailey."

I relented.

The vacation was something extraordinary and surprising. We left our harsher natures behind. It was as if I left my hard-charging and serious self right at the city limits.

We lingered in bed. We laughed. We talked. We strolled hand in hand on the beach. I discovered a deeper bond with this lovely man who had become my husband and was taking my life journey with me.

Elliott prepared truly simple dishes. At night, we ate fresh seafood, drank good wine, and explored new ways to please one another. Elliott mastered the lovely art of satisfying his wife. If I had left my serious nature behind, Elliott left his bad back issues behind. I could've gotten used to the honeymoon thing. But reality beckoned, appointments loomed, creative meals demanded to be fixed. We made promises to return. And for the first time in three days, I consulted my calendar. I had a rescheduled meeting the next day with a man who'd been described as "the new Danny Meyer." He had lofty ambitions and a big fat wallet. In preparation for our meeting, I had sent over my portfolio, which I'd updated before we left town. I was ready. New York loves "the next big thing." I intended to make him my latest client.

Chapter Thirty-Four

McClelland Whitney greeted me at the door of his forty-third-floor office. He was tall, dark, and handsome. And Southern. He shook my hand with equal parts firmness and ease.

"Miss Edgeworth, please, take a seat. It is so nice to meet you. I took the liberty of ordering you a cappuccino. I hope that's okay. You see, I've done my homework on you." The way he drew out my last name was as slow as molasses. He waited until I had sat down before he took a seat next to mine.

"Please, it's Bailey," I said. He was at least a full decade older than me.

"Thank you," he said as if I had granted him a favor. "I'm from rural Georgia. I will let you in on a little secret. I stared at all five of my best blue sport coats before deciding on this one. Your portfolio is impressive."

"Then your research failed you, Mr. Whitney. I am not sure I qualify as a real Southern lady." His little shtick somehow made me laugh. It felt like a release of something long forgotten after this exile imposed by my men. I wanted to get down to business, but I could predict what he was going to say next, and I wouldn't be disappointed.

"My daddy is Mr. Whitney. I'm just Mac," he said with effortless charm. "You're famous, Bailey. Your portfolio is amazing." Just the reaction I'd been hoping for when I assembled my now-plump portfolio.

"You will notice," I began, taking charge of the conversation, "that the green tab houses pictures of various venues I've decorated. The second tab, the blue one, hosts some of those same pictures with the corresponding awards I've earned for the projects. The third tab, the yellow one, should be of keen interest to you. It shows the profit margins of the restaurants after an article was written about me in conjunction with the restaurant. Because we both know it's not just about my accolades but about what I can do for you." I smiled. I noticed Mac relax back in his chair, allowing me to finish. "The last tab is a list of ten references regarding my work."

"I saw that. It is customary that a person generally sends three to five."

"Yes. But in the final analysis, do you choose customary, or do you want someone who goes above and beyond?" This was always my practice. I anticipated the next questions.

Mac nodded. "But the recommendation from Julian Palmer seems to be sufficient. After all, his opinion goes a long way."

"Yes. But you aren't hiring Julian Palmer. You're hiring me. I don't rely on someone else's name. Not when I have my own. I let my own work speak for me."

"I also noticed you do not include Elliott Graemmer's establishment."

"I make it a practice never to include my husband's restaurant. That wouldn't be professional." I was used to this Southern business of being charming, and I wanted it to stop. Mentioning a husband usually dampens those advances. I wanted his business. Nothing more.

"The Englishman, huh? That is late-breaking news. I know your brother and Griffin quite well," he said. The mere mention of Griffin's name jolted me ever so slightly. "Met them when I got ready to sell my establishments in Macon and Augusta—you may have heard of them—The Cotton Mill. My daddy made his money off cotton, and in a way, so did I." He laughed. Who hadn't heard of The Cotton Mill? He had made a killing when he sold his business to a couple of golfers who wanted vanity projects. "Anyway, I went up to Atlanta and met with your brother and Griffin. They both have pretty impressive business acumen. They even hooked me up with their attorney, Jake Fein, who was a shark. I'm surprised you didn't go back to work with them."

"Henry is the best at what he does. We do different things. To be the best in restaurant design, you have to work with the best, and at the time, it was Julian." My mind wandered back to my last feeble attempt to engage Griffin. I had texted Griffin regarding a bespoke cocktail, and his response was terse. "Ask your bartender. Not me." There had been a time when I thought Griffin and I would be together. For good. There was a time, and then Martha's Vineyard happened.

"I know they're biased, but they say you're the best. After seeing some of your work, I happen to agree. I was quite impressed by what you achieved with that French café on West Eighty-Fifth Street. They've garnered some high marks from those in the know. And the eclectic little bakery down in the village. I like the way you incorporate your style with that of your client. That is clearly on display with what you achieved at Ipanema."

I had enjoyed both those projects. Both had been small in scale, but each provided me with necessary income and good reviews. I was glad he had studied my portfolio.

I smiled as Mac continued, "I talked to Julian a long time about you."

"What about?" I asked.

"He's great, don't get me wrong. But when you see his work, you know it's Julian. He said that the pupil had surpassed the teacher. In addition, I like the way you incorporate whimsical and unexpected details. That's what I would want from you. Plus, you're much easier on the eyes than Julian." Mac just couldn't help his roguish behavior. While I loathed that sockless, pink-shirted frat boy so ubiquitous in the South, Mac seemed unaffected. Had he already made a decision?

"Where's your space?" I asked. "And what timetable are we talking about? Then, of course, the budget?"

"A lady that gets straight down to business. I like that. Let me put this out there. My two drawbacks: I am opinionated just like you are, and if I have an idea, I would expect you to listen to me. Feasibility-wise, I am not able to begin this project for another sixteen months, for reasons I would rather not divulge just now. If my ideas and my timetables don't scare you away, I would like to sit down with you again, look at your past projects in depth, have you explain the things you did and why, preferably over dinner. Strictly business. Okay? I'll show you the space, and then we can discuss numbers—yours and the project's."

"Okay," I said.

"Just for the record: I'm a harmless flirt. I have a wife now," he said.

This time, I smiled. I was ready for the comeback.

"None of my business, but is it you have a wife now or you have a wife *for* now? Prepositions are important."

Mac let out a laugh that was so hearty it could have shaken the whole building. "Well, damn. You are a woman after my own heart. You enjoy grammar. You will be happy to know I attended the University of the South, majored in English, and even wrote for the *Sewanee Review*. Daddy thought I was going to play for the other team. But my extracurricular activities told him otherwise. Did you name Elliott's restaurant, or was it one of those happy coincidences?"

"Both. It was his name, but it was my idea to capitalize on it." I relaxed, my confidence buoyed.

He pointed to my untouched cappuccino. "Not enough foam?" When I didn't answer, he said, "I'll work on that. By the way, I've eaten at your restaurant several times. I hope this doesn't come off as too stalker-like, but I watched you work the room. You sent me an amuse-bouche every time. I love the way you glided from table to table. You seem to value each and every patron. No table felt more important than another. It was as if you wanted each guest to feel cherished."

That touched me. It was the way I had always described my father. He made it look so easy. In reality, it was really hard work. But because I wanted everybody to feel happy, I had worked on my own presentation.

"So have I scared you away? Are you willing to meet with me in a few weeks when I get back? And don't worry, your matrimonial artillery is on full display," he said, pointing to my fresh engagement ring and wedding band. I found myself accepting another proposal with a single word: "Yes."

Walking into the restaurant that afternoon, I had a little extra spring in my step.

"Hello, wife," Elliott said and kissed me with a sense of urgency. I smiled. Never in my life would I have dreamed that the descriptor "wife" would find its way to me. We walked into his office.

"I'm starving. I'd do anything for food."

"I plan to hold you to that later." He sat behind his desk, preparing a list of the night's specials.

"By the way, husband, can I have a little money?" He thought I was kidding. "I'm serious. I've got to pay my health insurance, I need to get my hair cut, and sometimes when Penny and I are out, she likes to grab lunch at nice places. When you were so sick and I was running the restaurant, I had to turn down some big gigs."

"I can't believe you don't have much money left. We need to get you on my health insurance plan. I don't appreciate the dig at me."

"It wasn't. I just need a little until I get another job. And that may be rather soon." I always left details out. Mac Whitney might be on to something else by then. "Just for my health insurance and a couple of hundred for beautification and lunch money."

"You need to watch your spending, Bailey. I mean it. This will come out of our profits. We'll get this sorted out in the next few days."

He unlocked his desk drawer and wrote a check. He frowned when he handed it to me. For the first time in my life, I questioned my worth.

Leave it to Elle and Reggie to set me straight. "That man should give you anything you ask for. You saved his restaurant from going down in flames when he was sick, and you gave him the money for the new stove. He's begrudging you money for a haircut. Please. You better get things straightened out in paradise, honey." They both took turns serving me ample helpings of home truths.

Over the next few days, we met with Elliott's banker. If the ceremony on New Year's Eve didn't make it official, that day certainly did. I received my own debit card. Elliott put me on his bank account and the restaurant's and on all his credit cards.

"Now, love, everything I have is yours. So, if you need anything, within reason, you don't even have to ask me. But you may want to ask Lea since she's in charge of the books. If you need to get that long mane done to stay my beautiful Bailey, you can."

But something in me was cautious about using my new plastic. I didn't put Elliott on my account, and he didn't ask. Checking with Lea seemed like the best policy.

The flower arrangements returned. The little love notes on beautiful paper beside my morning coffee returned. Little trinkets returned. My work returned. Stellar reviews returned. And then congratulatory notes from the men in my life came. All but Griffin.

One such card read: "Would you believe someone just asked me if I was Bailey Edgeworth's brother? I am so proud of you. Henry and Hank."

"We need to meet ASAP. I want you on retainer to make sure you will have time for my little venture. You do still have time for me, don't you? —Mac." This one came with flowers. I removed the card, smiled, and remembered I had a jealous Englishman for a husband.

Out of the blue, a small note arrived in the mail. Even after all these years, I recognized the handwriting. I dropped my keys to the apartment, startling everyone in the mailroom. My heart quickened and I stopped breathing. The way my name, Bailey Edgeworth, stretched across the entire envelope, the unique way the *Y* looped and cradled my full name. The way he had written my name from the very beginning. When the room was empty, I carefully opened the envelope to not disturb the contents. My eyes drifted to the bottom first. It was short: "You made it in New York. Enjoy your moment and breathe. I'm sober. Griffin." The last one did more for my heart than any flowers ever could.

The following Sunday night, Elliott prepared a quiet dinner for us at home. It was reminiscent of the meals he had concocted before we were married. He opened a bottle of champagne and toasted us. "To my extraordinary muse who just happens to be my wife, my soul mate, and my partner in all life's most delightful endeavors." Lovely habits began to emerge. Drinking champagne. Laughing for no particular reason and touching for the same reasons. Even the playful habits in our lovemaking reemerged. Elliott preferred to take his time, removing each garment of my clothing himself and assaulting me with kisses in between.

Chapter Thirty-Five

The following Wednesday I received two calls while out scouting for three new projects. The first was from Lea.

"Elliott just went home complaining about his back. He said to call you." Damn. Not this again, I thought. I made my purchases quickly and turned around to head back. As I approached the restaurant, my phone buzzed. It was Mac.

"Hey, Ms. Bigshot. I'm back in town. Do you think we could get together next Thursday for lunch? I've got some ideas I'd like to run past you, and of course there's always the little matter of your retainer, which is probably sky-high by now," he laughed. It was the laughter of confidence that only old money, new money, and charm evoked.

I stalled. Next week would be fine if Elliott was back in form. "Let's tentatively say Thursday, and if something comes up, I'll text you."

"You're not playing hard to get now, are you?"

If only, I thought. "I'll text next week to confirm."

I entered the restaurant to see what crises confronted me. First thing, my clothes needed changing. I was dressed for scavenging, not greeting guests in a high-end restaurant. I needed to remember to keep a change of clothes in Elliott's office like I used to. The second thing—Rex was having a meltdown and threatening to quit because of his expanded workload due to Elliott's absence.

I called Henry at the restaurant to seek his advice. "Just deal with him. You negotiate every day in those bargain stores."

"But if he walks? I'm a bit of a chicken when it comes to negotiating things like this. We both know the restaurant would be royally screwed if he leaves. I have no backup chef." I heard another phone pick up on the line and it was Griffin. Just the sound of his voice did all kinds of things to me. I could barely concentrate on his advice.

"Just remember, it's your restaurant," Griffin added. "Pay him what you want to pay him." And just as quickly, Griffin hung up. For the first time, it occurred to me that as Elliott's wife, it really was also my restaurant now. So I did pay Rex.

"Elliott is going to have a stroke when he finds out," Lea said. I knew that and didn't care.

"Elliott isn't here. Can I borrow some of your makeup?" I asked.

"I don't know if the revenue can absorb that increase," Lea said, fishing around for her blush and lipstick.

"How's the new stove working?" I asked.

"It's great," she said.

"How much does one of those things cost anyway? I know they're expensive," I said, knowing we could look at Elliott's meticulous records to find out.

"A lot. It's a good thing the last one was still under warranty."

"Elliott forgot to fill out the paperwork and send it in," I said.

"Are you familiar with your anal-retentive husband? There is never an i he doesn't dot or a t he doesn't cross when it comes to that kind of thing. I'm sure of it," Lea said. I was suddenly anxious to look at Elliott's bank records to see where my check for fourteen thousand, mostly from Griffin, had gone, if not into a new stove.

I didn't tell Lea what I was doing. Elliott was still her boss. For the next few hours, I studied every record. I saw where the fourteen thousand dollars was deposited, but I didn't see any corresponding large deduction for a new stove or any equipment for that matter. Nothing. I did see multiple cash withdrawals on a fairly regular basis—two hundred here, four hundred there. No explanation for those. I was alone with troubling thoughts. My savings and Griffin's trip to Italy had vanished into thin air. Maybe Elliott was having a bad month and didn't want to tell me. I didn't want to fight about money.

One night in bed, I just lobbed the question, "Lea said you found the warranty for the stove. What did you end up doing with the money?" At least I thought it was casual.

He looked at me and jumped out of the bed and turned on the light. "What the fuck, Bailey? Are you snooping in my business? You're just like everyone else, carping about money." This abrupt change frightened me. I was navigating treacherous waters, and I didn't want to get Lea in trouble.

"Nothing like that. I just want to make sure that the restaurant isn't having financial issues."

"It is my business. My concern. You let me worry about that. We are not having problems. You just have no concept of how much it costs to run a restaurant." He stormed out. So much for my casual approach.

Chapter Thirty-Six

Lea's statement had shaken me. Elliott's reaction had shaken me. In my mind, given the popularity of the restaurant, Rex's raise should be able to be easily absorbed. But that was a worry for another day. I arrived at the restaurant in time to prepare for the dinner crowd.

When I returned home, the scene's familiarity didn't shock me. That alone should have scared me. A glass of scotch and a half-eaten bagel along with an assortment of muscle relaxers and pain pills were scattered around the living room. The blue, orange, and white pills formed a pharmaceutical charm bracelet or something resembling Chiclets on the floor. I took everything to the kitchen and only briefly considered how many pills he had actually taken. I found myself wondering whether, if he took just one more could he return to work. Why couldn't he be just a little more normal? Maybe Elliott just needed to see a different doctor. I hated those thoughts, and sleep punished me.

The next morning, I selected two of my nicest dresses, which Elliott had bought me at Bergdorf. I would leave them in the office for quick changes. My phone buzzed. It was Mac. "I need to go out of town for a few days. Can we reschedule for two weeks from Thursday?" I was relieved. With Elliott out, I had no time to meet with Mac. I made light of it. "Now who's playing hard to get? That Thursday is perfect."

"Thanks, Bailey. It's my mom's seventieth birthday. What kind of son would I be? I'll see you that Thursday." I returned to the restaurant to find a happy Rex and a nervous Lea. I didn't have time to address her concerns. I had to coordinate the dinner specials with Rex and get ready for the nightly crowd.

Two weeks later, it would be me who begged off. It was the first Thursday in the month and a big market day. I needed to go with Rex to see how it was done.

"Since we're not having such good luck with Thursdays, how about the Tuesday after next?" I offered.

"Done," Mac said.

"How was your mama's birthday?" I asked.

He roared with laughter. "Only a Southern girl would know that a Southern boy calls his maternal unit 'Mama.' Thanks for the flowers that you, Henry, and Griffin sent." I accepted the thanks and texted Griffin, remembering the flowers he sent Elliott and me on opening night of the restaurant.

He texted me back: "Mac is a good ole boy who loves his mama. Just glad you two aren't opening a restaurant in Atlanta." This was our first real exchange in months. I smiled, wanting desperately to text him back. For once, my cleverness escaped me.

Chapter Thirty-Seven

For five weeks in a row, Elliott remained in bed. His moods deepened with his pain. Our conversations dwindled down to one-word answers to questions. I made him go see his doctor. It was the same day I was to meet Mac. I watched Elliott get dressed in noticeable anguish. "Call me when you're done," I said, putting on another dress that Elliott had bought me along with the peridot earrings to match.

"Bailey, where the hell are you going dressed like that?"

"Meeting a client." I leaned over and kissed his cheek.

Elliott pulled me to him, demanding more, as if resurrecting some long-forgotten ardor. "I have to go," I said, pulling away. It would've been easy to surrender. It'd been so long.

"My doctor's appointment isn't for another hour," Elliott said inching closer to me. I continued to back away.

"To be continued. I have an appointment in thirty minutes," I said, combing my hair with my hands, scooping up my purse, and leaving before I changed my mind.

Mac Whitney greeted me with a cappuccino sitting in the chair next to mine. I noticed the circle of white skin on his left ring finger. I wondered if getting rid of a pesky wife had been part of his unfinished business. "Go ahead. Taste it. But be warned, I've consulted Griffin," he said, very proud of himself. Grinning from ear to ear, that dangerous smile either got him out of trouble or into trouble, I couldn't decide which.

"Better." It was improved but still not as good as Griffin's, who had apparently reserved a few secrets for himself. It reminded me that the restaurant business could be a very small world. "Did you make your mama a happy lady?"

"My mama is never going to be happy until I truly settle down," he said.

I laughed. Considering the rascal before me, it might be a while before his mom was truly happy. "Let's talk about the restaurant scene in New York. What are your thoughts?"

"This may sound crazy to you. I would really like to create the kind of establishment that's a cross between The Four Seasons Restaurant and the Ralph Lauren store on Madison."

"You don't have lofty ambitions or anything, do you?" I let my thoughts trail off, reconsidering this man.

"I want it to feel clubby. I would like part of it to be a drop-in-after-work kind of place for young professionals who like to drink a lot and converse. The back part should be a fine-dining destination. I want it to be a destination. Become a habit. Can you see that?"

"Hell, if I could conjure that up, I would've given that idea to my brother and Griffin. Or my husband," I added as an afterthought.

"Touché," he laughed. "But do you get the vibe?"

Before I could answer, my phone buzzed. Mac nodded as I took out my phone. I noticed he took the opportunity to check his own. It was Elliott. "Jesus, I hate doctors. He said the only thing he could really give me is that injection," he started.

"Elliott, I'm in a meeting right now. That's good news isn't it? No surgery. Take the injection. Let me call you when I finish my meeting." But Elliott had already ended the call. I tried not to think about how mad Elliott might be at me because I didn't hear him out. I turned my attention back to Mac.

"Where were we? Yes, your vibe," I said, more casually than I felt. I could tell Elliott was angry. I didn't look forward to dealing with that later. "Have you selected a space?"

Mac patted his jacket pockets. "Dammit." For the first time in our acquaintance, Mac looked sheepish. "This is a new sport coat, and I forgot to transfer my checkbook. I wanted to get our retainer out of the way. Always trying to impress the ladies. Vanity is the devil."

"Impress even the married ones?" I inquired.

"Sugar, you just never know." He grinned. "Here's an idea. Meet me at this address next Tuesday. Check out the space, and I'll give you a check for your retainer to feed our grand ambition."

When I reached the sidewalk, I called Elliott back. There was no answer, and I left him a message telling him I was on my way to the restaurant.

Lea met me at the door. She had a long list of unpaid orders and bills. We walked into the office.

"Is this unusual for Elliott's balance to get this low? And what are all these cash advances?" I asked, studying the accounts.

"It's always been like that. I was really surprised he could write you a check for fifteen hundred the other month. Do you have another checking account?" Lea asked. "As for the cash advances, I figured you were both withdrawing money."

"I don't know anything about other checking accounts. The restaurant and the personal checking accounts are it, as far as I know," I said, noting I had not withdrawn one red cent after Elliott's scolding about me needing to be more frugal. "Do you still have the checkbooks?"

"Yep. But Elliott still has the key to the drawers. He must keep cash in there," Lea added.

I looked at the bills and the balances. It was a mess. Something uncomfortable nagged at me. What the hell had I gotten myself into? It was scary. It had been as easy as . . . breathing.

For the next hour, Lea and I paid the bills that were due now. Then I reapplied blush and lipstick and buried myself in polite, meaningless conversations with our guests.

Elliott was awake on the sofa when I got home. "Thanks for checking in on me." His mood was obviously altered.

"I called several times. I was running *your* restaurant," I said. Biting my tongue had become an unnatural but necessary habit.

"Those injections hurt like hell, in case you were interested. But I think they did the trick. I haven't had anything to eat," Elliott snapped.

"Elliott, we need to talk about the restaurant."

"It is my restaurant. Everything is fine."

My mind entertained sinister conversations, but I restrained myself and didn't let the thoughts make their way onto my lips. Instead, I went into the kitchen to scramble some eggs with tarragon for Elliott. Later I noticed he had fallen asleep on the sofa without even touching them. I went to bed alone, hating myself for adding tarragon. And wondering how the hell I ended up here.

Chapter Thirty-Eight

The following Tuesday, I met Mac at the address he'd given me. It was a coveted address off Madison, a little higher than Ralph Lauren's. He was waiting for me.

"Am I late?" I asked.

"No. Just eager to see you and get your opinion," he said, leaning against the doorway.

"Well, I'm eager to get my check, so let's get to it," I said, which produced hearty laughter from Mac.

"I'll bet you are a handful for the people in your life," he said, still chuckling. He unlocked the door.

"Who says they're not a handful?" But my focus quickly shifted to this grand old building. I could really take a spin in here. "Have you already bought it?"

"The bank says it's mine all right. So, what do you think? Are you inspired? Do you think you could work your magic in here?"

I studied the beams and the intricate molding. With Mac's budget, this place could really shine. "I think this may be the beginning of a beautiful friendship, Mac," I said, extending my hand, but he was fishing in his pocket and handed me a retainer check.

"This should make our friendship bloom a little sweeter. That's your retainer until we can get serious." I'd say giving me a check of that magnitude definitely sealed a serious friendship. We shook hands but lingered in the building for a little bit longer. We talked and laughed in the way I did with my brother and Griffin. It made me miss them. I think he was pleased at my obvious approval. For the first time in a long time, my pulse skipped just a little faster with some long-forgotten joy.

I walked a block alone. The sky was darkening. I decided this merited a phone call. I called Henry. He was with Griffin who picked up the other line. "I got it!" I said.

"Just be sure a job is all you get from Mac Whitney," Henry said.

"Congratulations, Bae," Griffin said. He hadn't called me by my nickname since we had that wretched conversation on the telephone. Were we slowly reestablishing our footing or had it just slipped out, out of habit? "This might merit a repeat appearance on 40 Under 40. What does your husband think? It will be a lot of pressure," Henry added. A loud crack of thunder followed, jolting me.

Raindrops started as I was waiting for my Uber. I saw the awning of the bank Elliott and I used. The amount was burning a hole in my pocket and needed to be deposited. Later, I'd wish I had been more concerned about the math and a little less concerned about my dress. I would transfer the funds to my account tomorrow.

I hadn't even thought about Elliott. I hadn't thought about how or even if I would tell him. It could be construed as direct competition to Elliott. Although in my mind, we were looking at two different animals. Besides, Mac was just going to be the owner, the face—or as I would nickname him "Queenie" because he was the figurehead of the operation. Like Queen Elizabeth without the dowdy clothes. Mac had set his sights on a chef whose talents could match his ambitions to play with the big boys.

Chapter Thirty-Nine

The following morning, I headed toward the restaurant, deciding I could go by my bank at lunchtime. I overheard Elliott on the telephone. I had become suspicious and cautious about things in my very own life. It scared me. I heard Elliott mention my name. I moved closer to the door to listen better.

"Bailey is great. Of course, I'm deeply prejudiced. She is the most talented person I've ever met . . . " Was there a "but" coming? Who was on the other end of the line?

"I just get the feeling you're looking for a high-end vibe with a 'sky's the limit' budget. I just don't think that is Bailey's thing. Don't get me wrong. She's your girl when it comes to thrift stores. But if you are trying to evoke an old-money kind of vibe, I would definitely recommend Penny Prichard. She's the best. She has a quick eye. She has the best resources. And lucky for you, she has gotten into the restaurant business. She did my apartment, and I have never been sorry for one minute. I know Bailey is my wife. I just don't think her eye is sophisticated enough for what you want. If I had your kind of budget, I would totally go with Penny."

I just stood there. Listening. Disbelieving. Replaying in my mind what he had just said. All of a sudden, something in me broke. Broke free. Broke wide open. Broke apart in so many pieces they would never get put back together. Then I did something I hadn't done in three years: breathe. It felt so good I did it again. He was signing off his call with some pleasantries when I opened the door. I might willingly let Elliott wreck my life, but I'd be damned if I was going to let him wreck my career along with the help of that cutthroat Penny Prichard. However, she was the least of my worries.

"How fucking dare you? I cannot believe you. What the hell were you trying to do to me? Spouses are supposed to help and support each other, not kick them in the ass." I paused. So many thoughts were long overdue and demanding to be voiced. "First, is that what you really think? That I'm some two-bit hack? An amateur? What the fuck is that about, Elliott? Why the hell are you trying to sabotage my career?"

"As usual, Bailey, you are overreacting. You have to admit, and you have said it yourself, Penny is your go-to for over-the-top budgets."

I interrupted. I was just getting started. "For your information, Elliott, a 'sky's the limit budget' is easy. It requires nothing of the imagination. No cleverness. You just walk into a store and point your finger in the direction of your selection and give them an address. What I do requires real vision. Why am I even explaining this to you? I worked for Julian, and I've worked with Penny for several years, helping *her* with her clients for God's sake. So yes, I can do a 'sky's the limit' budget. I have done plenty of 'sky's the limit' budgets. What I offer is something more—talent."

Clearly there was some pent-up anger on both sides of the desk.

"When did you become such a suspicious bitch? Listening to every conversation. You are so damn prickly. Maybe you're not as good as you think you are."

I interrupted him again. "If I'm not as good as I should be, it's because I've been running this fucking restaurant while you've been in bed—for almost two years! Yes, I'm your wife. I did it because I love you. But I've gotten no appreciation from you."

"This is business. My reputation," Elliott said as if it were no big deal. I realized I had been carrying my hostility and anger at him around for a long time, toting it in my satchel and waiting for the right time to unload. It didn't feel sudden to me at all. If anything, it had gone on way too long. He threw a cookbook across the room. Not at me, but to show his own anger. Too fucking bad I wasn't scared.

"You are sabotaging my career. My reputation. That is a big deal, just like an affair. And frankly, I don't think I have been suspicious enough!" Before I could ask him about all the money, something else triggered in my brain. "Just who were you talking to anyway?"

"Mac Whitney. He called me to talk about prospective chefs for his restaurant, and we started talking about you." I would still be falling if the floor had not caught me.

"You do realize he just hired me and gave me a sizable retainer? Which now, thanks to you, I may have to return."

"Why would you even work for him? He's my competition. You're a disloyal bitch!"

"It's called a job. It's my job. However, my job does not involve running a restaurant. So, you can do that yourself tonight. Don't expect me home. I'll be elsewhere."

"What? Is Griffin in town? Are you going to crawl into his bed?" I was incensed by his remark.

I picked up a coffee mug and threw it against the wall. I turned on my heel and walked away. I was done with it all. Throwing the mug was like putting a punctuation mark on it. I walked out of the restaurant and texted Elle about crashing at her place.

When I arrived at Elle's apartment, I was greeted by an all-female welcoming committee. In addition to Reggie and Elle, Elle's baby daughter, Kendall, was there too. I reflected on this crazy year. When Elle announced last fall that she was going to have a baby, marriage was not even on the horizon for me. Now the baby was here, and my own marriage was on life-support.

My phone buzzed. It was Elliott. It was a one-sided conversation. "Love, come home. The apartment isn't the same without you. It doesn't sparkle with your spirit. The bed and I are very lonely without you. I promise I will make it up to you!"

"Elliott, this is not going to be fixed with . . . that." I hated that my friends had to hear the intimacies of our life.

"Darling, I will be better. I promise. It's been a few rocky years. I'll admit it."

I refused his pleadings and hung up. For a brief moment, I envied my friends. Their normal lives. The moment passed, and we turned our attention to unpacking my messy life.

"This is something I've always wanted to know," Reggie began. "Elliott hired you to design the restaurant, right? Was it a flat fee, or is he paying you now? Like a salary?"

I hated to answer this one. "It was a fee—"

Before I could finish, Elle interrupted. "Wait a minute. Are you telling us you've been running the restaurant for *free*? And Elliott has a problem giving you piddly money for your hair?"

"We've already had this discussion, Bailey. Months ago. But you've got bigger problems. You aren't even the hired help. Elliott is treating you like a slave. That's why you've lost so much weight. You're stressed out and overworked. And you're letting him do it!"

Both women listened. Lectured. Embraced me. Took turns dispensing tissues and pouring wine. I had been more comfortable with the boys telling me their version of the facts of life than I was with these women telling me the rules of marriage. How could I let this happen? I had so much confidence when it came to my work, but I'd given Elliott control over my life.

"That's why I got so mad at Elliott sabotaging my career with Mac. This is my profession, my livelihood. But it's also my life, and I'm good at it. Aren't I?"

"That man isn't sabotaging your career, Bailey. He's sabotaging you. You are not the confident woman we first met." This was not just a little tapas-serving of the truth but a whole fucking nine-course meal of it. We exchanged looks—a mix of anger, sadness, loss, and rage. Time had fallen away. It was well after midnight.

"Girls, I've got to go to work early in the morning," Reggie said, getting up to go home.

"I'm so glad Griffin and Henry don't know," I said. The women exchanged another look. My friends and apparently my traitors. "You didn't."

"You just haven't been listening to us. That stove thing pushed me over the edge," Reggie said.

A month ago, we three were out together and a little drunk, and I was so mad at Elliott that I had told them about the missing stove money. Apparently, they were so horrified they had discussed it with my men.

Reggie continued, "Whatever is going on with Griffin, he has been respectful. I think we all have our guesses on that. Your brother has been pretty vocal. He has very interesting opinions." The way Reggie said that made me shudder.

As she was leaving, my phone buzzed. It was Elliott. He was obviously very drunk.

"You really piss me off, Bailey. You should have more understanding about my back. What the fuck? Why are you on your little high horse? I had an opinion. You are not supposed to eavesdrop on my conversations. When the fuck did you get so suspicious? You're behaving like one of those bitches you hang out with. And I thought you were fucking Griffin." I hung up the phone and hoped they hadn't overheard Elliott. It was not his finest hour. One minute I was "darling" and the next minute I was "bitch." Talk about emotional whiplash.

"Then there's . . . those conversations." Reggie pointed to my phone with her hand on the door. "But me, I say nothing. I am the voice of restraint."

I laughed for the first time all evening. "Girls, y'all are a lot of things, but not so much restrained. What have you been doing the last six hours?"

"Au contraire. We kept our opinions mostly to ourselves for the whole nine months you've been married. Reggie, don't you agree?" Elle said. We all embraced.

Well into the night, I felt angry. I felt naïve. I felt stupid. Really stupid. I also knew that I had never seen a marriage up close. I never went over to friends' houses, and I had never had two parents. But I always came back to my strong suit. I was supposed to have vision. Why hadn't I seen this coming?

Chapter Forty

"You may not want to look at the papers this morning," Elle said. We were both getting ready to leave. I needed to go by the apartment to gather some things and then go to the restaurant. I wanted Lea to open the account information for me.

"What do you mean?" I asked her, and she handed me the paper.

"Don't say I didn't warn you."

Emblazoned on one of the pages in the tabloids was a picture of Elliott and me in his office yesterday yelling with the headline: "Kitchen Wars—Sparks Fly Between the Genius and His Muse. Is the Magic Over?" And then there was a picture of Elliott and a blonde. "I've got to get to the restaurant before Elliott does."

"Don't do something stupid, Bailey." Elle hugged my neck.

"I think it's too late for that. I think this paper makes me officially famous in New York." We tried to laugh, even though we both knew my troubles were just getting started.

Lea was at the back of the restaurant and motioned me to Elliott's office saying, "We don't have a lot of time. Elliott is getting ready to leave for the market. Here, before I forget." She reached into her pocket and pulled out a rolled-up hundred-dollar bill. "Leave it to Elliott to go with a big bill." She handed it to me. I looked at the thinly rolled bill in my hand, not exactly sure what I was looking at.

"What is it?" I asked, still stupid.

"Evidence," Lea said. "You may need it." When I still looked perplexed, she explained. "It's for snorting drugs, Bailey." From then on, I just followed her lead.

"First, I pulled up the restaurant's account. There is a lot of money flowing through this account—more than should be generated just

209

by the restaurant but with very little left over. So where is Elliott getting the money? And what is he doing with it? Secondly, look at your joint personal account. There was a big deposit yesterday."

I stopped her before she could link it to something nefarious. "I deposited that yesterday. It's a retainer for a new job, which I may or may not have to give back. I'm going to withdraw it today and put it in my business account."

"It's already gone. There was a huge cash withdrawal after the deposit cleared."

"What do you mean?"

"It means Elliott beat you to it."

"How did he move it that fast?"

"Are you kidding? You really don't know Elliott. When he's in his office, he is constantly looking at the accounts. Apparently, the business has been losing money, and he's had to use borrowed money to make payroll and do the business of running the restaurant."

"We made that much of a mess running the restaurant, Lea? We always have a full house. Do I even want to know what he is using this borrowed money for?"

"It's not our fault. Drugs cost money."

She then produced a key and opened the top drawer of Elliott's desk. There was nothing in the drawer except prescription medicine bottles, mostly empty. It was a sea of orange bottles and white caps. His drawer looked like a can of open sardines packed snugly and tightly. "I know what you're thinking. These are all prescriptions. Elliott could be buying extra drugs and putting them in prescription bottles to make it look legit. It is an alphabet soup of heavy-duty drugs, muscle relaxers, and vials. Have you seen him shooting up? By the way, all the drawers look like this. You should take some pictures," she said, like a true detective.

I felt sick. I felt stunned. I felt stupid. I had seen Elliott on several occasions injecting medicine into his stomach that he said was faster acting. I was in the middle of a nightmare. This should be someone else's nightmare. Not mine. "Elliott, a drug addict? He's so high-functioning."

"The world is full of them," Lea said.

"Did these cash withdrawals go toward buying drugs? Are you saying he has already taken my retainer?" She had already confirmed that, but the truth was having a hard time penetrating my naïve brain.

I ran my plan by Lea. I jotted down my destinations and inquiries for each institution and grabbed up checkbooks. About that time, Rex breezed in. "If you're looking for Elliott, he's meeting with Chip."

I had no idea who Chip was. "Who's that?" I looked at Lea.

She considered my question. It weighed on her. "Are you sure about that, Rex?" When he nodded, she proceeded. "Chip Esposito." When I showed no recognition, she continued, "Bailey, you really need to get out more. He loans money with high interest rates. His father is Tony Esposito." Again, I shook my head. "Really, Bailey? He is allegedly connected to the mob." Lea made air quotes around the word *allegedly*.

"Are you saying Elliott is connected to the mob?" I asked Rex.

"Can you leave me out of this conversation?" Rex said and escaped into the kitchen.

"No. Some people say Chip is a loan shark. And when he doesn't get paid, he tells Daddy," Lea said.

"Elliott has been borrowing money from this Chip." I was putting the pieces together. "And that is why there is no record."

I scooted out to our bank. As I walked inside, I felt like a cross between a criminal and a Kardashian. People glanced up at me and then glanced again in recognition, thanks to my picture in *Page Six* that morning. The bank manager escorted me into his office. He pulled up the joint account. He politely showed me where the funds had been deposited yesterday and been withdrawn by my husband this morning. It was already gone. My phone buzzed. It was Mac Whitney. For once, I declined his phone call. What if Elliott had talked him out of giving me the job and he wanted his money back? Not the kind of day I expected, to be dodging Mac's calls and possibly the mob. Dazed, I left the bank and thought of my next move. An idea popped into my head, and I texted Elle. Her advice, her legal advice, was to come to her office immediately and meet with one of her partners.

I looked down at myself. I had on a pair of wrinkled khakis, tennis shoes, and a sloppy shirt, and I remembered I hadn't put on makeup that morning. I didn't want to embarrass Elle by my unsightly appearance. When I tried to demur, she insisted. "Come on. We see distressed wives all the time."

Distressed wife? If you would've told the twenty-four-year-old version of myself I would be standing on a street corner with virtually no money, married to a drug addict who looked successful, and that I gave control and access to that same drug addict, I would've laughed. I was Bailey Edgeworth: visionary. Not Bailey Edgeworth distressed, destitute, and dumb-ass wife.

Elle escorted me into a conference room and introduced me to her senior partner, Larissa Tate. She walked to the head of the conference table and sat down with her notepad. I gave them a brief rundown of what had transpired, including the fifty thousand that Elliott had apparently taken from our joint account this morning. At first, Elle just looked at me in disbelief, like my friend, not like a shark lawyer. I showed them both pictures of the prescription bottles and the rolled up hundred-dollar bill. Larissa and Elle exchanged legalese.

Larissa turned to me. "Are you retaining my legal services?" My mind and my emotions had a bad case of vertigo. "Do you want my representation in a divorce proceeding?" Larissa asked slowly as if I were reading her lips. Elle looked at me.

"Shit, Bailey. This has been going on for a long time. His back pain? He's a drug addict. He has no money, and now he's stealing money from you. Think about the roller-coaster ride. The unpredictability. Don't you see? This didn't just happen yesterday."

I felt like a fool.

"He is a drug addict and thief. Don't forget the money for the stove. He may love you in his own twisted way, but he is using you. It is not safe to be around him. It's your decision. Is this what you want the rest of your life to look like?"

In that moment, I was very clear about what I wanted. What I didn't want. It felt sudden in a way, but I realized it really wasn't. I was confused by the people we had become. I didn't recognize either one of us at all. It broke my heart. I walked through the eye of the needle.

Chapter Forty-One

"Yes. I would like to engage your services," I said, refusing to use the *D* word. Larissa took my phone and instructed Elle to download the pictures of the prescription bottles in Elliott's office and the rolled-up hundred-dollar bill. I was going to have to pay her—money I didn't have. I fished out credit cards and started laughing. "Do you take Visa or Mastercard?" She nodded. I gave her Elliott's card because he boasted not only of a sterling credit rating but of the card's astronomical limits. His credit card was accepted. If Lea was right, Elliott would know very soon what I was up to.

"Elizabeth, you know what we need to do. We need to go to the magistrate office. Then we need to go to court with the restraining order in order to freeze this son of a bitch's assets. Find a favorable judge if you can. Maybe Sinclair."

"I can't go to court looking like this," I said, looking at Elle.

"You can, and you will," Larissa spoke.

"Are you going with me?" I asked Elle. When she hesitated, I realized my best friend was on the clock too. "No worries," I said. She was texting. Elle grabbed her file, and we all hurried out. A van met us and took us to court.

Reggie was waiting for us. She hugged me and said, "You're going to get through this. I promise." I was so glad at this moment to have good girlfriends.

"You are the best," I said and returned her hug while Larissa sat focused on her notes and phone, which buzzed.

"Good. We've got Sinclair. Let's move." For the next few hours, we were held hostage by the legal system in Manhattan. Reggie and I embraced occasionally while Larissa and Elle remained unflappable, getting the job done. I didn't have time for tears.

When we left the courthouse, Larissa checked her watch. "Are you good? Do you need anything from me? If you do, email me. I'll answer it as promptly as I can." I had no doubt about that. I felt reassured for the first time in twenty-four hours.

I said, "I probably should check in at the restaurant."

"Are you sure about that?" Reggie asked, worried. "I wouldn't go near the restaurant. Go to Elle's. You don't know what Elliott is capable of once he finds out you froze the accounts and hired a lawyer. I'll see you a little later."

I hated to admit it, but I was frightened of Elliott, of the man he had become. I decided to go back to Elle's. I needed to walk some of the way. It was one of those glorious "autumn in New York" September days. This time last year, I would've gladly breathed it all in, even the questionable smells of the sewer. The crispness in the air danced jocularly with the sun's warmth. I was its grateful beneficiary. Today I just felt old and weary. The elements nudged at me, but my smile and the lightness in my heart had already gone into hibernation. I was letting Elliott rob me of all my joys. My phone buzzed. Speak of the devil. I hesitated.

"Where the hell are you?" he said. "Forget that, I don't give a shit. I'm done with you, you temperamental bitch. Don't even try coming home. I've changed the locks." I didn't respond. I was numb. Elliott had rarely talked to me the way he had in the last few days. Calling me names only on occasion. Over money. Sometimes over Griffin. It dawned on me. Elliott was high.

❧✲

Chapter Forty-Two

Reggie met me at the door with a big hug, and the smell of comfort food wafted from the apartment. "Elle is feeding Kendall. I know it's not your usual gourmet meal, but I made a homemade chicken potpie for us to have tonight." It was the kind of meal a doting mother would serve her teenage daughter after a dramatic breakup.

I returned the hug and said, "That sounds perfect." And it did.

That night was different for us. We were very somber. It felt like a full-fledged death. They were abundantly kind and generous with their time, with their love and support. We all realized my marriage had unraveled. It seemed premature. It seemed sudden. It hadn't been.

We didn't talk about brevity, quality, or recriminations. We mourned. Grief must be fed. I finally allowed myself to cry in front of them. They didn't judge me. They embraced me. They forced me to eat chicken, carrots, and the peas from the potpie. I even tried one bite of the store-bought crust. It wasn't half bad. Both Henry and Elliott would still be blending cold water and butter and flour. "Is this a béchamel? It's delicious. And the baked apples are tasty."

"Oh honey, it's cream of mushroom soup and a little mayonnaise. I don't even know what a béchamel is. The baked apples are Stouffer's," Reggie said. "I think our little foodie is busted."

"I'm under a little duress, okay?" We managed to laugh, but I also thought of Elliott and the way he continually whisked together flour and that fancy European butter he used so it wouldn't lump together. How he loathed lumps. I had always loved his tenacity and talent with the whisk.

I appreciated the bond of women that night. They did not assign a value to death or divorce. They viewed it as it was: a premature ending that nobody was ready for.

Into another sleepless night, I reevaluated every memory with Elliott. Was there a moment that had been true? Real? Was there a time he wasn't altered? When we married on New Year's Eve, I had thought he was romantic and spontaneous. I had been so happy. Had Elliott just been high? I thought about his drawer full of prescription bottles. And the bank accounts that looked anemic. Money, scary loans, and pills comingled in a toxic cocktail. Had I been so willing to accept all of that? It had taken a blow to my career, an overheard conversation that had been the tipping point.

There would be no happy endings. No lifetime reservoir of treasured memories. No more shared jokes about Elliott's perfectionism, his desire to walk around naked, or my love of vintage shopping. Just an emptiness where completeness and joy once dwelled. My heart felt scraped up and bruised from the situation. I thought about Miss Havisham and suddenly felt her grief, her completely altered reality. She waited for her bridegroom who never appeared. I was waiting too. But neither of us was getting our happy ending.

Chapter Forty-Three

By the time I arrived at the restaurant the next day, it was late in the afternoon. Rex had told Lea that Elliott was meeting with his attorney and would be in later. I walked in with my head held high as if I had not spent the last couple of days complicating Elliott's life the way he had complicated mine in the nine short months we had been married. Lea had tucked the day's paper with yet another unnerving headline into her purse: "Wanted—A New Muse. It's Splitsville. A Kitchen's Hottest Couple Cools Off."

My phone buzzed with a text from Mac Whitney: "I read about you and Elliott in the papers. It doesn't sound too good. My daddy told me once never to get in the middle of a marital situation. Having just gotten out of one myself, I can see you are headed for some domestic turbulence. If you need me for anything, I'm there for you. In my opinion, no one can touch your talent. I still consider you my friend and partner." My inbox populated with other clients who had decided "to go in a different direction." Only Mac, and my beloved college cafeterias, didn't desert me. How was I going to rebuild my career and my life?

I strolled to the back of the restaurant with a false confidence. Lea followed me along with Rex. I pulled the accounts up on the screen. I started printing the pages. I wanted to add up the cash advances.

"I hope you're getting everything you need," Elliott appeared in the doorway startling me. "Bailey, Rex, and Lea: I'm just deciding which one of you three I will fire first," he followed.

"There's no need to get testy and no need to fire me. I'm not even on the payroll. Considering what Rex and Lea do around here for you, I would think seriously about your next step," I said, equally as calmly.

"Lea, you're fired," Elliott said as if I had never spoken. Tears welled up in her eyes, and I went over to comfort her. "Maybe you'll choose more wisely next time. Rex, we have a dinner crowd to get ready for. Work up the specials, and I'll see you in a minute. Lea, leave us alone—now." She hesitated but then left. My anger returned—so quickly it scared me.

Elliott patted his jacket pocket. "You'll be happy to know I was served yesterday with your little love letter. Divorce papers? Asset freeze? Nice move, Bailey. Let's see. You called me a drug addict, thief, and dangerous to your mental, physical, and emotional health. You'll never be able to make a case against me. I have never ever laid a hand on you. You have no grounds. And I can sue your ass for defaming my character and endangering my livelihood," he said. He sounded sure. So confident.

"If anything, you're the one who has defamed my character and reputation, talking to Mac Whitney like that. I wouldn't worry about your livelihood at all, Elliott. This city is full of drug addicts doing masterful jobs each and every day. No one gives a damn so long as you serve a five-star meal," I pushed back.

His mood changed. My heart pounded. "You disloyal slut. When I am through, you won't even have the clothes on your back. You've been such a busy girl over the last few days. Freezing assets? I suppose that was Elle's contribution."

"Not half as busy as you. I can't believe you took my money," I said, moving from around the desk, fear and dread creeping around the corners of my heart. I eyed the door, moving closer to it.

"Is that all you have to say?"

"No. You owe me my fucking retainer. And I want it back now," I demanded, my anger bursting free.

"Good luck with that. My attorneys are going to bury you. And if I can find a way, I am going to bury Griffin with you, bitch." He grabbed the papers out of my hand and threw them across the room. He moved so close that I stopped breathing. But I stood my ground.

"And I want the money I gave you for the stove, which you never actually used for a stove."

He was still moving toward me. I was shaking. But I wasn't breaking.

I heard a familiar voice, but its tones were unfamiliar.

"Bae, that's enough. Let's go." I turned to see Griffin. He pulled me out of the office, past customers, and into the night air where a car was waiting.

Chapter Forty-Four

I looked at Griffin for a minute. My eyes were having a hard time believing he was standing in front of me. "You're here. How?"

"Bad news travels fast. I drew the short stick. I lost."

"I'm in really bad trouble."

"I know," he said just as seriously.

"Who told you?"

"Both Elle and Reggie called last night."

"Elliott took my money."

"I am aware of the situation, Bae. Jake Fein has called Larissa. Elle calls her the barracuda. Once we are back in Atlanta, we will meet Henry at Jake's office, day after tomorrow. I'm going to take you to my hotel where you'll be safe. You can get something to eat. The girls and I are going to meet Elliott at your apartment to get your stuff." His tone was very businesslike.

Griffin's hotel room was a junior suite with a small sitting room with a sofa bed and French doors to the bedroom. He gave me the bedroom. I put my tote down and looked at him. Pent-up emotions and apologies tumbled out.

"I am so sorry," I started, but Griffin shook his head. I turned to the facts. "Be careful. I think Elliott is mixed up with some bad people."

"Yes, I know. I wasn't going to tell you, but we're meeting Lady Jane."

I stared at him. The news shocked me. "Lady Jane?" I asked.

"It's a long story."

I was suddenly very tired and very hungry. I hadn't eaten all day.

"I'm surprised you came," I told him.

"I wouldn't be anywhere else." I fumbled with what to say back to him. We were like awkward teenagers on a first date. Tentatively,

I walked over and embraced him, not caring where things stood with Alex. It was the kind of gesture couples exchange after suffering something traumatic. We finally pulled apart and I watched him leave. After I was sure he was far away, I started crying and felt like I would never stop.

Somewhere deep in the night, I woke up, not sure of the time or where I was exactly. I had been dreaming about Elle's wedding. But it'd been a nightmare. It's a bad sign when the nightmare you're living in is worse than the one you're dreaming about. The clock read three-thirty. My heart seized. Was Griffin back? I jumped up and headed to the sitting room. He was sitting on the sofa with his head hanging down toward his chest.

I just stood there a minute taking him in. He had come to me. Before anyone else. I leaned on the doorframe. It startled him.

"Bae?" He shook himself awake and began wiping phantom crumbs or drool from around his mouth. My heart was not immune to even this awkwardness. "What time is it?"

"It's about three-thirty," I said, staying put.

"You travel light for a girl," he said, looking at all my worldly possessions on the floor next to him. "I thought you would have more stuff." And then he looked at me. For a long time.

"Be glad it wasn't Elle," I said. He kept staring.

"You still have my flannel shirt?"

I looked down at the shirt I was wearing, the one I had appropriated from him so long ago. "I never leave home without it. It goes with me everywhere. Even fancy attorneys' offices." I sat beside him on the sofa. I rubbed his shoulder through the flannel shirt he was wearing.

"What? You want this one too?"

I thought of clever comebacks. Even tragic ones like, "I've taken everything else from you, why not the shirt off your back?" But sleep captured me and my cleverness and held me tightly in her grip.

Chapter Forty-Five

I woke the next morning to the sound of the hotel door closing and Griffin grousing about the quality and price of room service breakfast. Some things never change. And then I remembered. My life. I got up.

"I could use a cup of coffee," I said and watched him pour a second cup.

"This breakfast is not as good as the hotel we stayed in last time," he said. I lingered on the word "we." It was as if we were a married couple who frequently stayed in hotels and ordered room service.

"I am so sorry for all of this," I said.

"We can talk about that later. It's after ten o'clock. By the time we shower, get dressed, and check out, it will be time to go to the airport."

After we went by FedEx to mail my things, we headed for the airport, checked in, and boarded the plane. Both Reggie and Elle texted. Lea called. I checked my text messages one last time before turning off my phone. I reviewed the last message Mac sent.

"Domestic turbulence." He had put it so eloquently. If only my heart could be subjected to two hours of being bounced around, changing altitudes, and bumpy landings. I had stepped through the eye of the needle but was still bracing for the legal and emotional storms ahead.

When we landed, we went straight to Griffin's. Henry was waiting for us. Griffin deposited my bags in the spare bedroom. Henry hugged me tightly. "I fixed you something to eat. You need to keep your strength up. You have a meeting in the morning at nine with Jake. Be ready, it might not be pretty."

I had a hard time letting him go. I whispered in my brother's ear, "I feel like a colossal fuck-up." He squeezed me tighter.

"Don't worry. We've all been there," he said.

Chapter Forty-Six

As Henry warned, it wasn't pretty. Jake Fein's office was situated in the heart of Buckhead, very close to NOIR. I nudged Henry. "How convenient for you to be within walking distance of your attorney's office." It was too sarcastic considering my own legal troubles. The boys accompanied me for moral support, but I would meet with Jake alone. Jake's office resembled Larissa's in that it was a glass office building, but Larissa and Jake were different creatures. Larissa wore her hair in a neat bob. She had patrician looks and did Armani suits justice. Jake was younger, about the boys' age. Instead of a suit, Jake breezed in wearing a pair of gray slacks and a tailored shirt. Confidence followed him as assuredly as the smells of a turkey from the oven on Thanksgiving morning. He strolled to the head of the conference table as if it were a foregone conclusion. What he lacked in patrician looks, he made up for in charm and dimples. You could just tell this guy was a street fighter, and he liked it that way. As confident as I felt with Larissa, I felt that level of confidence in Jake. So, this is what it meant to be "lawyered up."

I started talking. "I want Elliott to give me my money back," I began.

"Understood. But before we get started, let me lay down the ground rules, Bailey," he began, as cool as the chilled cucumber soup Griffin served on July afternoons.

"First and foremost, I am Henry and Griffin's attorney for their businesses. If there is a conflict of interest in any way, I have to protect their interest first. Understood?" I simply nodded. "I hope there is no conflict. Secondly, I may need to ask you some embarrassing questions that I expect you to answer honestly." He looked at me, and I blushed. "I demand honesty."

"Yes, I will," I said. For the first time, Jake looked up and smiled and nodded, "Thirdly, my fee . . . "

I was about to run with my standard line of having no money, but Jake waved me off. "About my fee: I assume we will put it on your account for now"—as if we were in a bar and running a tab. "Does that work for you?" As if in a game of Simon Says, Jake nodded, and I followed suit. I realized in those moments that talk is not cheap. Jake was getting paid handsomely. He was not here to perform therapy but to get the best outcome. That meant answering the questions he wanted to ask when he asked them.

"Let's start with the timeline, Bailey." He picked up some notes that I assumed he received from Larissa. "You and Elliott married on New Year's Eve. We are now in September. Nine months. Not a good candidate for alimony." He paused. "What are your joint assets?"

"Just our joint personal and business checking accounts. I have a court order freezing those assets," I said in an effort to deflect my own feelings of incompetency.

"What about property? The restaurant? Your apartment? Are those jointly held?"

"No," I replied.

Jake reflected. "After conferring with Larissa, she will do the filing, but she has agreed to let us handle the daily stuff to reduce your expenses. We will do a quick search of New York law to see if you have any rights to those assets."

Damn. I had frozen those anemic checking accounts. That was the only thing Elliott and I held jointly. I'm sure Jake was used to representing Atlanta socialites who owned multiple homes in Buckhead and beyond.

"That's why I want my money back. Including the fourteen thousand for the stove," I started, and Jake waved his hand over his neck to cut me off from talking.

"Bailey, I do not need to know how or where you got that fourteen thousand. It doesn't constitute comingled funds. Don't mention it again. Is that understood?" I realized Jake Fein knew a lot more about my marriage than I thought. Including the provenance of that fourteen thousand dollars.

"Understood." I paused. "Can I just ask one question, Jake?"

He nodded.

"If Elliott has an apartment and a restaurant, why didn't he just borrow from an equity line? He's always bragging about his 'sterling credit.' Why did he have to go to some loan shark?"

"Good question," he smiled, ever so slightly. The dimples moved. "Wanda!" His paralegal appeared. I wished we were paying Jake by the syllables he used. He spoke to Wanda, and then she disappeared.

"Let's talk a minute about Mac's check. It is my understanding you put it in your joint checking account."

"Yes. But I was going to—" Jake gave me the signal to stop talking.

"When you did that, Bailey, it became comingled with Elliott's money. Therefore, making it half yours and half his, legally. I understand that was a check that Mac Whitney gave you to retain your services, but half of it legally became his property when you put it in your joint checking account."

I had a sinking feeling that things were about to get worse. Wanda dashed in and put some papers in front of Jake.

"Holy shit!" Jake said. "The reason Elliott went to the loan shark is because you cannot borrow against something you don't own." I looked baffled. Jake continued.

"Elliott doesn't own the restaurant or his apartment." I waited. "Lady Jane Turner owns the apartment. Elliott's father, Lord

Desmond Graemmer, owns the restaurant. Elliott owns less than you do."

"Elliott doesn't own them? I can't go after the restaurant or his apartment?"

"Not even if you put anything into either one of them. Apparently Lady Jane got the apartment in her divorce from Elliott, and he was renting it from her." I sat in complete shock.

"Larissa and I have talked briefly to Elliott's attorney. Apparently Elliott is worried about the negative publicity. Elliott and his attorney have already offered a preliminary proposal. He wants to play nice so we will unfreeze his assets and protect his reputation. His proposal is that you will get half of Mac's retainer back—and I will ask for the fourteen thousand, too, but I'm just not sure we can get that. We can structure it so it appears that fourteen thousand was a loan to Elliott, premarriage, from *your* money." In emphasizing the word "your," it dawned on me he was protecting Griffin. Jake didn't want Elliott linking that money to him. Elliott would love to sue Griffin.

"However, there are some stipulations to Elliott's kindness," Jake said sarcastically. My insides felt like a Mixmaster on high speed. "Here we go. Elliott's terms. He is willing to give you the retainer back, but your claims to the money are forfeited if you engage in 'cohabitation.'" He lifted his eyes to meet mine.

"But I'm staying at Griffin's."

"Elliott has been gracious to allow that. 'Staying with' is not the same thing as cohabitation. Cohabitation in this document is defined as sex." He looked up again briefly. I didn't blink. "You guys haven't already . . . have you?"

"It's only been three days!" I said. "Can you even put a thing like that into a divorce?"

"Divorce documents can be very individualized. Trust me, I've seen some weird shit. With pets. With housekeepers. With sex. You can put anything you want in it, as long as both parties agree. Have you 'cohabitated' under the terms in the document?"

"No."

"Just checking. It's my job."

"How can you even prove such a thing?" I asked.

"You will have to sign an affidavit for the court." He sounded serious. "Now for the last icky question." It sounded strange hearing Jake use a nonlegal term like *icky*. "Did you and Elliott ever have unprotected sex?" How much more personal was this guy going to get? I felt little pieces of my privacy and little pieces of my heart being slowly chipped away. By strangers. By people to whom we were paying by the hour. By a man I once—and still—loved.

"He was my husband, Jake."

"Understood. You'll need to get tested."

"Why? I haven't had sex with anyone else. Why would they want me to do that?"

"Elliott's attorney isn't asking for the test. I am." Jake stared at me. The brain cells I had left were having a hard time comprehending.

"Are you saying . . . "

"Get tested, Bailey." Five syllables, three words, let me know that my husband had not been faithful to me.

"I think I will be able to get your money back for you. But there's one last thing," Jake said.

I wanted to ask: Do you promise?

"As a final condition of the proposal, Elliott wants all of the jewelry he gave you, which has been itemized: your wedding ring and band, the sea pearl necklace, the flower brooch, and the peridot and diamond earrings." I could return everything except the earrings. My life was being stripped away little by little at an hourly billing rate. Everything was being picked at, not just in my heart but in my soul. Like leftovers. But they were *my* leftovers. The things that brought me pleasure I was having to give back. Jake provided an envelope for me to put all my worldly possessions that Elliott had given me into. The ideas of permanence and "forever" seem so shallow.

I stifled tears. "I just don't want you to think I'm some emotional wreck of a woman who married the wrong man."

"Because everyone who comes in here is looking to divorce Mr. Right." He smiled, and the dimples stretched out with great ease. He walked me to the door.

Griffin walked into the conference room and told me I could leave. Henry took me to a smaller conference room and hugged me.

"It feels like being sent to the principal's office a little bit, doesn't it?" Henry understood.

"If it makes you feel any better, I was a total disaster, and Jake's partner managed to get me custody of Hank. But if there are any skeletons in your closet, you'd better tell Jake now. He doesn't react well to surprises. Can I ask you something?" I nodded. The idea of personal questions and my privacy seemed of no concern to anyone. "Have you always been faithful to Elliott?"

I looked at Henry. "Damn, Henry, I was only married nine months." He looked back at me and waited. "Yes!" I said loudly enough for the receptionist to look at us. Henry looked a little surprised, and I tried not to hold that against him. "Do you have such low expectations of me?"

"No. I have really big expectations of you. With your clean record with Elliott, Jake should be able to make it rain for you. Jake loves that saying: make it rain. That means he'll be able to get you a favorable outcome."

"But Henry, you don't understand how little there is to split. Elliott has nothing but my money. Hard to garner much rain from that!"

Shortly after, Griffin appeared and took a seat next to Henry. I had purposely sat at the head of the table. I was still finding my footing with my men. Maybe it was because they were the men in my life. I felt a potent blend of disappointment, love mixed with a desire for independence.

"Thank you for coming to get me, Griffin," I started formally. "Please don't take this the wrong way. I appreciate you both."

"Oh no, here she goes," Henry said.

"You know me. I don't want your pity. I don't even want to be taken care of." I briefly looked at Griffin before I continued, "I am coming home on one condition. I hope you will meet my condition. You will let me redesign VERT. I'm not even asking you to give me the job. But think about it: VERT needs a facelift. What other restaurant designer do you know who has logged as much time in that restaurant as I have?"

"Your sister really is a kind of terrorist, isn't she? Talk about no good deed goes unpunished." Griffin managed a small smile.

"I don't want to be your project. After Jake gets paid, I can get an apartment of my own," I proposed.

"Just how much do you charge?" Henry asked.

"It's okay. You can stay in the other bedroom. You designed it yourself." I could tell he was annoyed with me. I was having a hard time expressing my gratitude. I knew I didn't sound grateful, but I had given all my power over to Elliott, and I wanted to gain some of that back. Certainly, Henry and Griffin would be better, but I was just discovering the mistakes I had made and how easy it had been. I wanted and needed them to see me as an individual. That had been a problem with Griffin and me all along.

"I see some things don't change no matter how dire your circumstances." Griffin was exasperated, but I saw a hint of a smile.

"You can go and come as you please," I offered, thinking about Alex. Henry looked at Griffin and laughed.

"Griff, you may be offering to send my sister back to New York before this is over." They looked at each other and asked me to leave the room. I went to the ladies room and surveyed my neglected appearance. I washed my hands. When I returned the door was cracked. I took another deep breath and found the tiniest strand of courage.

"I do plan to go back to New York. I don't have a lot, but I have some work. Like Mac."

"We expect a full-blown proposal after we give you the budget," Griffin said.

"I will treat you just like any other client," I said. I extended my hand to shake on our business arrangement. Griffin's phone buzzed. He excused himself, and I wondered if Alex was on the other end.

⸙

Griffin was gone briefly and when he returned, we left together. He drove past NOIR and VERT. He turned into a parking lot of a small clinic. He drove with the kind of efficiency of a homing pigeon or a prompt waiter.

"Where are we?" I asked, as my insides churned.

"We need to get your blood tested," Griffin said, like it was a common occurrence. I moved in slow motion. Once inside, a nurse took my blood in two vials. She said, "We'll let you know when we hear back from the lab on both the STD and HIV tests."

We walked to the car in silence. Griffin started the car. Leaving my home, my husband, my job, my friends, and my life behind seemed enough. And yet they wanted my blood to determine if I had some life-altering disease all because I slept with the man I loved? Everything had gotten so out of hand. How had this happened? I began to cry. Griffin didn't move. He didn't shut off the engine. He didn't reach over to comfort me. We just stayed put until I stopped crying. I thought about the absolute absurdity of my life. Courts, freezing assets, multiple attorneys in separate states, the horrible fights, and the bitter discoveries. I started laughing. My tears were mixed with uncontrollable laughter. I couldn't control either emotion.

"What?"

"Love, can't give you any money, but I can leave you with an STD," I said, forcing an English accent. "I think it's safe to say at this point that the wheels have come off the bus." Griffin reached over to touch my shoulder and left his hand there as we drove the rest of the way in complete silence.

Chapter Forty-Seven

The following day started with a flurry of activity. I had to go to the post office and change my address so that my mail would be forwarded to Atlanta. I had to go by my bank and change my address on my checks. Because I didn't own a car, Griffin drove me everywhere. We even went to Home Depot to change his locks—which I knew did not make sense, but Elliott had robbed me of the feeling of personal safety. After all that, it was four o'clock. We hadn't had time for lunch, so we headed to VERT. I fielded calls from Reggie, Elle, and Lea, who had made it their daily mission to check on me. Griffin brought me a bowl of cauliflower soup.

"Soup is love," Elle said, urging me long distance to eat. I sat in the best booth and looked around. With all my boundless ideas I had had for this place, inspiration did not show her face. Griffin brought over a glass of iced tea and some warm brioche. Soup is also comfort food.

"Eat," he demanded and shook his head when I asked for a glass of wine. I flipped open my laptop. My inbox had turned into *Law & Order* instead of quotes from vendors. I had emails from Larissa and her junior attorney. I had emails from Jake's junior attorney. And then there was all the back-and-forth correspondence between Jake and Larissa. It took me a minute to identify the cast of characters now populating my email. There were also forwarded emails from Elliott's attorney and ramblings from Elliott that were written around three in the morning. Griffin peered over my shoulder and said simply, "Ignore those."

I thought about abandoned female characters in books. How they wallowed in bed crying, sleeping, and eating ice cream. Who the hell had time for that? I had fifteen unanswered emails from the attorneys to deal with. I took my bowl to the kitchen, and Griffin just scowled at me. "No alcoholic beverages for you."

This place, VERT, beckoned me back. Every damn day. I sat in the best booth. I sat in the worst booth. I sat at multiple tables. I sat at the bar drinking coffee that Griffin poured himself. What if Elliott had been right? Could I push the bounds of my imagination past my own ideas? Could I improve on the vision I carried around for so long? Suddenly, none of my ideas excited me. Had I lost my vision? Some days I just got up without saying a word and took an Uber home.

One night, I decided to unpack the rest of my belongings. Griffin was right, I traveled light for a woman. As I got to the bottom of both boxes, I realized that none of my lotions or potions were there. No perfumes, no soaps, or creams. No candles. The smells that had given me pleasure and made me feel special had been stripped away too. Everything was gone.

It was clear Henry and Griffin were concerned about me, that they worried the burdens I carried would cause me to self-destruct. In the deepest and darkest pockets of my heart, I knew they were right. I wanted to go to sleep and never wake up. I wanted to drink myself into oblivion. I wanted to beat myself for being so stupid. I was tempted to take the noose of could-have-beens and might-have-beens, and wrap it tightly around my neck, stand on a chair and kick it away. I thought of Henry. I reflected back on the barren dwelling Julian and I had transformed into NOIR for my men. For NOIR and Henry, it took being stripped down in order to rebuild into something different, something better. The emptiness used to be my favorite phase because it was awash in possibilities and potential. But I was tired. So tired. I wondered if I had any vision left for myself. What if we are allocated a certain amount of creativity, and once it's gone, it's gone.

Chapter Forty-Eight

The nights produced the tears. I closed my door, and, alone, I wept openly. Griffin joked that he would allow one day a week for tears. If only. It was a really shitty time to discover I was truly a woman.

Sometimes Griffin came home early and knocked on my door saying, "Bae, I'm home. There's some hot chocolate by your door." Or, "Bae, I left you some soup and fresh bread." Or simply, "Bae, I'm here." He and I were still trying to navigate our way around each other. Even that made me sad.

Sometimes I walked aimlessly through the condo looking for hidden liquor; I envied Elliott's selection of pills. Sometimes the chasm of loss engulfed me until I fell asleep. Other times, I tiptoed onto the pages of Facebook. Facebook lives. My own page looked unfamiliar to me, hardly reflective of the life I was now living. I scrolled through other people's lives, other people's smiling family pictures and sundrenched vacations, perched on ski slopes. The app only opened a window to my envy. I shut it down.

The holidays approached. This year, they were just muted days on the calendar. I outsourced my gift-buying to Henry for Hank, Daddy, and Griffin. Even though Daddy's brain had been boarded up by dementia, he was sweet and held my hand any time we were together. The week of Christmas and New Year's had always been my favorite time of year. We were approaching my one-year wedding anniversary, which was really just a reminder of my failure.

I got through Christmas Day, but my sympathies threw in with Scrooge this year.

Reggie and Elle had talked about flying down for a few days after Christmas to visit me, and then Reggie came up with a plan. "Here's an idea. Why don't you allow us to buy your ticket, and you fly up for a couple of days? A belated Christmas present. It would be a whole lot easier for us to chip in on one ticket for you than for us each to buy a ticket and have the baby in tow. I know coming to the city might be hard. Just think about it."

I was learning two hard lessons: to let go of a married life I thought I had in New York and, perhaps the hardest of all, I was learning acceptance—accepting myself as I was and also accepting the help of friends. I went to New York. It wasn't as hard as I thought it would be.

Seeing Reggie, Elle, and Kendall was tonic for my soul. We found new places to dine. When we went out, I would just order an appetizer or a bowl of soup, and when the bill came, both girls would wave me away. "It's ten dollars. It is not going to break us," they repeated. One night, we just went out for drinks. I picked up the tab. Without the alcohol police, the three of us got tipsy and were so happy. I flew home on December 30. Griffin stayed home with me on New Year's Eve.

Chapter Forty-Nine

"I thought New Year's Eve was one of the biggest days for a mixologist like yourself," I said to Griffin as we were eating an easy dinner of grilled salmon, sautéed spinach, and quinoa—nothing like the elaborate New Year's Eve dinners I had had in previous years.

"Are you objecting? I think this is nice," Griffin said and produced a bottle of Perrier-Jouët. He opened it, and we both drank freely. With a little liquid courage, I got up my nerve to ask him a question I had been dreading.

"I haven't seen Alex. Is everything all right?" Griffin didn't say anything for a long time. I drained the contents of my glass. His eyes stayed focused on it.

"Alex decided to move on. Let's change the subject." We fell into an easy silence. I was starting to realize something. Our silences were always comfortable because we were terrible communicators. I let some time pass.

"I'd like you to do something for me," I started.

"Anything . . . within our legal limits," Griffin said as he refilled our champagne glasses.

"I want you to hire Lea. I think she could help us both around the shop. I have some other plans for her as well." My request surprised him.

"Wow. That's a great idea. We could actually use someone like her," he said as he smiled at me for the first time in so many months. We toasted to Lea. It almost lifted my heart to think we had gone through a whole bottle of champagne with something resembling a carefree ease. As the clock neared midnight, we made our way to the sofa. The idea of celebrating anything had seemed so far away a few weeks ago, but the idea of having Lea as part of the team, having just seen my best friends, and now the fire, the champagne, and my current company boosted my spirits.

"You're right. This is nice," I said to Griffin. We relaxed side by side on the sofa. I had to admit I loved what I had done with this room. It captured Griffin perfectly. We sank into a long-overdue conversation I desperately needed to have as we waited for the clock to strike midnight.

"I know you knew about the stove," I said. He nodded. "And the drugs?" He nodded again. "Really?"

"Your friends love you. They've been worried about you. It didn't take a genius, Bae."

"It shocked the hell out of me." I drained my glass and held it out in Oliver Twist-fashion, saying, "Please, sir." Griffin hesitated, but then he relented and filled my glass.

"That's because you loved Elliott. You saw what you wanted to see." He said this as softly as the embers burned in the fireplace.

"Do you think he ever loved me?"

He looked at me as if he were taking in each one of my features for the very first time. He took the champagne glass out of my hand. "He loved you the best he could. Addicts have a hard time with real love. Addiction is selfish." He paused. "Before you ask, yes, it is in the caretaker's handbook, chapters one through three." Without a champagne glass, I took his hand in mine and squeezed it hard. To my surprise, he let his hand rest in mine. "I really hated you for . . . " he paused, "a long damn time."

"I wasn't too happy with you either." I met his gaze, studying his features. He then returned my squeeze as if bestowing an act of benevolent forgiveness. "I feel so damaged. Like my heart made a fatal mistake. What's wrong with me that I picked Elliott? I had a fifty-fifty chance of choosing a good man, and I chose the drug addict."

"Nothing is wrong with your heart. It's been through an ordeal. A trauma. Your heart needs to repair itself," he said.

I lingered over the word he used. *Repair*. People had told me I needed time to heal, but no one had ever used the word *repair*. Maybe the heart was like a broken bone. It could be mended, but there would always be some tenderness where the brokenness once was. I let the word marinate. All good things benefit from a good marinade.

Our hands stayed connected as our bodies remained in repose. Firecrackers exploded far away in the evening air, announcing a new day and a brand-new year. He released my hand, turned to me, and took my face in between his hands and kissed me. Suddenly. Gently. Deeply. Tenderly. With a residue of stored-up passion. My insides crackled with emotion. Just as suddenly, he pulled away and stood up. He picked up the bottle of champagne. He kissed me on the top of my head and walked to his bedroom door.

"Happy New Year, Bae," he said and closed the door.

The word *repair* means "restore to wholeness." Right then, my heart felt so watery. Uncongealed, not solid. I was fixable, but it was up to me.

Chapter Fifty

It was fifteen minutes into the New Year. Good riddance to the old. Briefly I reflected on what I had been doing this time last year. Newly married, we were eating in that diner. I remembered the idea that swirled around in my brain while I was eating greasy hash browns. Another idea popped to the forefront.

I texted Mac: "You are probably engaged in a yuletide lip-lock with some beautiful woman in your orbit. Good for you. When you get back to business, do you mind sending me some bigger pictures of the space? I'm really interested in the molding and beams. Just give me the green light when you're ready. Thank you, Mac. Happy New Year. Bailey."

A video text came in from Reggie, Elle, and their men, who were spending New Year's Eve together. It was a video shot earlier in the evening of five-month-old Kendall toddling around with a noisemaker saying, "Happy Bae-Bae." I smiled immediately. I figured that would be my name for the next generation. I called them, and we chatted.

I was still under the influence of a five-month-old when my phone buzzed. It was a text from Mac.

"Ha. I am on a fishing boat down in the Bahamas with a bunch of ugly guys smoking cigars and drinking very old scotch. Why is a lovely lady like yourself working? Don't those boys in Atlanta know what to do with a beautiful and ambitious woman?"

"Domestic turbulence, Lily Bart, remember? Don't forget to send the pictures."

"Will do, Lily. Wishing you a better new year, Mac."

I settled into the quietness. Something caught my eye. It was a present wrapped in red and green paper. A leftover Christmas gift.

I picked it up. It looked like a wrapped book. It was for me, from Griffin. Questions arose in my mind. Should I open it? Why hadn't Griffin given it to me already? I ripped open the packaging. It was a book of poetry by Mary Oliver. There was a note:

> Bae,
> I know you like your vintage poets, but I think you will enjoy this woman. I do. I have marked my favorite poem: "Wild Geese."

> You do not have to be good.
> You do not have to walk on your knees
> for a hundred miles through the desert repenting.
> You only have to let the soft animal of your body
> love what it loves.

Tears welled in my eyes. It was the third line that fixed in my thoughts. I finished reading.

> . . . the world offers itself to your imagination,
> calls to you like wild geese, harsh and exciting—
> over and over announcing your place
> in the family of things.

Her words, Griffin's thoughts, and maybe the champagne made for a potent mix of yearning, longing, and sadness. It dawned on me. This book belonged to Griffin first. This poem had comforted and perhaps saved him after I chose Elliott, ironically, a year ago. It was a lamentation on acceptance and forgiveness—his and mine. Now he was repurposing these very ideas for me, with little fanfare and great kindness. The intimacy itself I had with Griffin was repairing. He had offered me some much-needed forgiveness to begin the New Year.

I reread it and found reassurance this time. I went to bed on the first night of this brand-new year keenly aware at some point I could stop repenting, love whom I loved, and rediscover my place in the family of things.

Chapter Fifty-One

The first week in January brought two deliveries. I received a large overnight envelope from Mac with pictures of the space plus one of Mac holding a huge fish over the bow of a yacht. The second came bounding into VERT like a welcome gust of cool air in the summer, delivered by my brother.

"Anybody here want the best cappuccino from New York?" It was Lea. It didn't go unnoticed that my brother had gone to the airport.

"Griffin insisted on going to market today," my clueless brother said.

Griffin came in from the back. "The gang's all here. Now, we have a restaurant to redesign," he added. A glimmer of excitement sparked in my heart. It had been dormant for so long that I hadn't known if it would ever show up again. Before I joined this happy reunion, I texted my high school friend Dexter Common who was now a prominent architect.

Lea helped me get the boys out of the restaurant so that I could meet with Dexter alone. I juggled so many little schemes that I often found it hard to know who was a part of which. It felt good to be a little devious. As Dexter found me in the best booth, I realized, plans were good. They signified hope.

He kissed me on the cheek. He had gone bald since high school. It made him look more distinguished, like the prosperous architect he was. He still was the best-dressed man I knew. Even in jeans and a sport coat.

"It's my day off. Your phone call intrigued me. I heard you were back in town. I also heard you were flat broke," Dexter said with a light touch.

"Both are correct. But I have a job. And I may have one for you."
I showed him the pictures from Mac that had sparked an idea for
the very place we sat. The molding. The beams. I pitched my idea.
Beams on the ceiling of VERT painted white. A change in the openings of the doors to archways. "I can see that. You want to round all
the entryways. You want to make the place a little more feminine."

"That isn't feminine. Just architectural interest. Do I have to
remind an architect of this? What do you think?" I still wasn't confident about all of the design elements.

"Your vision is spot-on. I made a similar suggestion years ago
to Julian. He shot me down. Not the guys. By the way, where are
they? I presume they are funding this project?" His confirmation
was validating.

"Could you work me up a drawing and let me know how much
we're talking about?"

"I get it. You're going rogue," Dexter grinned.

"I just want to get all my thoughts together before I pitch ideas
with price tags," I said. He finished making notes. Lea brought us
over two glasses of wine and an amuse-bouche, and we fell into an
easy game of catch-up. We were very similar. We both thought with
our eyes.

As he got up to leave, Dexter said, "I'll be in touch. It's been great
reconnecting. I'll never know why you didn't go with me to prom."

I shook my head. "Dexter, you're gay," I said. "By the way, how is
Mark?" Mark Upchurch was Dexter's partner of umpteen years and
one of the best landscape architects in town.

"So? We could've had a good time together, and neither one of
us would've gotten laid," Dexter said. "And Mark is doing great." He
smiled and passed Griffin on the way out.

"Just how many scams have you got running?" Griffin slid into
the booth with his coffee mug as I was savoring the Sausalito wine.
Food, wine, and memory blended together in nostalgic fashion. I

smiled at him. If I died tomorrow, the sight of Griffin clutching his favorite coffee mug might be one of my last images. Standing in a doorway after we had been together might be another. I would definitely go into eternity happy.

"Don't think I haven't figured out why you sent me to market today," he said, removing the wine glass from my grasp.

"Do you disapprove?" I asked, recapturing my wine glass.

"No. You seem quite pleased with yourself. By the way, you seem more relaxed. Getting sleep finally? I'm glad those three a.m. phone calls have stopped. What they do to you . . . I'm glad you told Jake about them."

"I actually told Jake's junior associate and Larissa's junior associate that if Elliott wanted to contact me and harass me, he better do so during business hours or I would sue his ass for harassment." Elliott had become notorious for calling me drunk and shouting belligerently. Being manipulative. Blaming me for everything. At first the phone calls affected me. I would let my emotions bubble like a simmering stew until I would either yell at somebody or dissolve into tears.

"Good for you. I'll send over another glass of Sausalito's finest."

Chapter Fifty-Two

Before I entertained my second glass of wine, I strolled into the kitchen. Aaron, the sous chef, was busy chopping ingredients for tonight's offerings. "Hey Aaron, would you have a minute to make me one of those grilled chicken and arugula sandwiches on sourdough with some of your cranberry and pear salsa?"

"Sure. Would you like fries or fruit?" Aaron called.

"I'll just grab an apple." I picked up a paring knife and a Granny Smith apple. Sometimes I liked the art of slicing an apple myself.

The glass of sauvignon blanc was waiting. None of that house wine shit for me. Life was too short.

It happened in a flash. The green of the Granny Smith apple bounced right off the table and onto the walls. My eyes followed. I let my vision roam up and down the walls. The color flooded the space and my imagination. I smiled the kind of smile that starts from within and spreads. Like a secret. Is this the way Sir Isaac Newton felt?

"I am going to need another apple," I said.

✻

For the next two weeks, I carried a Granny Smith apple everywhere I went. It went with me to estate sales, to newly discovered vintage stores and old favorites. It went with me to places selling art. Every few days, I either ate it or threw it out and went back for another. I had barely laid eyes on Henry or Griffin. At night, I would browse the internet.

The next week, Dexter was close to pitching a proposal, and I knew I had to meet with the boys. I sat them down in a booth to have a talk. It was reminiscent of one we had when I was thirteen, except this time I was in charge.

"First, I want to thank you for letting me reimagine the restaurant. I really appreciate the job and paycheck. But I really need you guys to tell me how much you're willing to spend." I said this with a nice blend of contrition and confidence.

"I already know we need to add some money to the pot since I saw Common around here," Griffin said. It amused me. My mind always went to the rapper Common. I'm sure Griffin had no idea who he was.

"Has he pitched you a proposal?" Henry asked.

"It's going to be my proposal—Dexter is a part of the plan. We're meeting next week. But I need to know what y'all have in mind. I've been browsing, and I would like to start buying, but I need to know my budget. I also need to know if you're prepared to close the restaurant for several weeks to accommodate architectural changes."

"In rethinking this, I think it is Henry and I who have the pity job. Paying for yours and Common's ideas. And we thought Julian had to be reined in."

"Just give me your number. I know damn well Dexter made a similar proposal years ago, and it was Julian that shot it down, not you guys." I held my ground.

Henry retrieved a piece of paper from his wallet. He and Griffin reviewed it. They nodded. Henry took out a pen and crossed out the original number and wrote something else. They slid the paper across the table to me. I realized they had been sitting this whole time, and I had been standing. I did not hesitate. I looked at their numbers. With the internet and a little legwork, I might pull it off.

"I need to know if you guys have any contingency money in case we go over budget."

"We need a contingency budget for all the apples you eat!" Henry remarked.

"A small one. Keep us in the loop," Griffin added. We all stood. At this point in a meeting, I would normally shake hands. Instead, I simply hugged my brother and looked into Griffin's eyes.

"Thanks. I've got awesome stuff to buy." And I left the restaurant wondering if I put a whole stand of green apples in the entryway whether people would know I had ripped off David Bouley.

Chapter Fifty-Three

A t exactly four o'clock on February 12, Dexter strolled in carrying an arrangement of flowers. I remember the date because it was two days before Valentine's Day. I was still in a place where I tried to ignore holidays and even dreaded them, threatening to trip me like uneven patches in a sidewalk.

"Either those flowers are a very early Valentine's Day gift, or your proposal is going to be so outlandish you're preparing for your funeral."

Dexter laughed and once again kissed me on the cheek. I nodded, and Lea brought us over two glasses of wine and a sample of the new mushroom and fig risotto under a small medallion of pork belly. "Neither. The glorious flowers are from some guy named Reggie." He sat down and added, "I love meeting with you. You always serve good wine and food."

"For your information, Reggie is not a guy."

Dexter encouraged me to look at the card.

To Bailey—Just Because—

"Life is too short not to be surrounded by beauty"—Bailey A. Edgeworth

We love you,

Reggie and Elle

I laughed. They were always making fun of my little phrases, especially when I stopped on the corner to buy flowers and would say that.

"At least you have good taste . . . in friends," Dexter emphasized. Getting down to business, he unrolled his drawing. I studied it before either of us spoke. My eyes ricocheted between the paper and the restaurant. He had taken my ideas and made some bold choices himself.

"I know I have changed the footprint. Before you even give me an opinion or any objections, I want you to sit with this drawing while the restaurant is in full swing. We can certainly tweak it."

"How much?"

He pulled out a sheet of paper. "I took the liberty of asking three different contractors to bid on this job. I studied them myself. They are fair bids. I remember how you bargained like hell at those vintage shops back in high school. I would be willing to say you could knock off about twenty percent if you negotiate well."

"This would be a high-profile gig for any of those guys. But I will reserve opinions until I take your advice and see it in motion. How long would something like this take? How long would we need to be closed? That is a lot of revenue for everyone to consider."

"That's where the negotiation comes in, Bailey. Everywhere I have been this week, there have been reported sightings of you. I'm almost as intrigued by what you have been up to as you are about these plans." Dexter picked up his wine, and we toasted to our collaboration. I heard Griffin approaching, and I turned the prices over and rolled up Dexter's plan.

"It looks like you two have been busy," Griffin said and shook Dexter's hand. I could tell they liked each other.

"The risotto is divine," Dexter said, then kissed my cheek. "Will be in touch."

"Bye, Dexter. Happy Valentine's to you and Mark," I said.

"Nice flowers," Griffin said.

"No worries. They're from my girls. Are you jealous?" I poked him in the ribs.

"Considering Dexter is gay and the court has ordered a kibosh on your cohabitation antics, I'm good. By the way, I'm taking the night after tomorrow off."

"That's Valentine's Day, Griffin. Another important day for a mixologist. Do you think I'm going to completely crumble if I see couples kissing, spontaneous engagements, planned engagements, or serious PDA? I would rather see that than warring parties in a divorce proceeding. Besides, I have lots of work to do. I plan to be right here sitting at the bar in the middle of things working."

"Valentine's Day can be brutal, Bae." Griffin held my glance. I linked my hand in his to express my thanks for his consideration, knowing he had to endure Valentine's Day last year.

"I need to head out to this florist who is going out of business on the other side of town. Some vases there caught my eye. If I'm not back by tomorrow morning, send the search party."

"Not funny."

Two hours later, I was the proud owner of sixty uniquely shaped vases for less than a hundred dollars. I thought the Tiffany blue of the vases would pop against the green walls. The florist suggested orange flowers because orange and turquoise blue mix and mingle so happily together. She gave me a list of all sorts of orange flowers. I would have to modify my green to a leafy green or mossy green. No matter, I was cooking. I had learned that visions, like life, require adaptability.

Chapter Fifty-Four

I hadn't expected it. I thought I was stronger. Better. Valentine's Day buried me in those treacherous contractions of could've beens. I observed the massive arrangements, boxes of chocolates, festively wrapped presents, cards, and small boxes. I reflected. All that was mine last year. It had all been illusory. Fleeting. I watched from my perch at the bar. I noticed a blind spot. I texted Dexter.

"You realize every time you text Dexter, it costs money," Griffin said as he placed a second drink at my place. Before I could react, a beautiful blonde with enough makeup on to last until next week gushed up to the bar.

"Hey, Griffin. I'll take the usual," she said, her attitude as proprietary as a cat marking its spot. Within no time, Griffin had produced a pink drink for her. "You are the cutest bartender in Atlanta." She took a sip and continued, "I heard a rumor that you and Henry were about to revamp this place. Are you going to get Julian out of storage to do it?"

"Not this time. We're using Bailey Edgeworth."

She interrupted. "The sister? I hear she's a giant train wreck. I heard her life imploded on her, and she is destitute and getting a divorce!" I couldn't tell for sure, but I think the word "destitute" was the worst crime in her mind.

"Annabel—" Griffin started, and I interrupted.

"What Griffin is trying to tell you is that I am the sister," I said with air quotes. When the world knows your riches-to-rags story, what the hell does it matter anymore?

"So sorry, Bailey." She was already inching away.

"No worries. It's all true," I answered with something bordering on satisfaction.

"I'm meeting friends. Griffin, I would love to interview you after your grand reopening." The name finally clicked, and I realized she was the editor of *Buckhead Magazine*. She always wrote those inane articles about my men.

"Anything for you, Annabel." He smiled, but I knew it was for me. "I'll send over some drinks when your party arrives," he said with a wink.

When she left, I said, "Don't encourage her."

Griffin chuckled. "Go easy, girl. I meant to tell you. Some things are going right for you." He paused until he caught my full attention. "Henry and Lea both requested that Lea work at NOIR because Henry is doing a seven-course tasting menu and needed her expertise. But I can tell it is going to be a trend. Happy?"

"I'm not in the mood."

"Stop being a 'glass half empty' kind of girl. It's not your style," Griffin said, refusing me another drink. Before I could contradict him, my phone buzzed. It was Dexter.

"Great idea! I'll work on it."

We closed the restaurant and Griffin and I drove home together. We were both a little tired and wired at the same time.

"Would you like some hot chocolate?" he asked. It was cold and raining.

"And a fire?" I asked. He nodded and went into the kitchen. He carried mugs of hot chocolate. Memories crackled like the flames in the fire. So many.

"I love the rain," I said.

"Really?" It was hard to believe we were still learning things about each other. He looked at me.

"I love the sound. It was raining the first night we were together."

"It was?"

"Yes. It sounded so sweet. I remember waking up in the middle of the night and just listening to the rain. Occasionally it thundered. I looked over, and you were sleeping. I thought to myself that if I died that night, hearing the rain and being with you, I would be happy."

"Really, Bae?" He smiled and touched my arm.

"Yes. Then I thought, if Daddy were to find us, he would probably kill you and you could join me sooner rather than later up in heaven." We both laughed. But then I became serious. "Griffin?" I began a hard conversation.

"Hmm?" He settled in.

"I'm so sorry about the money for the stove. If I had known . . . I'm sorry you haven't been to Italy." My emotions frayed.

"Take that off your list, Bae. That was my choice to give you the money. That's all on me. I could've said no."

"And for the disaster that was my marriage."

He smiled. "I could've expressed my feelings better." The enormity of what all my actions had cost him bore down on me like the rain outside. We were quiet for a long time.

Then it dawned on me like a puzzle piece I had just discovered. Griffin had never said he loved me. Not like Elliott, who said it often. Griffin was a caretaker. He took care of the people he loved. Henry. Daddy. He took care of me. With every sidecar he made, every case of Sausalito's finest he had delivered, every cappuccino he blended and hot chocolate he steamed for me, he was saying it. Griffin had shown me time and time again. It was tattooed on the topography of his heart. The realization recalibrated everything. I looked at him.

I saw the little crinkles around his eyes. The years stacked up and fell away all at the same time.

As was our custom, we began kissing. Easily. Naturally. Lovingly. My tears began falling to match the rain. The terrain of his body had always felt like home to me. I pulled away and got up and walked to my bedroom. I sat on the bed and turned on my lamp. He appeared next to me, and I made no effort to turn him away. He sat down next to me. He ran his hands over my thighs, my shoulders, and my face. He wiped the tears away and kissed them at the same time.

I had loved him before anyone else. I supposed I would love him after everyone else too. I kissed him back gently, which quickly turned to urgency. He laid me back on the daybed. He looked up for just a moment.

"Who the hell thought a daybed was a good idea?" he asked. I laughed through tears and kisses.

"It's good for one person," I protested, since it was my idea. The confines of the bed were not a deterrent. He was finding every part of my body that he had been denied for so long. Something snapped in my brain. My thoughts landed on all his sacrifice for me. With one grand push I shoved him off me. "Stop!" I said. I got up, trying to put my boobs back into my bra. I started buttoning my shirt. I moved toward the living room. Neutral territory.

He reluctantly followed, buttoning his shirt in a lopsided and haphazard fashion. I wanted to go over and correctly button his shirt for him. It was so endearing. We were both out of breath. He sat on the arm of the sofa. I stayed in the doorway.

"What the hell, Bae?" he panted.

"Jesus, Griffin. I have asked you to do a hell of a lot of stuff for me over the years, but I'll be damned if I ask you to commit perjury for me," I continued, adjusting my clothes.

"I don't want that money back," Griffin protested.

I continued, "But I do. This was Elliott's little game. He wanted me to stay with you so this would happen and he wouldn't have to give my money back."

"I don't care about the money, Bae."

"It's mine. Griffin, you were right about one thing at Martha's Vineyard when you said we're too old. I could sneak around with you at eighteen or nineteen. But we're too old for that now. I'm tired of sneaking around. Besides, when you and I are finally together, I want to be free. I don't want to worry about Elliott. Or attorneys. Or courts. I want to be yours. Free and clear. I want to be able to look at your face and say 'I love you. I loved you before anyone else. I will love you after everyone else.'"

Griffin said nothing.

"I just told you I love you, and you have nothing to say?"

"Always did. Always have. Always will," he said with a smile.

"Really? Can I ask you something? What was that whole Martha's Vineyard thing about?"

He weighed his words carefully. "I don't know, Bae. Several years ago, Elaine invited me to the opening. I went, and I thought the place was magical. I couldn't wait to bring you. I wanted to tell you then how much I loved you, and maybe if things had gone really well . . . "

"Oh my God. Did you have a ring?"

Griffin laughed. "Oh no. Nothing as elaborate as that. I was just going to tell you what you meant to me. But you looked so sad, and I thought you were wishing Elliott was with you instead of me. I thought we could be together one last time. But then I didn't want to put that guilt on you."

A flurry of emotions swirled around, and nothing was staying put. If only . . . For some reason, Griffin's gesture of protecting me hit me a different way this time.

"Well, we could have saved ourselves a shitload of money on attorneys if you had." I turned on my heel and slammed my bedroom door behind me.

"Now there's my feminine flower." I heard his door close soon after. I couldn't tell if we were fighting or flirting.

Chapter Fifty-Five

I greeted Griffin the next morning as if the earth hadn't shifted. "What are you doing?" I asked, coming up behind him as he was writing a check.

"Writing you a check. After last night, Elliott wins. I'm making you some French press."

"Close your checkbook. Elliott is not winning anything," I said, checking the timer on the coffee. I had so much to do today.

"Okay, Bae. I'll be good," Griffin said.

"You don't have to be too good." And with that, Griffin scooped me up in a kiss that contained a lifetime of memories.

When he released me, I said, "I need my coffee to go."

Griffin looked appalled, "This is not a Starbucks drive-through!"

"Which reminds me, I need to borrow your car. I'm picking up some things that have been on hold for me for the restaurant."

"How long has it been since you drove anywhere?" Griffin asked.

"About five or six years," I smiled, making his case for him.

"I was much more willing to commit perjury for you than I am to let you drive my car," Griffin said, fishing around for another set of keys. "Remember, I was there when you were learning to drive. Here, take the RAV. It's easier to navigate and will give you plenty of storage. And I am religiously opposed to French press coffee to go."

I took the keys and his favorite coffee mug and grabbed up my satchel. "Well, I can't help it that I was more distracted by other things. I'll see you later."

Around four-thirty that afternoon, I pulled into the parking lot of VERT. I had several boxes of the blue vases I had purchased, a can of remixed paint, some flowers, a painting, and a change of clothing.

I might have been destitute, but I didn't have to look it anymore. I asked a couple of the guys to help me unload my largess.

I met Henry and Griffin, who were conferring at the bar. I embraced my brother. "Henry, how are you?"

He ignored my question. "What is all this stuff, Bailey? I guess Griff and I are paying for all this."

"It's within your budget parameters. May I borrow your office to throw up a can of paint to see if the color is right, Griffin?"

"Do I have a choice?" he said to me.

"Hey Henry, how's Lea?" I smiled and disappeared into Griffin's office. It felt good to be plating barbs with my men.

Alone in Griffin's office, I opened the paint. It was a moss green, warmer than the Granny Smith apple color. I instantly liked it. It played beautifully with the greens and blues and yellows in the painting. I cleared the small table and staged my design. I put the tablecloth on the table along with a blue vase and some orange flowers with the painting on the opposite wall. It was like the colors were bouncing around on a trampoline and joined hands in midair. I opened the door and went to get a glass of wine before taking it back into the office. I sat down at the makeshift table and thought about my color scheme and the vista. I sipped my wine. "I like it," I said.

I changed into the dress I had brought with me. It was the last one Elliott had bought. I studied the layout. I wanted to go back to the gallery to buy two additional paintings that were complementary. They were pricey, but VERT was worth it. I texted Dexter to see how the revisions were going and asked if Mark had any time on his schedule. The revised green was deeper. More robust. I wanted to carry that theme outside into the courtyard. I let go of my long-held ideas about this place. Reimagining requires letting go, but in the process, you gain something even better. It was all so bittersweet. Griffin knocked on the door. I stood up, zipped my dress as far as I could, took a deep breath, and opened the door.

"Sit down on the sofa. What do you think?" I asked him in regard to the miniature restaurant I had created.

"You look beautiful," Griffin said.

"Not me. This," I said as I spanned my hand around the panorama of his office. Then I sat down next to him. I wanted to see what he saw. In the silence, I picked up my wine. He took his time. He considered my efforts. I appreciated that about him. Even now.

"It's different from Julian's vision. It's deeper. Richer. Fresher. I really love the painting, Bae. The vases are the exact color of the dots of blue in the painting." He looked into my eyes. "It's better."

"I want to order linen napkins one shade darker than the vases. I'm pondering that."

"Sitting here, the wall color is really growing on me. It's not the cool colors of the restaurant now. It's soothing. It's a very sophisticated vibe, Bae. Mature. Very assured but very welcoming." He stopped, sitting with his thoughts. Was he just describing the restaurant? He seemed so reflective and serious. Were we ruminating on the same question: would I have put this together ten years ago?

"We need a bartender out here," Charlie said. It broke the sweet reverie.

"I guess I need to get to work. I hope you're not planning to do anything with my couch." Griffin leaned into me. "It holds some very happy memories," he said and smiled. "You're unzipped. Shall I unzip you the rest of the way?" The moment and memories blended together to form an elixir of might-have-beens and possible maybes.

"I wouldn't think of doing anything with this couch," I smiled. "Finish zipping my dress."

"I would rather not, but I will." Griffin let his hand rest on the zipper. "I like it. No, I love it, Bae."

At that moment, I was happy. I lingered over my color combination. I touched my earlobes and realized they were naked. It made me sad. I smoothed my dress and even applied some lip gloss.

I made myself focus on Griffin's office and his compliments and joined him at the bar.

My drink was not alone. Next to it sat a pink concoction belonging to Annabel. I hesitated. I did not want to wear my weakness in front of someone so put-together. I breathed. I walked steadily and sat down next to her. She gazed at me.

"Wow. You certainly clean up nicely. Is that Armani?" Annabel asked.

I noticed Griffin moving away from us. "Yeah," I said. "My ex-husband bought it for me before the wheels came off the bus. Long before I hit domestic turbulence." Annabel laughed out loud.

"Sorry. That's funny. I've never heard anyone use that phrase except for my brother, who is getting out from under his own domestic turbulence." For a moment we just sat there, drinking our drinks, keeping company with our own thoughts.

"Oh my God!" Annabel exclaimed. "You're *her*." I wasn't sure who I was, but I was pretty sure I was guilty of it. "You've been all over *Page Six* in New York." She said it as if New York were a foreign country. It was as if the scandal and my divorce had followed me everywhere. Like those pesky commas and prepositional phrases that kept linking me to Elliott. I simply nodded. I took a rather big gulp of my drink. It was starting to dawn on me who she was. "I'm Mac Whitney's sister. Annabel Whitney Monroe."

"Well, shit." I smiled despite myself.

"Mac told me all about you. He told me how beautiful you were in an understated way. He came in here trying to poach Griffin's cappuccino recipe. For you."

"I'm hungry. Let's get a table." I realized my notoriety was appealing to some folks. Griffin seated us in a booth and brought another round of cocktails over.

"My brother is an outrageous flirt, but you made quite the impression on him. He appreciates your talent. He refers to you as

Lily. All I could think of was Mac was crushing on some married woman named Lily." She paused, weighing her next words carefully like one would do between fast friends. "He knew you were married, but I think he was much more worried about a certain bartender in Atlanta." I smiled, only because it was strange to hear Griffin referred to as a bartender. I told her about feeling like Lily Bart. "Now you've piqued my curiosity. I'll be very interested to know what you have in store for VERT." I told her that I liked to assume different places in the restaurant to understand the visual benefits and drawbacks. She referred to these placements as my "perch."

Over the next two hours, plates of food arrived and disappeared, wine replaced cocktails, and conversation sparkled between us. Wit and attractiveness must be Whitney family characteristics.

I told her a lot about Daddy and how his motto was "women don't belong in the kitchen."

"So, you don't cook?" I shook my head. She continued: "I wish I could get Mr. Monroe to adopt that motto." It took me a minute to figure out she was referring to her husband. Now, that was someone I would love to meet after meeting the wife. We fell into relaxed conversation. She peppered me with questions like I was the subject of one of her magazine articles. Through our conversations, I understood her profession better. I understood how Annabel got people to tell her personal things like what they ate after sex.

"Favorite vacation?" she asked. I told her that some families may take beach trips, some may visit national parks, but mine wined and dined our way through a city. "Ironically, my favorite family trip was when I graduated from high school and all of us, including Griffin, went to New York. I think that solidified my desire to move there. The food was heavenly and exotic to me." I smiled, unearthing a treasured memory. My father had been in his prime then, not lost in a quicksand of brain inertia.

"That begs the question, what's your favorite New York restaurant?"

That was easy for me. "I love the whimsy of cotton candy being served at a fancy restaurant like The Four Seasons. But my favorite all-around for food, flowers, ambiance, and the clever names of dishes has to be Bouley. We went to lunch there on that trip. I couldn't decide between the porcini flan and braised branzino. Who comes up with a name like porcini flan anyway? It impressed me that the waiter brought me both saying, 'A young lady should never have to decide,' so I had about ten courses that day. That man has to be a fucking genius to come up with clever names to match his exquisite dishes. It was at his old place, not the new one. But I love the new one too." Had I revealed too much? I suddenly became cautious. I allowed myself to dive into the memories of that trip as Annabel talked about her many New York experiences.

Back then, prom had just happened. Griffin and I had just happened. How we were able to peel away moments to be together still escapes me. Being the only girl and having my own room helped. I smiled. It juxtaposed the way I ended my New York adventure with Elliott. As we parted, Annabel insisted we *must* do this again.

At home, I permitted that sadness to creep in. I replayed the years with Elliott. Tears came. My heart wasn't fully repaired. I thought of my daddy and how he had allowed me to have sips of every wine he tasted and how I was nearly tipsy when I left Bouley. But joyful. I had floated through the streets of New York. Our best memories are often tinged with both happiness and sadness. In the end, we choose to focus on one. I was ready to choose happiness.

Chapter Fifty-Six

I met Griffin the next morning while holding my head. "In addition to being Mac Whitney's sister, Annabel can drink anyone under the table," he announced, handing me a mug and two Tylenols.

"Thanks for the heads up. That girl can drink. Where were you, my alcohol police?" The mug had water in it, and I swallowed the Tylenol. "Coffee, please."

"I'm an owner first. Hell, Annabel picked up the entire tab on your little drinking foray." Griffin handed me a plate of eggs and toast. Sans tarragon. "Here, this should help." He sat down across from me and began writing checks.

"I told you before you're not writing anybody a single check," I said, scarfing down some of Henry's brioche and feeling better already.

"Well if you're going to walk around like that . . . I'm not impervious to you, Bae."

I looked down at my T-shirt, "You still really want me like that? Even after all these years?"

"I'll say it again, Bae. Always did. Always have. Always will." Griffin smiled handing me another third of my design fee.

It was more money than I'd seen in a long time, especially during those later months when I worked for Elliott in the restaurant for free. "Do you want me to pay you rent?"

"And negative on the rent. You are earning your money fair and square."

"Wait. You and Henry have saved me by giving me a job," I started. He walked over to me so closely I could hear him breathe.

So closely I could see the kiss of freckles on his nose. So closely I could smell that he had freshly showered and shaved.

"You kind of demanded we offer you the job." Griffin was serious. He continued, "Henry and I did not save you. With your résumé and your talent, you would've gotten on your feet. Mac hired you. If anyone saved you, it was you. It was your talent, your vision, and your hard work that saved you. You need to believe that." I did. But it was nice to hear him say it. He stepped back. As if the seismic truth of it all needed to land on me and me alone.

My phone buzzed. Twice. The first text was from Mac: "Two of my favorite girls together. Be still my heart. Be warned, my sister does not play when it comes to alcohol consumption."

The second was from Dexter. I gasped, "Oh my God, I forgot I was supposed to meet Dexter and Mark this morning!" I said, reading Dexter's text. "Good. They want to reschedule for later."

"Let me guess, they want to meet around lunchtime. Why are you engaging Mark? He's a landscape architect. What are you doing, gutting the patio?"

"I'm doing my job," I said. For the first time in a long time, I believed it. I kissed him on the cheek like a punctuation mark at the end of a declarative sentence and headed for the shower.

Over the next month and a half, I shopped in out-of-the-way vintage stores where I snapped up undiscovered treasures. I tweaked plans, searched the internet for everything else, and perched myself around the restaurant to study.

On many nights, Annabel would show up and ask, "Where's our perch tonight, Bailey?" She would gamely sit at the bar, the worst table in the restaurant, and even on the patio on warm April nights knowing my concentration was divided between her and my plan. Annabel took it in stride. I learned a lot about her in the process. Like her brother, she had an affinity for the English language, having attended the University of Georgia and majored in journalism. In Annabel's words, she "minored in jocks."

"The golfers could get you into the Masters, the football players could get you tickets to the bowl games, and the baseball players, well, aren't worth shit. Sitting nine innings outside in the heat and humidity is hell on the hair." She had the same easy humor as her brother. "I married a jock. That pretty much cured me of that habit."

I laughed. I learned she was lonely. I learned how to pace myself around her. One of those evenings sitting on the patio, I came up with a plan.

"Annabel, would you take me to some of the most happening spots? I want to understand their vibes. The restaurants and the bar scene." Annabel's eyes grew wide. She threw a hundred-dollar bill down on the table, grabbed my hand, and we were off.

I loved going places with her. Because she was the editor of the big magazine in town, everyone knew Annabel, and people treated her like a celebrity. I was content to be "just Bailey," Annabel's friend.

I could study these places unrecognized and undisturbed. We were like two newly twenty-one-year-olds darting in and out of "hot" clubs and dodging stodgy adults at every turn. I would sneak in at night as if I had missed curfew. Griffin would be "working on the restaurants' books," but I knew he was waiting up for me. After that first night, I limited myself to one drink per night. I needed my wits about me to figure out the "why" of the vibe. Some nights, I would kiss his cheek in the same fashion as I had in the mornings. He would often lean into me for a deeper kiss. Other times he would be on the sofa with his laptop, and I would quietly sit beside him, linking my arm in his and enjoying the companionship of our shared silence. There were times our mutual longing overpowered us both until he would pull out his checkbook and I would pull away. That checkbook served as an aphrodisiac suppressor for me.

As we headed into May, I knew I had to pitch my ideas to the boys soon. Under my plan, the restaurant needed to be closed at least a month, potentially six weeks. I had already talked to Dexter, and if the boys were on board, we could close the restaurant the last week in July and all of August, when summer was dead in the city. Closing during that time wouldn't mean a big loss of revenue. I realized one night I would rather make a pitch to strangers than these two men who had placed so much responsibility and hope into my hands.

I refused sleep. Instead I rehearsed my plan over and over in my head. I had wanted to reimagine VERT from the start, and I had gotten my wish. Anxiety crushed me at times. Henry and Griffin being underwhelmed was my nightmare. Fear comes with age, like maturity and wisdom. As children, we are often immune to the contours of fear. In our twenties, we are fortified by our own ambition. The shadow of mistakes and might've-beens has not found us yet. My own insecurity with the two of the men I loved most shocked me.

Then I got a call from Elliott. He was curt.

"Bailey, who makes the paint color on the walls, and where can we get it?" His aloof manner undid me. He sounded like a stranger. I gave him the information, and the phone went dead. Hearing his voice coupled with my anxiety balled me up in the corner of my room. I did not need that today.

My phone buzzed. It was Dexter saying the plans were ready. He had made three copies and put them in a folder. He could drop them by tomorrow so I could study them before my presentation. My thoughts landed on Henry. And Griffin. These plans involved a big ask from them as well. I texted them and set up a meeting. My thoughts shifted to Griffin's tattoo. *Breathe. Breathe. Breathe.*

I texted Lea. I wanted, no needed, her blithe spirit. We met at a Starbucks equidistant from VERT and the place she was increasingly calling home, NOIR. "It seems like you have been seeing more of my brother than I have lately. How's Henry?"

When Lea blushed, I instantly knew. Their happiness sliced into my anxiety. "He's good. Hank is just adorable. I'm sorry I haven't been there much," Lea said.

"Ah, new love takes time." I knew my brother well. Now, this I had envisioned perfectly. "I'm going to make the pitch tomorrow afternoon to the boys. I'd like you to be there. I have to tell you, I have been scouting out potential office spaces. Ideally, I'd like you to come to work for me at least part time. But there's something I would like you to do first."

Chapter Fifty-Seven

By morning, my fear had receded. Excitement had taken its place. The kind of excitement that blends anxiety and hope together. It looked lumpy and messy like me. All me.

I visited Daddy. He didn't talk much anymore, but his face brightened when he saw me, as if inside his boarded-up brain there were glimmers of light and recognition of love. I grabbed his hand, and he rubbed his fingers over the wedding ring he had given my mother so many years ago. He was a safe repository for my hopes and doubts and even my dreams. I had a few of those left. I got up to leave and kissed his cheek. His hands still gripped mine.

"Beauty," he struggled to say. I realized that my own motto of being unapologetic about being surrounded by beauty had simply been a derivative of his. In the end, we hold on to love, then beauty. I had been trying to do this all my life. Now I would try to convince the other two men who mattered most that I could bring fresh beauty back to VERT.

They were there when I arrived. I had worn one of my nicest dresses. They looked up, startled by my appearance. They were sitting in a booth, and the sight of them and their familiarity was reassuring to me. Henry and Lea sat close, and Griffin clutched his coffee mug. He fumbled with his bracelets, and I knew he was nervous for me. Before I handed them my proposal, I looked at them and smiled. My brother, who had been through his own struggles but had never deserted me. And Griffin. There weren't enough commas, prepositional phrases, or ellipses that could adequately define that place he occupied in my heart. What we become is the only thing we can ever truly take credit for. I was about to become Bailey Edgeworth, visionary of VERT. I took a sip of water and started.

"Thank you for giving me this job." It may have sounded hollow, but I meant it with everything I had. I opened my preliminary notes. "Before I get to the nitty-gritty of my proposal, I want you to stop a minute and think about what the color green conjures up for you.

"For me, the color green represents limitless possibilities. It is, the color of lush fields and the leaves that surround fragrant flowers, the color of robust lawns awash in new growth. It represents spring-time when everything blooms anew. Green is the color of hope rewarded after a brutal winter. It is the color of Daddy's eyes—yours, Henry—and my own. Green is not a color of stasis but rather one of seizing opportunities and momentum. Green signifies beauty." I paused and set down the proposal in front of each of them.

"I have not only studied this place but other successful restaurants and bars in town. The first thing you'll notice is that I've changed the footprint of the bar." Griffin looked up. I continued, "I did this for two reasons. I have added additional seating in the bar area. Some people like to just come after work with money in their pockets and an Uber app. They want to drink, maybe have a bite to eat, and watch some sporting event on TV. Henry, I want you and Griffin to put your heads together and concoct a dynamite new bar menu. A five-to-seven menu with drink specials, food specials, and some neat offerings. The other reason I changed the footprint around is because I want those same people to be able to look out into the restaurant and see how much fun everybody is having, to see the beauty and interesting food passing by, and think to them-selves that this would be a great place to come on a date or to bring their family."

No mutiny yet. I continued. "Currently, the bar is blocked off by this wall. I hate not being able to look out and see the panorama of the restaurant. There's no vista.

"The other big architectural changes I'm proposing are to add ceiling beams and paint them a distressed white and round off all the doorways into arches to soften the lines and create an inviting feel. The last structural addition I would make is to plump up the landscape to make the patio more inviting and delightful. Green applies to both flowers and foliage. I've eliminated the additional walkway, and by doing so, I've added six extra tables to the patio. With heat lamps, it will be a great place three seasons of the year, and we could rent it out for parties." I sensed Griffin's eagerness to look at the cost page. He humored me for now. "Now if you could join me in Griffin's office, Lea and I have created a mock-up of the restaurant with the new color scheme and décor." I managed a smile. My brother and Griffin did too. Lea did the honors and led both men to the sofa and makeshift table.

"I've purposely made this the worst table in the restaurant. Now pretend you are on a date."

"Sorry little sister, Griff isn't my type," my brother joked as he sat.

"Bro, I'm wounded," Griffin said. I smiled. My serious side reared its demanding head. I needed their hijinks, their ease with each other, their playful banter.

"You don't have to marry each other. Just pay attention to the girl in the dress," I scolded. "I've taken the liberty of painting the walls the green I suggest. If you allow your eyes to scan the vista of the room, you will see how the green and the blue dance happily together, especially in conjunction with the paintings. You will notice I have added about six new pieces of artwork to the walls when we walk around the restaurant. Again, to make it homey and to give an unexpected amuse-bouche for the eyes. I want this place to be a treat for all the senses." I had two final things to show them. I removed the big tablecloth over Griffin's desk to reveal an antique white enamel and green teardrop chandelier I had bought at an estate auction. I wanted it to go in the ladies' room or the hallway. It reminded me of my beloved earrings.

"The last thing is from me." I opened a box to reveal some festive green cocktail napkins for the bar with the letter "V" in white. I noticed Griffin cracked a smile. The "V" had a soft line at the top of the left line to match their logo. "These are just a few pennies more than the white ones. It just steps it up a notch. Now Griffin, the part you've been itching to see. The next page is a proposal from Phil Richards of the Richards Group outlining the cost of the construction, which if you look at the bottom line, is within your parameters. Also, I have already talked to him, and he has carved out the last two weeks of July and the month of August to do the renovations. I wanted to go ahead and get it on his books because that's the best time since Atlanta is dead. Now we can walk around the restaurant, and I will show you where those paintings would hang."

As we moved around, Griffin asked, "You've already lined up Phil Richards?" Henry and Griffin exchanged looks.

"Sure. If you want to move forward, not only do we need numbers, but we need availability. Mark will handle the new foliage. I want the color and the robustness of the plants to catch the eye of passersby. Now, I know this is a lot for you guys to take in. Just take your time." We walked around the restaurant in silence, each counseled by our own thoughts. We circled back to the original booth. I reviewed my notes to make sure I hadn't omitted anything.

"One last thing. If you do approve this renovation, we will want Lea to be here for a while until we get things really cooking," I said and paused. "So to speak."

"Griff and I will go back into your mini restaurant to talk things over and see if we have any questions," Henry said. I watched them go back in Griffin's office and close the door. Lea and I were left alone.

"Wow, Bailey," Lea said, clearly impressed.

My thoughts drifted to Elliott and his throwaway comment to Mac. Would I have pushed the boundaries of my own imagination so relentlessly if it weren't for Elliott? I decided, yes, I would have. I had challenged myself. I had undergone repair. If anything, those childhood years with and without my men, those dog-eared design magazines and empty lunch tables made me who I am.

I observed how the light glided in through the windows and provided a great assist to my color palette. I didn't know whether Henry and Griffin would accept my presentation. I wanted them to like it. In the scheme of things, it just didn't matter. I knew in my heart I had made a damn good presentation of a damn good proposal.

After a few minutes, I gathered my notes and stood up. "I think I'm leaving to have a proper conversation with Reggie and Elle and then to find a little watering hole."

Shock stole Lea's face. "You're not waiting for the boys to get back?" she asked.

"Nope. I've done my best, Lea. It's enough. Text me if you need me." I walked out into the sunshine.

⚘

When Griffin got home that night, I was curled up on the sofa trolling Etsy on my laptop. I glanced up at him.

"I hope this is not indicative of the way you manage a project when you're in charge, by leaving early." I met his eyes and watched him sit down next to me. He closed my laptop. We exchanged smiles. The kind of smiles that lead to other rooms and other antics. He shifted my whole body until I straddled his. Another dangerous move. Our faces were so close they revealed everything. Our love and longing bobbed like blue veins under the incandescent skin of an elderly person.

We held one another's gaze. A lifetime of conversations passed back and forth silently. I leaned into Griffin. He leaned away from me, denying my advances. For now.

"You impressed the hell out of me today, Bae," Griffin said and was silent again. Personal and professional feelings blurred then blended together. "You sure as hell impressed your brother. And we both know Henry does not impress easily." He gathered his thoughts. "No one, not even Julian, has given us such a detailed proposal. It was brilliant, Bae. We love it. When we came out to celebrate, you were gone. We called Phil Richards, and he told us you were a terror about negotiations. You wouldn't take no for an answer. He was impressed by your reputation, by your name."

"You forget, I've lived in New York for ten years, worked for Julian, and spent half my life shopping and negotiating in vintage stores and estate sales."

"In your absence, Henry and I brainstormed new recipes. We came up with some ideas. You and Henry are geniuses. I just mix drinks."

"When someone needs a good basil-infused margarita, they're not looking for me or Henry." Griffin smiled. "By the way, I had you with the green cocktail napkins, right?"

"You had me long before that." He paused. "I loved your little soliloquy on the color green. It made me think." He continued, "Annabel came by, and I told her the news—that she was going to have to find a new hang out for the month of August. She suggested BLANC. If we decide to open it at night, that is. I suppose you've trained your vision on BLANC next." His smile lingered.

"I always have a pocketful of ideas, Griffin. Sara Beth's in New York started out as a breakfast place, and now they have a nice nighttime crowd. I received texts from Lea, Annabel, and Mac, who is ready for me to start on his place. They were all congratulating me on my new gig. News travels fast. Nothing from you two."

"We were too busy trying to rise to the occasion to match Henry's sister's standards. Speaking of rising . . . You're going to have to get off my lap, Bae, unless I can use my checkbook," Griffin said rolling me off his lap.

"Never," I laughed.

"This is going to be fun." He winked. "I love what happens when you are the guinea pig for some of my concoctions." I knew he meant the sidecar and the Bing cherry hot chocolate. "VERT is going to be amazing and beautiful," he said, bestowing a long-awaited kiss. I ensnared him for just a little longer.

"Amazing and beautiful. That's what I was going for. Good night, Griffin." He grabbed my hand. I turned around. He said it then. Unequivocal. Unadorned. Without preamble.

"I love you, Bae." He released my hand, and we went to our separate rooms.

Chapter Fifty-Eight

I blinked and summer had dwindled to one little month. August. September loomed—the grand opening. We were all busy. NOIR had recently garnered another award. I marveled at how Henry could create dishes and redefine and adapt his creations. He was always tweaking, rediscovering spices and recipes, and adding a new flair. He had done that in himself and in his kitchen. He had dedicated his life to it. As I performed my own life tweaking, I realized Henry and I were very much alike. We both needed Griffin and Lea to add balance; they were key ingredients to us, and without them, we could go haywire.

We were at home one night when I broached the subject with Griffin that I had been avoiding.

"You know, after this, I have to go back to New York and work for Mac. I discussed it with Jake. He thinks it's a good idea for me to rent a corporate apartment. Unless you don't mind me living with Mac." I dodged making eye contact with him.

"I don't think so. Can't you just stay here?" Griffin asked. But he knew the answer.

"It's who I am. I can't change that about me. I don't want to. Just like you can't change being a caretaker. I understand that now." I paused to let him think about it.

"My work is everywhere. But I will always come home to you. You are my person, Griffin." He had waited a long time to hear me say those words. He finally smiled and embraced me.

Chapter Fifty-Nine

Opening night, I surveyed every inch of VERT like a new mother examining her newborn. I had to admit, the deeper paint color anchored everything else. It turned out even better than I had hoped. Henry and Griffin's bar menu sizzled and introduced nuance. I accepted that a beautiful restaurant wouldn't be anything without offering clever and interesting dishes. Reggie and Elle had texted big well wishes and sent flowers to the restaurant. I was there when the arrangement arrived. I set it on the bar. I had handpicked my own arrangement for the hostess stand to complement the colors in the design. We had invited a number of special guests, including Annabel. I hoped she would bring her husband. I was dying to meet "Mr. Monroe," as she referred to him. I couldn't even remember his first name anymore.

I had gone home about three o'clock to shower and change. I was wearing my salmon dress to complement the new VERT. It was part of the Elliott collection. I heard Griffin also getting ready.

"Griffin? I need to see you before we head out," I called. I had purchased two gifts for him to commemorate the night. I just couldn't decide which to give him first. He came out with a towel wrapped around his waist. It took all of my willpower to stay put.

"I'm not impervious to you either," I said, hoping he would stand there just a little while longer.

"Good. As you can see, I'm not wearing a checkbook." I blushed. "Just remember to breathe, Bae." He then threw the towel at me to reveal his full-frontal tattoo in addition to other parts of his anatomy. I tried to breathe while snatching glances at him. He returned to his bedroom to finish getting ready.

He strolled back out in dress slacks and an open-neck shirt and his favorite sport coat. My gifts were on the table. "Why didn't you tell me you had presents?" He surveyed the two gifts. One was in a square box and the other a tie box. "You think I should wear a tie tonight?" he asked, picking it up first. "I would be a little over-dressed for a bartender."

"A mixologist," I corrected. "And you can open the other one first if you want." So he did. It was a coffee mug. The kind he liked. I had special ordered it in green with his initial "G" in white in the VERT font. I could tell he loved it. "I'll use it tonight. This is so thoughtful."

"Don't worry. I ordered two dozen for you. There are a dozen mugs here and the rest at the restaurant."

"Let me guess. You got some sort of discount for ordering two dozen," he grinned. "Well I guess that merits wearing a tie for you. I love the vintage paper." He unwrapped the other gift, revealing a Neiman Marcus tie box. He looked up at me. I was eager to see what he thought.

"You darkened the doors of a mall? You must really love me," he said, observing the box. "Did you buy this today when Annabel took you to get your makeup done?" He studied my face. "They certainly did your makeup very natural."

"I wiped all that stuff off. Holy shit. Who's ever heard of brown cheeks? I looked ridiculous."

This brought spontaneous laughter from Griffin. "I think they call it bronzer, Bae."

"Are you going to critique my makeup or open your present?" I asked. We exchanged one last conspiratorial look before he opened the box and examined its contents.

"How?" he asked.

"Well, I talked to Mac. The delay over the permits got handled, and he's ready to do the restaurant. I've been saving, but I had to wait until the last installment yesterday, and then Annabel helped. She knows everyone."

"You don't have any money."

"I have a little more than I used to. They're real tickets, but Annabel suggested you might kick in a little bit for an upgrade."

"Tickets to Italy, Bae." He seemed overwhelmed.

"Better than a tie?" I asked.

He leaned over and kissed me. It was a kiss that matched my generosity. "You really shouldn't have."

"The way I see it, I'm just giving you back something you should've already had." He was about to protest, but I continued talking, "Now I can have sex in a foreign country with you before anyone else and—"

"If you keep talking like that, it won't be my checkbook I pull out." Griffin pulled away from me. He straightened up. "I can't believe you did this for me."

I was very pleased with myself. I stood up to leave.

He took my hand. His gratitude could not touch my happiness in being able to give him Italy. "Wait." He continued holding my hand. I sat back down next to him on the sofa.

"I have something to say. When you came home, you had really lost your way. You lost yourself, Bae. I want you to always know that no matter how often you feel lost, you always have the ability to find yourself. I wanted to give you a tangible reminder that even though some things look lost, they are merely misplaced." He reached inside his jacket pocket and pulled out a box. I recognized the box immediately.

I took it from him before he offered it and opened the lid. Looking up at me were my own peridot and diamond earrings. "How?"

"Because I listen, too, Bae." I smiled at him and remembered the phrase about listening being the most basic forms of love. I put them on my ears.

"Tell me you did not give Elliott the satisfaction."

"Nah. Lady Jane and I have actually developed a fairly cordial relationship. She isn't keen on wearing the replacement wife's earrings. By the way, they suit you, Bae." He leaned in to kiss me.

"Thank you, Griffin."

"Thank you, Bae. All of this, and the excitement of an opening night still awaits."

⚜

Henry scowled at us when we walked in. "You picked a great time to be late. Here." He thrust the new menu at us. I had already seen it. It was sublime. A creative tour de force. Henry's generosity and talent was evident in the new menu. I knew some of the offerings were things he would've normally reserved for NOIR, like foie gras with saffron foam on a plate dusted with ramps and poached lobster salad with hearts of palms flown in fresh from Hawaii. The creativity reminded me of Elliott. I still thought of him, more often than I would've liked. But the weight of the emotional anchor of those thoughts dropped into increasingly shallower and calmer waters around the sea of my heart.

I allowed my eyes to scan the room one final time. I took pictures of the flowers Reggie and Elle sent and texted them to my girls. They sent back thumbs-up emojis. The crowd trickled in, and I smelled the familiar perfume: Annabel with her plus one, Mac.

For once, she did not greet me with a clever bon mot. Her face revealed everything. It pleased me. She embraced me as if seeing me for the first time. "Baby, Mac did not do you justice. This is amazing." She took out her camera and then hugged me again. "I hope Griffin was appropriately appreciative of his gift!" She gave me a wink and, not missing anything, she pointed to my earlobes. "I see that man reciprocates appropriately." She nodded approval.

"Where's Mr. Monroe?"

"Tonight is the Georgia versus Auburn game. I couldn't get his attention if I was standing naked in front of him. You'll have to be content with my big brother." I laughed. This Mr. Monroe still intrigued me.

"Hey, Mac, thanks for coming." I leaned over and hugged him.

"I wouldn't miss it. For the record, you look like more than two rungs up from Lily Bart," he said—a reference to my domestic turbulence. In a conversation immediately after I had left New York, I had told him that I felt about two rungs up from Lily Bart in *The House of Mirth*. He had laughed at that.

"Just barely. There's the little matter of our financial connection," I said.

"Honey, what's a huge retainer between friends?" Mac laughed easily.

Emily, the new hostess, brought over two menus and whispered in my ear, "Table thirty-four." I realized tonight I was the master of ceremonies, not Daddy. The moment overwhelmed me. This was Daddy's gig. I allowed my thoughts to wander to him, wished he were here, and hoped he was proud of his children. This was Hank Edgeworth's legacy. The three of us. I swallowed hard and took the Whitneys to their table. Lea swooped in right behind me to take orders. I said another prayer of gratitude for her. She had saved both of Hank Edgeworth's children in different ways.

"I was going to ask where your perch was tonight. I see you are the grande dame," Annabel observed.

"Didn't I tell you Bailey is amazing?" Mac added.

I saw Griffin motioning for me and excused myself. He moved around the bar to join me.

About that time, I saw them: Elle and Reggie. I looked at them and then back at Griffin. I'd been texting with them all day. "How?" I asked him.

"Because they're your best friends. They should be here," Griffin whispered in my ear. I turned to him, and in the room full of people, I took his face in my hands and kissed him, not withholding anything.

They approached us. "Can you believe Griffin flew us in this afternoon?" Elle said. Their hands were waving in the air ready for hugs. Forgetting myself, my duties, and everything else, I embraced them. For the first time in my life, I squealed. They had transformed me and my life.

"Table thirty-seven," Griffin said. I looked at him.

"That's our best table," I whispered.

"They're your best friends," he countered, kissing me again. "I'll take over. Sit down with the girls for a while," Griffin encouraged.

We slid into the booth, and six-year-old Hank in his white cook's jacket placed two amuse-bouches in front of them. "Swordfish over fig risotto," he announced. Both women extended compliments to our young chef.

"That was some public display of affection we just witnessed," Reggie said. Elle said nothing. She was privy to the terms and true limits of our affection.

"Public is the only sort of affection we are allowed to have these days," I said to Reggie.

Griffin appeared with a tray of drinks. "Your white wine, Reggie. Pink lemonade for you, Elle. Something a little different for you, Bae. I call it the Sideways." So many things to comment on. Griffin sat down for a moment.

"Pink lemonade?" I asked. "When is the baby due?" Our easy rhythm was restored.

"April Fools'," Elle said, and we all laughed. "Griffin booked us a fancy hotel room, and you're spending the night."

I was torn. I wanted to be with them, but I also wanted to be with Griffin to recap the night. Griffin had done this intentionally.

We had commemorated every opening in some form of horizontal fashion. I just looked at him. Then I looked down at my drink. It looked the same, but it was different. The orange color was not as robust. A slice of lime had replaced the usual orange garnish. Griffin had arranged the lime artistically, pushing out sections to look like the petals of a flower.

I raised my glass in a toast. "To great expectations," I said. I clinked glasses with everyone before taking a sip. It was different. More nuanced than my regular sidecar. I took several tastes. "Lime juice. What else?"

"I went old-school. Courvoisier, simple syrup, triple sec, orange juice, lemon juice and lime juice, and a little something. Can you guess?" He waited. "Sprite to give it a little effervescence."

"I love it, Griffin." I toasted to him. I always associated Griffin with sidecars, never Elliott. "You need to say a few words to our guests," he told me. "Henry and I will join you." A couple years ago, public speaking intimidated me. But because of Elliott and his "illness," I had learned to mix and mingle with guests in his restaurant. Henry stepped out from the kitchen with a glass of sparkling water, Griffin did the same, and I joined them in the middle with a glass of champagne. Henry clinked a table knife against the side of his glass to get everyone's attention. When they quieted, I knew that was my cue to speak.

"Welcome to VERT reimagined. We hope you feel at home here. It's a gathering space just like your kitchen—except with a lot more tables and no food fights or boring uncles. We hope." There was laughter and applause. "This is, after all, a family business. When you're here, you're part of our family. I may be partial, but my brother, Henry, is probably one of the best chefs in the country. And if you will allow me a personal privilege, his restaurant NOIR just received another prestigious award, their first Michelin star. The first Atlanta restaurant to garner such acclaim. I've always said Henry is a virtuoso in the kitchen, and he isn't a bad brother either. His partner in crime, Griffin Hardwick, is the most talented and creative mixologist around. To celebrate or to drown your sorrows, he has a concoction to soothe the soul. I hope you'll keep us in mind whether you are having a family gathering or dining alone. We want you to feel welcome, truly like part of our family.

"Oh, I am Bailey Edgeworth . . . the sister. But I am also the visionary behind the new VERT." I smiled as I said it and glanced over at Annabel. Tonight was not the night to worry about commas. Or prepositional phrases. Just ellipses.

"Let us know if you need anything." I kissed the cheek of these two men who had been in my life from the beginning. We had been through a lot. We had finally repaired our relationship. We were always better together.

Chapter Sixty

In the weeks to come, traffic was steady. I still enjoyed my perch at the bar to keep an eye on things. I loved the new layout. My eyes could span every inch of the restaurant. I would also walk around to mix and mingle with our guests. I realized I had learned so much from Daddy on those precious Saturday nights we had together. I also had to admit, I owed a lot to Elliott. On those many occasions he was out, I would be the one to circulate.

"I noticed you're having the special. What do you think?"

"I hear you're celebrating an anniversary. Which one? I'll send over something special and complimentary glasses of champagne. Thank you for celebrating with us."

"Do you like the poached lobster? It's my favorite dish."

And always, but always, I would end with the most oft-heard question in a restaurant: "Did you save room for dessert?"

※

Several weeks in, I knew VERT was a success. It teemed with people and whirled with activity. It no longer looked dilapidated or sounded subdued but hummed with happy noise. About the same time, Annabel asked Henry and Griffin for an interview for her magazine. She had never interviewed them together. On Tuesday night, she looked in Griffin's direction and said, "I'll see you in the morning at ten o'clock. Don't cancel on me again. It would be nice if Bailey was there."

When she arrived at Griffin's, it was clear that Annabel was not a morning person. Sunglasses covered her eyes, and she plopped down in a chair as one would at the end of an exhausting day.

"Annabel, can I get you some coffee?" Griffin offered. "And an apple scone?"

"Griffin, you're an angel." She flipped open her notebook. Griffin poured coffee into three of the green mugs I had given him, and we each saluted before Annabel got down to business.

"What are you wearing, and who makes it?"

"Brown corduroys. I have no idea."

Annabel glanced up at me and I shook my head. She asked Griffin silly questions, but she also asked serious ones like, "Why revamp a successful restaurant?" Unexpected questions yielded unexpected answers.

"Who influenced you the most and inspired your love of food and libations?"

Without a breath passing, Griffin answered, "Easy. Hank Edgeworth. He was a true master."

"That's what Henry said," Annabel replied. She gazed up at me, and I nodded in accord. All of us were influenced by the same man. He had taught the beauty of cooking and plating food to Henry and Griffin. I inherited his desire to be surrounded by visual beauty.

"What would our readers be most surprised to learn about you, Griffin?" Annabel asked. Griffin thought about this one for a minute. He must be in a reflective mood this morning. "I read poetry," he said, and I smiled. "Rumi and Mary Oliver are favorites."

"I'm drawing a blank," Annabel said.

"She was a poet . . . " Griffin reflected again, looking at me, remembering.

"Of the three, which is your favorite restaurant?"

"I think I'm most at home at VERT. Don't you agree, Bae?"

At this, Annabel put her pen down. He had her full attention. "Bae? You call Bailey that? Is that her nickname? I never pictured you for an 'on trend' kind of guy."

Griffin, confused, looked back at me for clarification. I moved into the circle of conversation. I sat on the arm of the sofa next to him.

"What is she talking about, Bae?" All those times Annabel and I had sat at the bar, Griffin was mostly silent, and Annabel did most of the talking. I took charge.

"Well, Griffin, nowadays the kids use 'Bae' as a term for best friend, like BFF. It literally means 'before anyone else.' Like I tell you my secrets before anyone else. I do things with you before anyone else—"

Griffin interrupted looking squarely into my eyes. "But you kind of are that, aren't you?" My heart softened, quickened, and stopped all at the same time. It was a delicately beautiful moment I had no intention of sharing with greater Atlanta.

In all the years of doing these interviews, Griffin was about to have an unguarded moment of candor. Annabel was our friend, but she was a journalist first, and I just could not let her write a story titled, "The Mixologist and His Muse." My heart had barely repaired itself. I was not ready to go public. I loved him so much at this moment.

I stepped up. "Hell, Annabel, sitting at the bar, I'm everybody's best friend!" They both laughed. My breath had been suspended for minutes now. I exhaled. Griffin got up and poured another cup of coffee. He leaned into the doorframe.

Annabel turned her attention to me. "Was this always your vision for VERT?"

"Actually, my vision evolved over time, and I adapted. Just like with lots of things, it's all about adaptability. Henry adapts his menu to trends, and Griffin introduces cutting-edge drinks. Vision is a lot like maturity. It improves over time." My serious side burst through.

"Well said. You're a vintage shopper. What are some of your favorite places?"

"And have my favorite stores inundated? No way," I said with a smile. At this, Griffin interrupted.

"Ask her what her favorite vintage item is," Griffin offered Annabel. I looked at him. I had just saved his ass, and he was feeding me to Annabel. I knew what he wanted me to say: a flannel shirt.

"Good question, Griffin. Bailey what is your favorite vintage item?"

"One that I bought? Or one that I already had?" Two could play this game.

"How about both?" Annabel asked.

"I bought a great Chloe off-the-shoulder silk blouse I just love. And a Lanvin evening clutch I bought for a song," I said.

"And the vintage item you already had?"

Griffin moved in closer. He thought he knew what I was going to say.

"I would have to say my mother's engagement ring and wedding band," I smiled in utter delight and thrust my hand at Annabel. Griffin let out a big laugh. He was having fun.

It was as if the strain of the last year had finally lifted. My situation had taken its toll on him too. Annabel took out her camera and took a picture of the rings. She continued her questions.

"Is there anything you would like to do? A secret ambition?"

"I got this idea around New Year's Eve last year. I would love for the guys to open a diner. A city café like my Daddy's. The menu would be populated with old-school dishes like macaroni and cheese and then new-school dishes like lobster, capers, and grilled asparagus or reimagined spaghetti. Hell, menu planning is not my forte, but it is the boys'." I didn't tell them that it was on my wedding night when Elliott and I were eating in that greasy spoon diner that this first came to me. "I would opt out of the color wheel and call it Edgeworth's. I would love to vision that restaurant."

Griffin walked over and just looked at me and mouthed, "Really?" I smiled and nodded. He continued enjoying this banter.

"Wow, Bailey. It looks like you have projects out the wazoo, with Mac's restaurant, the place in Chicago, and I know you want to get your hands on BLANC." I'd told Annabel that in confidence. Griffin rolled his eyes in amusement.

"Griffin said he liked bananas Foster French toast after sex. What is your pleasure?" This time I laughed. The morning after our first time, I was the one who ate bananas Foster French toast that Griffin fixed.

"I'd have to say peanut butter on toasted brioche," which was always Griffin's go-to answer and what he had eaten that morning after our first time. We smiled at the revision of our shared memory.

"I know about your love affair with Bouley, but I'll ask you the same question I asked Griffin. What would the readers be surprised to know about you?" I took my sweet time with the answer. Griffin waited with anticipation.

"I have a tattoo." I smiled. Take that Griffin. His eyes about leapt out of his head.

"Since when?" Griffin asked. Even Annabel looked intrigued. No doubt she assumed Griffin knew the unabridged version of my anatomy.

"What is it? Where is it?" Annabel asked.

"That's on a need-to-know basis. If I'm not going to divulge my vintage stores, I'm sure as hell not going to tell you where my tattoo is!" I looked up at Griffin, who was mentally surveying every inch of my body undressed. His eyes stopped and clouded. He had not seen me naked since Martha's Vineyard, before I married Elliott. For all he knew, I could have "Elliott" emblazoned across my ass like the teenagers have "Juicy" across theirs.

"Kids, I could visit with y'all all day, except we know I'll probably see you later perched at the bar," Annabel said, gathering up her things. "I've got to get this all down while it's still fresh," she said as she left.

Griffin grabbed me and held my gaze. "Where?"

"Mystery is a good thing in a relationship, don't you agree? I'm meeting Lea to look at potential office space. Do you think she might reveal her secret that she and my brother are dating?" I said, trying to wriggle out of his grasp.

"I'm not letting this go, Bae. And if Lea does say anything, try and act surprised," Griffin released me. "You and I both know how fast 'Eye Candy' works. It ain't just in the kitchen."

Chapter Sixty-One

About two weeks later, Griffin returned home after his marketing expedition. Typically, he went straight to work. His unexpected presence filled me with dread. "What's the matter? Is it Henry?" I had become accustomed to bad things happening.

"Nothing's wrong, Bae. Annabel's article and review of the restaurant is out on newsstands. I wanted to share it with you before anyone else." He did not approach me. Nor did he scoop me up in his arms in congratulations. He stayed put, not coming near me. Had I poisoned Henry and Griffin's winning streak? Had my bad choices and bad luck tarnished them? My lungs constricted even though I fought desperately to breathe.

"Before we look at it, show me your tattoo," Griffin said.

"Really? You're holding the magazine hostage so you can take a peek at my lady parts?" I asked.

"Well, it has been a really long winter. I just need to know if I'm going to be looking at Elliott's name for the rest of my life," he said. I figured.

I played along. "It isn't Elliott's name," I said. "It isn't yours either." Now, he really looked perplexed. "It isn't my name. Or Daddy's name or initials. It isn't even some long word like 'breathe' that has my initials embedded in it."

"You figured that out," Griffin said.

"Our yoga time was really a sweet one for us," I said, turning serious.

"There have been more good times than bad, Bae." The man's generosity touched me. I wanted it to linger in the air a moment longer. I took a few steps toward him.

I tugged at the waistband of my pants. I pushed it down ever so slightly to reveal on the opposite hipbone, done in the color green with the VERT font, the small word *repair*.

"Happy now?" I asked. I smiled. I was. After everything, we were.

"Not by a long shot," he said grinning.

"Now show me the magazine."

He turned it over to reveal the cover, which looked like a collage of images. It looked like the paperback edition of *The Great Gatsby*. It was purple with the words "Buckhead Magazine" in our green. It showed a barstool, a martini glass filled with orange liquid, and a rather large, real picture of a human eye. Looking closer at it I realized the eye belonged to me and the drink was a sidecar. Underneath it, splashed across in green letters, was the phrase: "The Visionary."

"It's about me?" I reached out to grab the magazine, but Griffin raised it above my head. It dawned on me then that he had already read this thing from cover to cover.

"Fuck you," I said, still reaching.

"That is particularly amusing given the title of the article," Griffin said. He turned to the page as if there were a hidden bookmark. In small letters it read "Sometimes it takes . . . A WOMAN'S TOUCH."

"Shit." I pouted and started to read.

A New Edgeworth Claims Her Place on the Culinary Scene

A reimagined VERT blooms anew, thanks to Bailey Edgeworth returning to her roots. The restaurant now offers a visually stunning atmosphere, has introduced an incredibly inventive and impressive menu, and created the hippest bar and bar menu in town. The "Color-Wheel Boys" are back big time. Their major achievement just may be bringing aboard "The Sister."

I smiled. A huge grin broke across Griffin's face. He was happier than I was. The article was peppered with pictures of me sitting at the bar with Griffin and my cocktail, pictures of me throughout the restaurant mingling with guests at different tables, pictures of me sitting alone in a booth scribbling notes and looking pensive. There was a picture of me laughing with Lea. Accompanying the pictures was an extensive article that Annabel had woven together from our outings over the last months. The article about me was linked with an enchanting review of the restaurant. My eyes darted from picture to picture and word to word.

"Sit down, Bae. Read the entire article."

Annabel asserted I had saved VERT, but in my estimation, it was the other way around. The truth bobbed somewhere in the middle. A section titled "Small Bites" had a picture of my mother's ring and some quotes I had given Annabel that day.

"In case you're wondering, Annabel gave Henry and me the tapas version. We share a page toward the back of the magazine." I didn't think I could've been happier. Griffin always had a knack for improving things. He sat down beside me. "Do you know what today is?" I shook my head. I've always been bad with dates. "You have been a free woman for exactly three days. Your check from Elliott and the papers arrived day before yesterday."

"You mean I'm free? We can—Why didn't you tell me?"

"Because. You were enjoying living." We tarried together on the sofa in happy silence and togetherness until Griffin got up. I looked at him.

"I'm going out to get some warm brioche and peanut butter," he said. I just looked up at him, at this good man whom I had loved before anyone else and would love after everyone else. I smiled and grabbed his hand and pulled him toward me. "Brioche can always be toasted. Later."

Chapter Sixty-Two

The beauty and crispness of the November weather suited the occasion perfectly. An outdoor wedding. Thanksgiving loomed. Togetherness dwelled. Happiness floated like the white clouds overhead. The reality surpassed even my vision.

My brother looked so handsome. Hank served as the ring bearer. In a fitting role reversal, I served as Henry's best person. Griffin had another duty. He would walk Lea down the aisle as Henry, Hank, and Lea became a family.

In the weeks that followed Annabel's article, I heard from Reggie and Elle. Mac and I exchanged texts including: "Thank God I've got you locked in already. Rest those pretty little eyes of yours." I had a raft of possible new clients calling and emailing—including an Ivy League cafeteria!

Griffin and I slipped into couplehood seamlessly and privately. We christened every room. Griffin took to saying, "before anyone else!" Except, of course, for his bedroom, which had been occupied by others before me. I couldn't nitpick on this one since I had gone off and gotten married. Perhaps all the times that Griffin and I had come together, we were creating our own version of married sex.

We always showed up for each other when asked, when needed, or when wanted. We showed up for each other at the unexpected death of parents, the loss of a beloved home, splashy openings, troubled times, on Tuesdays or Wednesdays, and on rainy days that offered themselves up to us and our imagination. We approached each other in kindness, without questions, and with gratitude.

Occasionally my thoughts would wade into dangerous waters. What if I had never left Atlanta? And all those should'ves, could'ves, and would'ves regarding both Griffin and Elliott. There's a significant difference between contractions and commas. Contractions may shorten phrases. Yet, contractions caused me to remain stuck. Emotional quicksand lies beneath the surface of those little words. Commas and prepositional phrases can go on and on like an infinity pool.

When I was twenty-one, I was ready to take on the world. I had the deepest desire to chart my own destiny. I had misgivings about being "just" Bailey Edgeworth, daughter of, sister of, and friend of. Why had I limited myself like that? At twenty-one I didn't know shit.

In nine years, I had become so many more things. Some good. Some not so good. I had added some astonishing roles to that short and rather naïve list.

I was Bailey Edgeworth, surrounded by good men and good food, devoted friend to some treasured women, vintage shopper, learned apprentice under Julian, girlfriend, muse, lover of the right man, lover of the wrong man, awesome aunt to Hank, unapologetic aficionado of beauty, cappuccino connoisseur, guinea pig for creative cocktails, bridesmaid, wedding planner, recipient of 40 Under 40, enabler, caregiver, liar, reluctant hostess, ex-wife, colossal fuck-up, tabloid fodder, motherless, destitute, and lover of the right man—again. And I was Bailey Edgeworth: visionary.

Who said there were no "do-overs" in life? We were planning a trip to Martha's Vineyard in the spring to visit Elaine's. And to Italy.

I was less concerned about the Bailey and Griffin in that alternate universe than the ones looking back at me in the mirror. I knew enough now to know the commas and prepositional phrases would keep coming. Some might just knock me off my feet with joy, causing circumstances to change in a big way. Others might produce tears. But they were mine. I claimed the whole damn messy, awful, wonderful paragraph of my life. By claiming it all, I could move on

and continue with my life. I could add another word to my repertoire: *survivor*. I had no idea what the future held for me and Griffin.
I didn't know whether a day like today awaited us or if we would
just eat a lot of peanut butter and grow fat and happy.

Acknowledgments

In many aspects, the day to day job of writing is a singular effort. In the main, it really does take a village to write a novel.

And, oh my, do I have a wondrous village!?

I have my beloved committee. The ones that read everything and I do mean everything many, many times over. A single scene. They may read it three or four times to make sure that I had it right. And while they are beloved, they can be brutal and honest in their remarks and then turn around and supplement that with kindness and hugs. They are Melissa Walker, Cindy Grim, Amy Royal and Lew Burdette (every committee needs a handsome and Well-Read Man).

There are the cheerleaders. These are no ordinary cheerleaders either. They have Impressive Powers with a pen and paper offering unimpeachable criticism and unfailing suggestions. All the while showing enormous generosity. I call you the Super women of Sewanee: Margot Livesey, Gail Hochman, Christine Schutt, Cheri Peters, Karin Davidson and Amy Greene. Sewanee is my happy place where creativity and kindness dwell together. Rounding it out are Kevin Wilson and Richard Bausch. Once again, a cheerleading squad needs funny and articulate men that sometimes get a bit rowdy!

But every cheerleading squad needs a head cheerleader. The head of my squad has feisty and indefatigable pom-poms. She NEVER let me give up. And goodness knows, there were times I felt like I would be "up in heaven," before my manuscript saw the light of day. There are not enough adjectives in my repertoire to describe my feelings of love and admiration for you, Jill McCorkle. The bricks have been removed.

Some other wonderful people that have aided in my writing career:

Tracy Curtis (how could someone be so beautiful and so funny. Damn you), Betsy Thorpe, Kim Wright (nobody can touch your query letters) Colleen Oakley, Patti Henry, Lisa Barr (When do y'all find time to sleep?). Judy Goldman, Susie Almon, Regina Romine. And Wyatt and Barbara Prunty (Again, there are not enough adjectives to describe my beloved family at Sewanee).

But I also need to extend some big thank you' s to the book bloggers. Bless you. Bless you all. You have been so kind and helpful to me as I entered the world of Instagram. You embraced me and BAE with fierce love and devotion. I am SO grateful to you all.

Some other tireless villagers that helped BAE take flight. Miriam Maloney, you worked your magic with the camera and made me so much more attractive than I am "IRL," John and Meg Maloney helping me with so many things including the necessary cappuccino and bourbon as needed. Kim Brattain and Brattain Media, you and your sweet and patient team did your best to make me camera ready. You made me feel comfortable, welcome and like I was doing a good job in front of the camera. Chelsea and Andrew, we still need to go out and toast you.

My village is not complete without my fairy godmother and fairy godfather. Stephanie Beard and Todd Bottorff. Little did I know when I met you at Sewanee, Todd, and when you called me in February, Stephanie, how profoundly you would change my life. Again, adjectives and words of thanks fail me. But it was like that from the beginning. You took BAE and loved her and turned her in to something "ready to go to the ball." You introduced her to Heather Howell who to my knowledge never sleeps and is an editor extraordinaire and Kathleen Timberlake, who was always available and with good humor and enormous patience. They answered all my questions day after day after day. And just like Cinderella you gave her the most exquisite book jacket. The wickedly talented Emily Mahon your beautiful design made me cry happy tears. Thank you so much for whatever you saw when you thought of Bailey and her world. I landed on the word "beauty," and you took it to a whole new level. You are the best.

I owe a debt of thanks to Lauren Langston Stewart for your meticulous reading and editing once I thought BAE was finished. The joke was on me. Or you.

And to Annie Grim for introducing me to the concept of BAE.

In my village there are some wonderful restaurants that let me just hang out, ask questions, take notes and were hospitable enough to invite me back. Bailey's best days were spent with you. And to those legal eagles. I hated having to get to know you, but you treated me with the utmost respect and care.

And last but never least, the people of Leslie Inc. You and the men in white coats kept this bargain-basement body afloat during hours of stress and working late. Don't worry, you'll get a whole memoir devoted to your efforts!

And to Joy GSD (get stuff done) Bennett. People think I am your boss . . . Little do they know you're the boss of me. Finally thank you to my family: Robert and his family and Sandy and her family. Thank you for propping me up when I was so weary. And to the rest of the village of GOOD friends, who may not fit into a nice paragraph but do fit perfectly into the chambers of my heart. Each of you always gave me a generous smile or ask about my work like it was something REAL other than just a hobby. Those smiles and inquiries kept me going on many occasions.

Any mistakes, grammatical errors or weaknesses belong to the one lone village idiot . . . Me.